THOSE THAT MATTERED

THOSE THAT MATTERED

Barbara Angle

CROWN PUBLISHERS, INC.
NEW YORK

Permission to reprint "Battle of Jericol" on pages ix–x by Mary Lou Chandler.

Permission to reprint lyrics from "Walk Like a Man" on page 234 written by Bob Crewe and Bob Gaudio. Copyright © 1963 Claridge Music, division MPL Communications, Incorporated. International copyright secured. All rights reserved.

Published by Crown Publishers, Inc., 201 East 50th Street, New York, New York 10022. Member of the Crown Publishing Group.

Random House, Inc. New York, Toronto, London, Sydney, Auckland

CROWN IS A TRADEMARK OF CROWN PUBLISHERS, INC.

Manufactured in the United States of America

Book design by June Bennett-Tantillo

Library of Congress Cataloging-in-Publication Data
Angle, Barbara.
    Those that mattered/Barbara Angle.—1st ed.
        p. cm.
1. Women coal miners—West Virginia—Fiction. I. Title.
PS3551.N468T48 1994   94-6828

813'.54—dc20

                                              CIP

ISBN 0-517-59799-3

10 9 8 7 6 5 4 3 2 1

First Edition

This book was written for the rank-and-file
of the United Mineworkers of America

A special thanks to Tom Bethell . . .
whether he wants it or not.

ACKNOWLEDGMENTS

This work has been supported by my Union Sisters, particularly Carol Jean Niland; and by Betty Jean Hall, who initiated the Coal Employment Project, which encouraged the efforts of women in the mining industry. I owe Paul Mahon, my agent, who took the trouble to listen to what I was saying, and Jane Cavolina, my editor, the lady with the difficult job of cleanup, which she managed with humor and style. Jonathan Saxon Angle, my son, was always the irritant who kept this work moving, and a skeptical brother, Gary Angle, kept me ever-mindful of the need to do it.

BATTLE OF JERICOL

Bless the Fathers, Bless the Brothers, Bless the Sons
 who pass their time
Standin', waitin', watchin' upon the picket line.
You can see their thoughts written on each face as
 they watch that L&N roll,
And as they see the trucks run by each day takin'
 scabs into Jericol.

Bless the Mothers, Bless the Sisters, Bless the wives
 and daughters too,
Who stand behind the miners, Lord, tell them what
 to do.
They can't sit back any longer, you know they've got
 to take a stand,
'Cause the women in Harlan County want to make
 it a Union land.

Bless the veterans and disabled who can't work in
 the mines any more,
Yet keep on laborin' for those strikin' men though
 they be old and poor.
'Cause the Union they built for thirty years they
 can't stand by and watch it die.

*Though their hands are worn and their lungs are
    spent, they'll fight till their final sigh.*

*Bless the miners who are buried in the coal fields of
    these great hills.*
*Lord, their spirits are among us. Oh how could they
    be still?*
*On the mountainside of a non-Union mine, how
    could they peaceful lie?*
*If there's a reason for the rich to rule, then please,
    Lord, tell us why.*

*Bless our struggles and our trials in the Battle of
    Jericol.*
*Bless our demands that only Union men mine our
    homeland's coal.*
*May our safety crew be miners, may our pension
    plan be written down,*
*Or in the pits of Sigmon's Jericol, may the walls
    come tumblin' down.*

M. L. Layne

THOSE THAT MATTERED

PROLOGUE

After forty-odd years, most wanna-be adults get around to leaving home. Not this good ol' girl. I did meander a bit, hither and yon. *Yon* is a comfortable word, having the ease of going and the softness of staying. But basically I am a hither person: homebound.

Still, yesterday's lost possibilities track me. Most mornings I don't deal with them. The new light is too blinding to confront memories. Besides, in the morning I must plot my days with righteousness. By evening, righteousness has grown thin and I am too tired to peruse worn goods.

Another barrier to memories is my smug todays. Life has meshed very nicely, thank you. I live and teach, quietly and efficiently. I appreciate the tedium that is my element. Yet in some shadowed mental coves, yesterdays persist in trying to define themselves, stalking me through white sleep, teasing with moldy odors, pungent touches. The drab light of early Mass is shattered by the hacking cough of miners marking time with the Lord. Carbohydrate-stuffed women finger food stamps with a placidity that I know is resignation. A wizened man leans against his car, coal dust written in his pores. He is waiting, perhaps for his old lady; perhaps for time to pass. A maimed claw manipulates match to cigarette.

Remembered pain has its value, confirming a prior existence. But I cannot get too close. I am older now, more vulnerable, even to usage at a distance. . . . I will not, must not, be shattered. Hence, a buffer, the invulnerable third person, will speak to you. Her name is Portia Crowe.

1 The girl intently studies the splay of hairs across her smutty big toe. They are upside down, a curiosity rather like seeing oneself wrong ways in a spoon. As her other toes offer no such phenomenon, she abandons this line of thought and stretches her ambiguous fourteen-year-old length across the front porch, oblivious to its ingrained soot. Positioning her head to one side so fingers can worry an erratic cowlick, Portia Crowe turns her mind to the town beneath her.

In the manner of coal towns, Cogan's Bluff, West Virginia, follows a cornucopia of hills dipping to the West Fork River. Dowdy fringes of row houses straddle these ridges, descending into a tattered business area fringed by the brick homes of extinct coal barons, now mostly serving as apartments. The mine itself is at the lowest point, humping the river, but one can never escape its domination over the town it defines. The Crowe residence is positioned on a corner lot at the high end of town, a section referred to as Hooper's Hollow.

Daniel Crowe, Portia's father, has versed her in the history of Cogan's Bluff: how a cluster of company houses had been built near a wool mill constructed by a man named Cogan at the time of the Civil War. Cogan, it was said, arrived from Ireland in the proverbial rags six months before the rebels figured out Fort Sumter was an eyesore. Within three years he made a million selling uniforms to Lincoln's army, uniforms that fell apart in a light rain but that sold because of Cogan's uncanny knack of reading palms. Cogan had moved on by the time the coal operators discovered the area's potential, but they shared his entrepreneurial spirit and the Bluff flourished. When the company houses erected by the benign coal barons were fifty years old and it was no longer profitable to deduct enough from a miner's pay to cover the cost of repairs, management sold the strings of uninsulated shells to their employees, who were proud to become owners of the homes they had already purchased many times over.

A rigid row of lights beyond the town's erratic boundaries marks the track of Cogan Number Two Mine's beltline. The coal-glutted caverns beneath expand silently into corridors known only to those humans who work them. In the gathering darkness, wandering blimps indicate the movement of men and machinery while an occasional brief flare marks the spot where a miner grabs a quick smoke before going back under. Sometimes a cap light rises toward the Hollow as the man contemplates the hovering houses with their eventual promise of ease and sleep. Lifted higher, the beams bounce against the darkness of the coal-scarred mountains overhanging the town.

Neighborhood screen doors begin to slam as the women come out for the evening air, acknowledging one another with explicit silent nods. Mornings were for fence talk, the idle pleasantry of discussing a husband's latest quirks, a child's most recently acquired evil, and the fate of the world as determined by food prices. Now they settle on porch swings, quietly resting on what has been done, what has yet to be done, and what would most probably be done again tomorrow. Socialization was left to the men with whom they had little discourse.

Second shift is still underground while night shift attempts a few minutes of sleep before the midnight change. Daytime had been released from the mines about four o'clock. The bleary-eyed men have washed, leaving drifts of soot around the tub, then eaten frantically as if to satisfy a need beyond hunger. Now they move within the twilight, hosing down the work clothes that kill Maytags and tinkering with pickups. Many drift to neighbors' to swap hunting stories. Others plug radios into porch outlets, listening to the Pirates. Umpires' calls are followed by church keys snapping on Old Germans and the arguments possible in the early Sixties before instant replay. Some few Yankee fans isolate themselves in their inner sanctums to follow the team's forbidden rites. They are not missed.

On the pavement, children romp at tag or such, drifting among the streetlights' orbs. At about the age of twelve, some hormonal urge moves them to hang around the adolescents, mingling in the shadows of the advancing game of boy-girl. Giggling females stalk pubescent males whose hands leave their pockets only long enough to trace the oily tracks of their hair.

From within the Crowes' clapboard home, a replica of twenty others strung along the street, comes the clink of dishes and a cupboard slammed with finality; signs that Ida has finished with cleaning up and is coming to the porch for her sit. Portia does the dishes along with her older sister, Harriet, but Ida is the one for spit and polish: wiping smudges from the counter, drippings from the faucets, and collecting dinner's few unusable remains for the dog. Later, lunch buckets will be packed and the coffeepot primed, but these are night things, as are the few defiant pin curls Ida always rolls before retiring. Now damp and apronless, this crisp husk of a woman settles onto the porch swing, working it gently, allowing the rise and fall of the night breeze to catch her. Portia moves closer and her mother's fingers seek her cowlick, restlessly twisting it as the two of them study the street and the fledgling couples.

"So young, and already they're at it. They see the excitement, the security they think comes from another. Can't see the price of it. I remember . . ."

Portia squirms beneath the worrying fingers. She has heard this many times and does not want to hear it again. But knows she will. "Your daddie, when I met him . . . He had such a look about him. He made you wonder . . ." This sentence is always left unfinished.

"We met at the Wander Inn. Wasn't really a bar or nothin'. You could get beer but I just had Cokes and couldn't afford many of them 'ceptin' there were usually boys enough to buy them for me. I'd had my eye on Daniel and finally moved him around to askin' me to dance. He was wearin' an argyle vest; had this thick wave of hair fallin' into his eyes. Always a cigarette danglin'. Some women like men who seem to promise them nothin' but trouble and I was fool enough to be one."

Sometimes she would stop there, but tonight Ida is troubled and the purging monologue continues. Portia visualizes the two of them dancing beneath a caul of Sammy Kay and Lucky Strike Green gone to war.

"Once we got together, that was it. Pearl Harbor had just happened and all the boys were struttin' round in uniform. Your daddie would have to enlist, and I took a job at the sewin' factory, started savin' money for us. I'd write him every night, how good things was goin' to be for us; how good we were goin' to be for each other. Daniel kept after me to move in with his parents 'cause things were hard at home, what with nine of us. That was my mistake. I shoulda never done that. Tom and Pansy have been good to me, signed over this house to us when they bought the new place. But when Daniel came back after the war, we were two different people and, because I was livin' here, we was stuck with marrying each other."

Portia asks no questions, knowing Ida will go on. She attempts to distract herself by studying the ongoing street play whose tempo has changed. The aimless wanderings of adolescents have settled into distinct couplings, while the shunned younger children begin frantic games of hide-and-seek, merging with the darkness and often with those seeking the seclusion of the shadows. "Bobby Moore! I'm goin' to kill you. Now, get out of here." Younger children converge on their parents with desperate pleas for money as they hear the bell of the approaching ice-cream truck. Still Ida's low monologue overrides the whole and Portia sighs, letting herself be sucked back to the story.

The woman regards her worn hands, mapped with liver spots, and her voice is laced with new wistfulness when she speaks. "Oh, I wanted to marry him, all right. I wanted Daniel because so many others did. Felt like I'd won something for the first time in my life. But he was a man with a man's doings. You four kids came fast, and after losing little Andy, things was hard on me. Dan changed so much. He was tight, kinda twisted. Always tensed for something. He took to drinkin' heavy after he went in the mines, kept havin' nightmares, wakin' up screaming. He'd mumble about some woman. Helen. I knew he'd done some runnin' around overseas. Probably an army woman. Them types always goes into the service to get a man. Or another woman."

Portia averts her face, contemplating a well-scratched mosquito bite on her shin. She knows this Helen, having found her picture in a bruised Air Force photo album under a tool drawer in her father's workshed. Pleasant faced, with a broad-hipped air of lusty possibilities, Helen seemed to recognize Portia, returning her study with bemused curiosity. Briefly she tried to imagine the woman as her mother, but Ida had conceived, carried, and birthed her. That demanded loyalty. She never mentioned finding the album.

Ida gives her exit line: "Any woman who marries is a fool if she can get around it. But there's not much avoiding it in this world. You have to have a man to survive. But pick careful. When you pick a husband, you get his way of life. Stay away from miners. Mining is hell on women."

Ida's monologue having run its course, she studies her daughter, thinking what an odd child she is, tall for her age and lean, with angular elbows and a frizz of red hair riding freckled skin. She doesn't look real, the woman thinks. She looks like one of them Saturday cartoons. But the girl's smart as a whip, skippin' the third grade in school. Only fourteen and already a sophomore. She knows things that are beyond me and is in too big a hurry to use them. Ida recognizes that this instinct isn't sexual sophistication, but is unaware that it is her own complaints that have neutered any budding interest in males. "Your daddie thinks he's still sixteen. I can't be puttin' up with his foolishness anymore." Portia had heard that one before she understood that the foolishness had to do with the pleas that penetrated the floorboards separating the sisters' rooms from their parents'. The complaints were either silenced or followed by whining bed springs. Lately these episodes have become more infrequent and her father's increasing frustration is quieted under a pall of drink.

The old man frequently speaks his epitaph: "Yep, Mama wanted me to be a preacher. All I woulda had to done was give a little bullshit and pass the plate. Not this man. I had to be a big-time coal miner. So look at me. Arthritis. Black lung. Drinkin' myself to death and too damn ugly for any woman but the old lady to look at. A man's gotta know when to quit. That's a big part of livin'. Knowin' when to quit."

He has the miner's black spittle, spewing coal-flecked mucus accumulated from years of working underground. He always keeps torn squares of cotton around that he dissects from the kids' discards. Spitting his poison phlegm into the upper half of the cloth, he will fold it neatly, the next time soiling a fresh surface and so on until the cotton is too small to use. Monday washes are flagged by these colorful clusters fluttering from the clothesline, where they have been gathered by a single pin. But the old man won't use a hanky. His lungs would ruin a hanky.

The two women watch the street for their men as activity begins to diminish. The tinkle of the ice-cream truck fades and mothers reclaim smeared children. Adolescents drift homeward. Harriet pries herself from a giggling clatch and drifts toward the porch with cultivated casualness, ignoring her mother's sharp look. The slamming screen door scatters insects, and with a put-upon sigh, the woman resumes her vigil.

"I wish they'd be gettin' home. A little time hangin' out with the boys after work is fine, but it's eight already. They'll be fussin' loud enough when five o'clock comes around in the morning. Dan may be up before that if he gets to coughin'. And I don't know how Robert can be seein' a baseball in this dark, though after a few blind months underground, seems he can see through lead."

As if sensing her growing agitation, Daniel appears from the dimness, perching himself on the porch steps. Portia moves to sit beside him, sniffing his aura, heavy with sulfur and beer. He mumbles something about having tossed back a few with his father and Pansy's resulting displeasure, then releases a squirt of tobacco juice onto some anemic petunias. Ida looks at him with disdain. "It makes them grow, woman."

Robert ambles toward the porch, fist pounding into his baseball mitt until he sees the family assembled, then veers quickly toward a group bent over a pickup. By tacit agreement, the Crowes are left alone of an evening. Although not averse to a few beers, neighbors are well aware of Daniel's fondness for liquor. The family can sense him wanting another drink. The women silently fight his thirst, and he stalls.

"Payday tomorrow, Idee."

"Good thing. I got the makings for one more day's lunches and it'll be Spam for dinner. Lord, I was scrapin' bottom tonight."

"Fried corn mush sits good with a man. Sticks with him. Wouldn't mind a couple slices in my bucket."

Ida snorts. "Trash food. And that's with two of you workin'. I don't know how people makes it."

"They don't." Daniel showers the petunias with a well-placed arc of tobacco juice.

"Do things look to be pickin' up any?" The eternal litany of a miner's wife.

"Well, Idee, I don't know. Company's not about to tell us what's happening, and that union shit that's runnin' things don't know nothin'. If you can call what we have a union. They mighta cussed ol' John Lewis in his day, but if the man was a crook, he was a damn good one. He knew the only way to keep coal sellin' was to bring in the machines, keep it cheap. But now the government is yellin' 'clean fuel,' which means takin' money from our pockets and givin' it to those damn Arabs." He shakes his head and jams another hit of tobacco into his swollen cheek. The porch swing stops and Daniel accurately reads accusation in its silence.

"Christ, woman! Don't blame me. I take all the overtime I can and I'm gettin' too old for that. We could always move to some damn city. That would kill all of us." Restlessly he shoves back the dank remains of the lock of hair. "I always said I'd shovel shit before I'd shovel coal. Now it just seems I do both."

The air is heavy with his wanting a drink and her resentment. Rising, Ida stalks into the house, the screen rattling loosely. Daniel glances at the girl beside him, who is trying to sort out her confused loyalties. "Ah, Portia, she can't help it. No more than I can. Just don't pay us no mind."

Night's blackness has swollen full, congesting in the hollows, isolating the mine from the town. The tipple's lights take on a hardened hostility. Men abandon their porches, meandering in purposefully aimless ways that will merge at Whetzel's, the town's prime watering hole. Daniel and his daughter are both acutely conscious of these movements.

"Gettin' late, Portia. Why don't you head for bed?"

"I'm not tired. I'll sit up with you awhile."

"Nah. You got school tomorrow and I feel like a walk. Gotta go see a man about a horse." Winking broadly, he moves into the dark, following a trail of hacking coughs and flickering cigarettes. Sleep is already clogging the house as the girl climbs to the small attic she shares with Harriet. Passing the door of her parents' room, Portia momentarily watches her mother stroke her sparse hair with an equally scant brush. Ida's eye catches her daughter's in the vanity mirror. Neither speaks.

2 Time passes, persistently nudging the family to redefine their lives, but some things maintain continuity. The Sundays of Portia's diminishing childhood continue to be a thing of the senses rather than the calendar. Although Ida invariably reminds her family the night before of their need to fast for Communion, Sunday morning announces itself in a tangible easing of the week.

The Crowes attend the six A.M. service, the "Miner's Mass." Daniel ignores the Lord's allocated Day of Rest if there is overtime to be had, but even on holidays the family is programmed for early rising and attendance. In summers, awakening comes as a crackling spurt of energy, but in winter's dark dawn, the family needs extra urging to shed sleep's cocoon. Then the streetlight refracts ice flowers onto the girls' striated floor as Ida's voice ascends the stairs: "Time for church. Let's be getting ready." Hearing the familiar sounds of her mother moving about, stirring subtle sleep, Portia pushes deeper into her blanketed burrow. Harriet will move first. Despite her propensity for sleeping in, Harriet's recently developed pubescence demands grooming time and she rises quickly to stake out her bathroom turf. Although she's only two years younger than Harriet, Portia's toilet is still limited to basic hygiene, a brief procedure she simplifies when possible. Summers Ida demands she poke herself into a starched dress, but in today's

November frigidly, Portia merely camouflages her nightgown under a long coat and, buffered by this comforting layer of flannel, huddles next to her siblings in the old Chevy's backseat. The family sits, knowing they must wait. Daniel always forgets something: change for the newspaper, the car keys, his lunch bucket if he is putting in Sunday time. Back stiffened, Ida stares at the plastic Jesus on the dash. "I don't know why," she mutters as her husband climbs into the car, the night before written in sagging face and trellised eyes.

"Don't start in on me, Ida. We've got plenty of time."

Hands clinch and still. Each knuckle meshes into a splotch of white as Ida grimly maintains the Sunday peace. Church women ritually arrive at St. Bernadette's as early as possible to watch the congregation gather, see who is there and who isn't, who comes with whom and who is left at home and, by surmise at least, what they were up to the night before.

Harriet is also fretting to go, being in the throes of first love and eager to see the object of her affections. Youthful crushes are not taken lightly in coal towns; many a marriage has been wrought by the flicker in an adolescent girl's designing eye. Harriet's chosen, seventeen-year-old Joey Zanzucki, is prime material. The only son of liberal Catholic parents who do not see the value in a parochial education, Joe moves within the superior social bracket of the public-school system. He is a blondish boy with faded blue eyes, and his appearance on good days, and most of his are, is of a diluted Tab Hunter. Joey does not have sufficient imagination to have other than good days.

The Catholic Church does not assign pews, but families acquire a specific seat by regular habitation. Any unknowing visitor who inadvertently trespasses is subject to hard stares and throat clearing. The Crowes wedge themselves into their slot, Robert stumbling over the kneeler in his haste to find obscurity near the wall. As Ida hushes him, all eyes are drawn to the family. Portia squats down on the rough kneeler, some initial appearance of prayer being required. As always she is disoriented the first few moments inside the sanctuary, where points of garnet light stir dusky depths, calling up sacred icons that haunt the shadows. Beeswax, Simoniz, and incense intermingle. Throughout her life, Simoniz would be the odor of sanctity.

Beneath the figures huddled over pews, miners' buckets gleam; rolls of work clothes are stashed by the ushers' benches. Many of the men are working today and will go directly to the mine. Most would have gone without the Church's blessing except for the iron discipline of their women. Yet despite the bitter early hour, the Mass is comforting, binding miners with families, friends, and an obscure God who hovers above the high altar. Although the life He prescribed often seems unreasonable, few doubt His presence. Miners cannot afford such presumption.

Harriet begins to stir restlessly, a sure sign that young Zanzucki has entered the church. Dumb bitch, Portia thinks, then hastily crosses herself with an eye to the statue of the Blessed Virgin. She does not seem perturbed. Her sister has chosen stupidly, chosen a company man's spawn. Men's voices grow respectfully resentful when they talk of Joey's father, Steve Zanzucki, general mine foreman and chief union ass-kicker, reportedly a tough man in the tradition of men who fill this position: hard worker, hard drinker, and hard-nosed with the union "scum." Harriet's girlish crush could bring warfare onto the family turf. Portia knows this is not some romantic notion pilfered from reading; this is a hard fact of coal-town life.

A tinkling bell ushers the priest into the sanctuary. Raising his palms to the vaulted ceiling, he intones, "I will go to the altar of God . . ."

Black and white altar boys prostrate themselves on cold marble and respond, "The God of the joy of my youth."

And there is joy then. Youth buffers the realization that not all mothers are worn out, edging toward oblivion in their thirties. That fathers are not always stooped men with clogged pores and hacking coughs. That a roaring tipple does not dominate every community, and that a half-moon of coal dirt under the fingernails would be noticed in some places. In Appalachia's world, sulfur paints streambeds into a dull orange that mocks fool's gold. Heavy rain sometimes washes the dust away, turning the ground brackish. Women spend a goodly amount of time desperately seeking the color white. Dirt congeals in the eyes and grit in the teeth. Miners are tolerant of these discomforts. Since the Earth graciously allows them to hack a living from her, female idiosyncrasies are forgiven. The men ritualize their relationship with her in hunting, fishing, and gardening. They respect her power and unpredictability.

"Holy, holy, holy . . ." The priest's monotone drugs Portia into a half-sleep and she struggles for an appropriate degree of consciousness, spending the remainder of the Mass assessing women's varied hats and deciding how she would have her eggs fixed on the one morning she would be asked. When the dismissed congregation finally stumbles into a half-light clogged with morning, the girl goes with Daniel to get the car, leaving the rest of the family to mingle with the gossiping worshipers. From beneath sleep-heavy lashes she watches Joey Zanzucki cross the church steps to where Harriet stands with a group of girls. Receiving his unspoken message, her sister subtly edges away and talks to him. What they say is written on their faces.

Daniel pulls the car to the front of the church, and now it is his turn to sit resignedly, waiting for the family to conclude their respective pleasantries. Harriet lingers with Joey while Robert stands at the fringe of a blustering cluster of union men. Getting into the car, he preaches the gospel of unity.

"Pops, you goin' to the Local meeting this afternoon?"

"Haven't given it much thought. Whose ass they after now?"

"Looks like Ol' Man Wilson's. Gonna shut down that scab outfit of his from haulin' our coal. And if Blanchard gives us any shit, we'll shut down the whole mine. Knock him out of his fat superintendent's job."

"Another strike, huh?"

"If that's what it takes."

"There's enough want right now, boy. Think you kids would learn how good you got it, just havin' a job. You young bucks, you live at home and make the big paycheck. No responsibilities. So you hotheads get a few dollars ahead and the urge to go huntin', and end up shuttin' the mine down over nothin'."

"Oh shit, Pop! There'll always be want as long as there's old shits like you willing to let anyone step in and take a union man's job."

"Robert, you know I got 'union' written on my ass, same as you. But it used to count for something. Now—"

"Now it don't? If so, people like you need to answer for that."

They quiet as the two women bundle into the car, scattering fresh snow over the interior, but the old man starts up again, knowing his wife won't let it get far. "You know you ain't accomplishin' nothin' by strikin'. So what's the point?"

Ida's face freezes. "Strikin'? I can hardly manage now. For God's sake, don't start with that talk."

"We gotta stand up for ourselves. You know damn well where the company would put us if we didn't. Back hand-loadin' for fifteen cents a ton and nothin' to show for it. But we'll win. Little by little we'll nibble away at those fat sassy bastards, and if they keep pushin' us . . . Well, the blood is on their hands."

Ida ends it there. "Blood, is it? That's enough. No such talk. It's Sunday and I won't be hearin' it."

The engine crackles placidly as Robert regroups. "Makin' a little time there with young Zanzucki, weren't you, Harriet?"

His mother glances at him sharply.

"I mean, he was being attentive."

"We was talkin' a bit." Silence. "He asked me to go to the movies with him this afternoon."

"The movies!" Even Robert is impressed. Unconsciously he expresses Ida's thoughts. "Comin' from him, that's almost a statement of intent."

His mother quickly silences him. "Watch your mouth, Robert."

Sitting behind her, Portia can sense how Ida's mind is working. The Zanzuckis aren't religious but the boy seems stable enough. And they have money. More money than anyone else in the parish. That house, the old man with his big Buick . . . The boy even has his own car. Maybe they could get by with two hundred at the wedding, but the reception would have to be larger. Daniel's daddie lives like trash in that row house on the bottom, but he and Pansy have a bit stashed away. They should be good for a loan; glad to see the girl better herself.

Robert rattles his tobacco pack, a flagrant defiance of Ida's oft-stated views on chewing. "All I gotta say, Harriet, is keep that scab out on the porch. I don't want his kind sniffin' around."

Ida whirls on him. "The girl has a right to her friends. And from what I've seen of some of yours . . ."

"That ain't the point, Mum, and you know it. If he starts hangin' round, we'll have to be watchin' everything we say lest he carry it back to his old man. I'll have every union man in the valley on my back."

Harriet's tears are artful. "Joey don't care about union stuff. He starts at the university next fall."

Robert chews reflectively. "I'll tell you how it is, Sis. He'll give school a go, but his old man will tighten the money belt and get him back in line. The only school Zanzucki believes in is the school of hard knocks. And you'll never get him away from that mother of his. Miss Peg's gonna have a fit when she hears about her boy's new love interest."

"There's nothing wrong with me."

Daniel answers. "Nobody's sayin' there is. But, honey, the boy's right on this one. Mrs. Zanzucki ain't gonna like the fact of you none. She's gonna want some big shot's daughter from Pittsburgh or Charleston for her boy. We're union trash to her."

"Union! I'm sick of union."

Ida emits a quiet fury not to be challenged. "All of you, just shut up. Lord knows, if this girl can . . ."

Everyone understands what is unsaid. The rest of the ride is completed in silence.

3 Moving into adolescence, Portia discovers this new stage of development has certain advantages. Adults don't credit her with deductive thinking and consequently are not careful of what they say. Listening to their conversations, she learns that most individuals flounder through life as confused as herself and without hormonal excuses.

Clambering around for an identity, she begins to borrow personality traits from others, not only threatening her own individuality but alienating the role models who sense her felony. She also develops the knack of thought control, finding that hard concentration can move a person to behave as she desires. Portia does not quite understand this trick but quickly sees that people sense the manipulation and she pays a coin in hostility.

Whetzel's bar is the forum for some of her best humanistic research. Originally a shanty, it was converted into a bar by a disabled miner. There are half a dozen like it scattered around town, but some spore visible only to miners has made Whetzel's the unofficial union watering hole. Fights long forgotten have shattered most of the windows, which have been replaced by battered beer signs. Coming in from the intense cold in the winter of '61, a man must adjust his eyes slowly to the dim light. The bar itself is a relic of the few Republic movies Portia has been allowed, a length of scarred wood polished by sliding mugs and supported by a brass footrail. The mirror running its length reflects decanters of booze: amber, white and russet, square and shapely, half-empty and full. Clusters of miners are thickly reflected in its smoke-hazed surface on weekends and at shift change.

Ida had started her daughter's trips to the bar when she used the time-honored ruse of sending her to shame Daniel into coming home. He responded by sitting her in the corner with a warm bottle of Coke until he was ready to leave. The next time she wandered in, Dan salvaged a cold bottle. Time had made her an accepted fixture, although her impending maturity would end such visits.

The union clientele is inbred, knowing what can be said to whom and most of a man's thoughts before they were spoken. Company men generally frequented places with a little more class because when a man became management, he needed visible reminders that his status had been improved. But on any typical day, if Whetzel's regulars weren't at home or at work, you could be reasonably sure they were ensconced in one of its murky corners. Daniel Crowe and his father, Tom, were regulars, either drinking together or with friends, talking union, hunting, cars, stud tires, and the subject that always comes up after a few drinks, layoffs.

The voices of fearless men were underlaid with fear when they spoke of joblessness. Times were strange. Coal demand had risen but not enough to give miners any confidence in tomorrow. For every man with a job, there was another one looking. These either hung around the bars or disappeared to Cleveland, Detroit, or any of the other outports of Appalachia. They came back for visits, bringing strange ideas. Sometimes they stayed when there was work, only to drift on again with layoffs: last hired, first fired. Portia heard coal cursed along with the people who owned it, some of the people who mined it, the Arabs, and those who had forsaken black gold for cleaner fuels. Much of this bitching occurred at Whetzel's, as the miners' wives wouldn't tolerate it at home, sick of hearing it and frightened of its possibilities.

Portia comes to know Tom, her grandfather, on this alien territory. A crease-stained pensioner whose eccentricities are accepted (breeding goldfish and collecting saltshakers, no pepper), he is infamous for his endless monologues, which most try to avoid. When Tom can't hold the attention of Dolly Sod, the bartender, or another unconditioned listener, he indulges himself with his granddaughter. Invariably he tries Dolly first.

"You know, I got this little grandkiddie here and she's a baby doll, but I ain't ever seen nothin' as cute as little baby turkeys."

Seeing it coming, Dolly frantically looks around for a patron needing attention.

"Now, that's a fact, Dolly. Took my gun out to Jordan Run the other day, lookin' to see somethin', and was all hunkered down under this stand of bushes when out they come. Six little turkeys struttin' onto a saplin' branch in front of me. And they was havin' a time, just like a bunch of kids. The ol' hen, she was a smart one. She knew I was there, so's she stayed under the ridge a bit. I could see her bouncin' around, keepin' an eye on them birdies. And they was carryin' on. . . ."

Moving down a patron or two, Dolly gives his head a shake to demonstrate his affection for Tom and his perception that the old man might not be dealing from a full deck. After his futile attempts to snare Dolly, Tom moves to Portia in her darkened corner behind the woodstove. The hand holding the shot glass has two fingers gone and his breath is heavy with whiskey.

"You know what they was doin', girly? They was jumpin' up and down, tryin' to break them little branches off. One of them fuzz balls would squat on a twig and take to chatterin' and carryin' on and they'd get the whole thing rockin', and it'd snap right off. Then they'd go to the next one. Cutest little devils . . . Most as cute as you, hon." He stretches a taut curl, allowing it to relax on his finger.

"You're gettin' to be a right pert little girly. Of course, I'm just your old granddaddie talkin', and there'll be plenty enough young bucks to tell you that, give a couple more years and a little more flesh. You get your red hair from me, in a manner of speakin'. I made your mum eat all them carrots when she was carryin' you and they went straight to your head."

He slugs what is left in the shot glass. "Don't mind me, hon. I got more shit than Carter has liver pills." Ambling back to the bar, he holds his glass up for Dolly's attention, leaving Portia with questions about red hair and Tom's participation in the birthing process.

Fighting talk was high that winter. Many of the new mines being punched into the Earth were scab holes, with high wages and few of the union safety rights. Bitter complaints to UMW Headquarters in D.C. brought little response; if anything, a form letter from the President full of legalistic garbage and signed with a rubber stamp. Trying to organize these mines, the men fell back on skills learned in whiskey-running days. A pistol could often persuade a reluctant scab to turn union, and if an owner toughed it out, his equipment was likely to meet an untimely end. Truckers were forced to dump their loads, and though this hijacking was usually done in remote areas, if the union men were sufficiently riled, the coal could become a roadblock in the middle of town. Pensioners immediately rallied with shovels and buckets at the chance for free fuel, and as the one policeman in Cogan's Bluff had three sons working union mines, he was disposed to look the other way. But despite a few successful skirmishes, the miners knew the war was being lost.

An hour or so after he was discoursing on baby turkeys, Tom is half a dozen whiskeys down and laying into the coal companies.

" 'Mountaineers are always free,' they say. Got it right up there on the state motto, writ in Latin. Shit! Free! You're free to leave, free to starve, and free to die. Them goddamn coal companies got all the other freedoms. They come from New York and such, drivin' big cars, buildin' slick roads we can do without, use our taxes, and then they mine us out. Work us till we die while they sit in some fat-cat office suckin' whiskey tits. Miners ain't ever gonna have shit till we have a say in what goes on in our mountains."

"What's left of 'em." A young miner speaks.

"They've destroyed most of them. Stripped 'em bare."

Strip mining brought a special anguish to these men so intimate with the Earth. Though not one of them could have been called an environmentalist without putting up a fight, they knew strip mining ate the guts of the land. Strip operations were generally scab, but the real indignity was the mutilated land and fouled streams.

Tom sometimes talked of the low coal he had worked in southern West Virginia where the thirty-inch seams required a man to lie on his belly and the only way to move was to crawl—through mud, muck, and death if need be. A man couldn't run when he couldn't stand.

When they talked of death, the litany began: Monongah, West Frankfurt, Centralia. Lost two brothers in that one. My father. Let me tell you how this leg got took. Call the roll. Gone. Gas. Fire. Cave-in. Damn machinery. Crushed. Burned. Mutilated. Suffocated.

Young miners personalized these losses. "We don't have to take this shit!" When they left Whetzel's or wherever, they were usually hunting their own justice and inflicting it relentlessly on the increasing number of scab miners and truckers. "Dump her, Bud." The Blue Diamond Department Store stocked ski masks year round.

Daniel's opposition to this strong-arming infuriated his father and confused loyalists at Whetzel's. At first they wrote it off to a whiskey brain, knowing the boy was as staunch union as old Tom. "Gettin' burnt out," they'd say. "Losin' it. Don't understand how things are." But now Cogan's Mill was very aware that Harriet was "keeping company" with young Zanzucki and miners had taken to watching their words around Daniel. Talk dropped off whenever he entered the bar. Fewer drinks were shared and some men moved if he sat next to them. While the situation embarrassed Robert and drove Tom crazy, Daniel was complacent, almost smug.

This Sunday being the last union meeting before Christmas, Local 1830's idealism has risen with their intake of holiday refreshment at the union hall. They arrive at Whetzel's early and Portia slouches back into a corner as her brother enters, knowing she will catch unshirted hell if he sees her. Daniel has been at the bar since after Mass and he is past giving a damn. Coal-stained bodies quickly fill the room and Dolly draws beer with both hands, letting bills and change stack on the bar.

"Herbert didn't show up today. He never misses a meeting."

"Didn't you hear?"

"What?"

"His ol' lady decided to get pregnant and he stayed home to get in on it."

"Shit."

"So, what are we goin' to do about those scabs of Wilson's?"

"Shut 'em down."

"Gonna take hard balls to get that bunch."

"We're the boys that got 'em."

Tom goads the youngsters on while his son stares into a flat beer, his lack of enthusiasm a blatant taunt.

"You wouldn't be knowin' about that, would ya,

Dan? Hear your daughter is sportin' around with Zanzucki's boy. She breedin' yet?"

Daniel continues to be transfixed by the lack of bubbles within his brew, adding a dash of salt for stimulation, and leaving Robert to deal with the slur. "You inferrin' something, Clyde?"

"I ain't got no quarrel with you, boy." He flashes a bill at Dolly. "Here. Set them up. The old man, too." Three mugs of beer slosh down the bar, stopping precisely in front of the Crowes, who ignore them. Clyde leans forward contemptuously.

"You see, boy, it's just that your daddie's way of thinking confuses some of us."

Daniel looks at the miner, spits into the proffered beer, and walks away. The miner's face flushes, veins exaggerated, as he yells at the departing back. "Crowe. C'mon back here. I'm tryin' to talk to you."

The bar's sudden silence momentarily disorients Clyde, but he is too far into it now. "Why don't you just explain yourself to the boy here, Danny. I'd sure be enlightened. I know you've been a union man some twenty years or so. We stood a lot of picket lines together. But you ain't makin' much sense these days."

Daniel walks toward him, albeit a bit unsteadily. "Clyde, I ain't gonna argue with you over bein' right about organizing. It's the union's lifeblood. And I don't owe it to you or no one else to be explainin' how I feel. But I'm gonna give you an idea.

"I've been a member of the United Mine Workers

of America for twenty-five years, so you're right about at least one thing, Clyde. I've been talkin' union for as long as you knowed me and long before you ever knew a number four from your asshole. Every goddamn mine in this country should be UMW. Right? Bet your ass that's right."

He pauses to draw on his beer and the silence holds for him.

"And it ain't nothin' but words. Ya gotta have somethin' behind those words, Clyde. Gotta have brotherhood behind them. Not this hate and destruction and killin' we got. You're making violence part of union law. You're sayin' it's all right to kill and destroy. You're old enough to know better, but our sons . . . My son is buyin' it. He's makin' violence a way of life and it will turn on him. It will destroy him."

Daniel steps back from the bar, visibly shaky. The men are grumbling, their rising voices steaming the mirror, prompting Clyde to become more vocal. But on his best day he would never have the old man's way with words.

"You sound awful goddamn holy for a man who swore by every word John L. ever spoke, Danny. I never saw no halo over that head."

"Nah. There wasn't no halo over that head, but there was a hell of a brain inside. He never did a thing without knowin' exactly where it was gonna take him. They say labor gets the union it deserves. Well, this fuckin' industry has tried to kill us for the better part of a hundred years, and John L. knew how to fight fire with fire. Even when I knew he was wrong, I supported him. And I support Tony Boyle because we elected him, even though the man's got a stink to him. But Clyde, by God, nobody elected you to nothin', so take your shit and pack it."

"I don't get your point, Dan. You think we ought to just bend our backs to those scabs and take their shit. That's what you're wantin', ain't it? You're gettin' old and you're tired and you've lost your pride, and what you're wantin' to be givin' your son is an easy way out."

Drink is having its way with the old man, warping his tongue with frustration. "I want my boy to be proud. And I want him deservin'. He ain't gonna be neither with the union we got today. You can smell fear on our boys. They're runnin' like animals. I'll tell you what I want. . . ."

"Fuck what you want, Mr. Danny." Fred Robinson, a man Crowe's own age, faces him off. "This ain't our war. Them coal companies started it. We didn't put guns over the portals; they did. But by God, we'll finish it and we can do that without the likes of you, a company-suckin' shit fartin' all this pretty stuff about brotherhood."

Daniel attempts a lunge at Robinson, stumbles, and Robert catches his shoulder, motioning to his grandfather. "Help me get him outa here, Tom."

"Oh, c'mon, boy. He ain't that drunk. I've seen him drunker. And that woman of his would kill me as soon as look at me. I expect you can manage. I gotta be gettin' back to Pansy."

As Robert looks futilely around the room for help, his eye catches Portia crouched behind the wood burner. She breaks for the door knowing she will have hell to pay at home.

4 The girl takes the hill at a run, grunting against gravity's pull, and slams the Crowe door to quiet the furies behind her. The kitchen is tranquil, heavy with the odor of boiling cabbage as Ida calmly proceeds with stirring and seasoning, unaware of the fast-approaching crisis.

"About time, girl. I need some help here and Harriet's still out somewhere with that boy. I can't keep track of her these days." This is obviously not a complaint. "Them males will be gettin' back from Whetzel's any time, probably in their cups and needin' something on their stomachs."

Hearing the faint edge of the din coming from Harlan Street, Portia edges strategically toward the steps.

"And where are you goin', missy? I just told you to help me."

"Gotta hang up my coat, Mum."

"Well, get right back here. I can't be doin' everything myself, despite what you all seem to think."

Portia is only halflistening, her attention on the voices beating against the kitchen door. A blast of cold air penetrates the stuffy kitchen and Robert comes in, supporting the old man. Ida's voice abruptly changes tempo, turning shrill.

"Not again, Daniel Crowe. Can't you leave that stuff alone, even for one day? Merciful Jesus, Mary, and

Joseph! Then staggerin' home for the whole town to see. Robert, you know to keep an eye on him."

The boy positions Daniel on the chair with blatant disgust. "He ain't the only one doin' the disgracin'. You should keep a better eye on your daughters, the both of them. Little Joey doesn't waste no time, does he? Harriet's out there neckin' like common trash. No better than a—"

"Robert!"

"You know the word, anyways. What would you have me call her? November and her out there lovin' that scab all up."

"You were the one told her keep him on the porch."

"I gave her credit for sense. She'd probably have her clothes off if it weren't for the weather."

"I'll tend to Harriet, Robert. You just watch your mouth in front of Portia."

"That one! Mama's little girl. She'll come to it soon enough. Hangin' round bars at her age."

Seeing Ida flinch, Robert pushes his advantage. "Hearin' God knows what kind of talk from them miners. Not to mention Pappy Tom down there crawlin' round like an ol' booze hound."

"Dan, has this girl been hangin' round that bar with you?"

The old man hangs up his jacket and muffler with great precision. "Well, Idee, you sent her there. Remember?"

"My God, that was once last year. Has this been goin' on since then? People will think I'm allowin' it. I'm shamed to show my face."

"There's no harm done. She stays quiet, which is more than can be said for most women. And I'm less afraid of what she'll hear at Whetzel's than the shit you ladies throw around the front room when your sodality meets in the name of the good God."

Ida's head sinks into her hands, a posture she affects when lesser efforts to control her home have failed. Daniel ignores the strategy while Robert throws up his hands in exasperation.

"Well, I've had enough of this shit. I'm movin' out."

"And just where would you be goin'?"

"To hell, I guess. I don't know. The boardin' house."

Ida resumes her slump in genuine horror, confronting the loss of a paycheck and, secondary, the possible corruption of her son. "That hellhole! Eatin' God knows what. Hangin' out with God knows who. Catchin' diseases from the toilet. And you talk about your sisters bringing shame. Merciful Jesus, Mary, and Joseph." The sob that follows is half rattle, half wheeze, and truly shakes the family. Robert kneels, encircling his mother with his arm.

"Ain't no other way, Mum. Harriet's gonna hang round with that scab even if you did try and make her stop. Which you won't. Dad . . . half the guys at the mine are harassin' me now because of him."

"Son, it'll kill me." Ida's pallor gives her melodramatic words credibility; still Daniel merely snorts as Robert helps his mother to her feet.

"Well, I can't stay here. I can't condone—"

"You can't what, boy!" The old man's lethargy vanishes. "You can't condone? Who are you to be condoning anything around here? I'm the son of a bitch who put this roof over your head. I did the work and the breedin', and believe me, neither one was easy. You just get the hell out. I don't have to apologize to those sorry bastards at Whetzel's, and I don't have to apologize to you, except maybe for bringin' you into this sorry world."

"I'm tired of you shittin' on me, old man."

Portia flinches, expecting her father to give him the back of his hand, and in drawing away, she touches damp jeans. Harriet stands in the stairwell. In the kitchen, Daniel is slackening from the battle, hands grinding at his temples. "All this yellin'. I'm getting a headache."

Ida takes her opening. "Yellin', is it, Daniel? Drinkin' is the problem, and me fightin' to keep food on the table. Drinkers never see their money. Then takin' this child to the saloon with you. You ain't got no decency, Dan. I've put up with a lot with you over the years, but you ain't draggin' Portia into your ways."

"You think you've put up with a lot over the years, Wife? C'mon. You've given me damn little to put up with. Why do you think I drink, Ida? There's always a reason. I drink to forget. I drink to get numb in my head so I can't feel what you won't let me use." Daniel balances himself against the table, a hand cupping his crotch. The others avert their heads as Ida visibly wilts. Seeing everyone immobilized, Portia takes matters into her own hands, throwing herself facedown into a puddle on the linoleum.

"Portia, baby." Ida pulls the girl up, wiping the

muddy smudges from her face. "Now, see what you've done, Daniel Crowe. You know she's high-strung, and yet you haul her around those drunken miners." Looking up, she sees her elder daughter cowering in the stairwell. "Harriet . . ."

"I don't care what any of you say about Joey. I'm going to see him whenever I can."

"Please, hon . . ."

"I'm not a little girl anymores and you can't stop me. I will not stay in this house with you all talkin' about him that way." Turning, she runs up the stairs and they hear bureau drawers opening and shutting. But no one takes this seriously. Harriet is fifteen. The world beyond Cogan's Mill is closed to her, and the world within won't open a door.

"Well, it's for sure I'm getting the hell out of here." Robert takes the steps in turn and there is a crash from above as he empties his suitcase of its stash of *Playboy*s. Daniel ignores the din, sipping the cabbage broth on the stove and smacking his lips. "Pretty tasty. Think a man could get something to eat around here?" He sits at the head of the table, regarding the two women detachedly. Ida walks to the stove, studies the mess congealing in the pot, leans over, and spits into it.

5 Portia uses books to dilute her pubescent disgust with humanity. Fictional characters are invariably interesting. If their life becomes tedious, the author obligingly supplies them with some relieving drama. And if one book doesn't satisfy, she can always shut the cover and choose another. Saturdays are spent at the library, an imposing structure of Doric pillars and fierce gargoyles at the opposite end of town. The grilles on the building's windows are not to protect it from desperate residents who might break in during the night to steal a copy of Wolfe or Twain. Rather, the structure was once a bank erected by a calculating optimist who believed the town was bound to grow to the west and that when it did, he would have a central location. His plan was foiled by Wall Street's demise, and by the time Roosevelt got things going again, grass was growing between the cracks of the marble steps.

Twenty years later, the silent brooding wife of one of the mine foremen died in strange circumstances, having slit her wrists over a copy of *Main Street*. She bequeathed the town a surprisingly large number of books through her husband (who wanted them out of the way). The Jaycees put them into the bank building and opened its doors. Gradually the library was expanded, supplementing whatever education students had inadvertently received in school, but most days Portia has the building pretty much to herself.

As a child she had entertained herself during these ambulatory excursions by lowering her eyes and navigating according to the sidewalk. The first stretch of path was packed dirt, littered with beer cans and gum wrappers. The debris thickens at Westfall's corner store, where mothers send kids to pick up that odd item they've forgotten at the supermarket. Like most miners' families, the Crowes have a charge account there to tide them over the last few days before a pay.

Next came downtown, marked by cracked cement pavements splotched with brown spittle. This was followed by precise diagonal bricks fringed with grass tufts. Suddenly the grass was trimmed, and if Portia counted to two hundred, she was in front of the library.

Older now, and at fourteen, beyond the ways of a child, she has altered the game, studying the homes she passes and pondering the lives of the people within. The stately edifices at the other end of town are particularly fascinating, heavy of brow and long of porch, mantled with crusted towers and gables. The architects of the Nineties would say they made a statement, and make it they did. The precision of lawns is marred only by gazebos and statuary. At one time, most of the front gates had been guarded by little black boys encased in cement and jockey attire, clutching lanterns and hitching rings. Moses Redman, a black miner, had liberated these sentinels one evening after he left Whetzel's armed with a Lou Gehrig slugger and a substantial amount of Stroh's. Moses got away with decapitating his brothers because a hard rain was coming and most of the elite were engrossed in their six o'clock repast behind drawn curtains. Trudging home from the library, Portia had gratefully accepted a ride from the man who interrupted his work to save her from a drenching and explained en route that he didn't take kindly to his kin standing in mute sentry before the houses of fat-cat company scabs. Their secret was always good for a Coke and a grin from Moses whenever he saw her. The fat cats got the message and the sentries were replaced by plaster deer, though these proved a hazard for estates on the town's fringes when they were stalked by frenzied miners during hunting season. Moses kept the Lou Gehrig behind the seat of his truck for years, being prone to shatter a lawn ornament on occasion.

The Zanzucki abode is at the bottom of the street where some of the older mansions have been torn down to make room for a bevy of split-levels supported by hollow columns. The patches of grass mottling its sooty yard are broken by grazing flamingos and an undecided tree. Portia always lowers her eyes when passing, offended by its gaucheness.

The librarian, Edith, greets her as one of the chosen. Edith is another stereotype that flourish in small towns, seeming elderly, frumpish, and imbued with a vestal virgin's dedication to guard the realm of literature. Portia figures her to be seventy if a day, and years later, reading her obituary, finds that when Portia was fifteen the librarian was thirty-six. The woman frequently warns her protégé of the dangers of becoming addicted to books.

"You can't be thinkin' life's like what you find in books," she'd say. "Too much reading spoils a person." Picking up a ruler, she whacks a volume for emphasis.

"There's intensity in books. Has to be to keep your attention. You get used to being on the edge. But life's not like that. Life can't hold your interest and that makes for depression. Suicide."

Whap!

"Life's a bore."

Whap!

"And then, when you run out of books, that's it."

She lets this statement dangle ominously, ruler aloft. Portia finally gets the nerve to ask her what exactly will happen if she runs out of books.

"Different folks takes to different things. Some drinks. Some smokes that marijuana. Some get religion. Some even die. It's all frustration, one way or another. Everydayness starts eating at you and you've got to find something to do with your mind to take away the sharp edges. Elsewise they cut right through you."

Whap!

"Did you ever think about writing a book?"

"Of course, dear. Everbody's got a book in them. I probably got several. And I'll get on with them someday. Just like everybody gets on with everything. The trick with writing is you have to do it. You learn what's inside your head by putting it down on paper and sticking with it. Most folks find that too hard. They don't have the discipline and they don't like what they write. Another problem is we're latecomers. Most of the good words have already been used. Shakespeare. Agee. Willa Cather. Hard to find good stories, good words."

"How do you know what to write?"

"Words come unbidden. They come in dreams or sometimes they get locked into your head, like someone reciting to you. You may not always like what you hear, but write it down anyways. I keep a notebook by my bed. Use the thoughts in letters if nothing else."

"Would you write me if I left?"

"Sure. I'd put you on my list." They both know she would never write. "Now move on, girl. I gotta get these books on the shelves. Look at the way they come back." She eyes Portia accusingly. "Tore up. Pages gone. Underlining. Ice cream on this one, if not something worse. Town doesn't deserve a library." She regards the young woman, severity fading into wistfulness. "Start yourself a diary, miss. That's the way to get into steady writing."

For a while Portia religiously keeps a journal in a marble-backed copybook. The "while" is about a week. She misses a day. Then a couple. Then she forgets about it. The predictable repetitiveness of her life depresses her when put on paper. Besides, there are still enough books to go around.

Usually Portia leaves the library early on these December Saturdays when one can sense the night shifting in on a four o'clock dusk. Sometimes the old man stops to pick her up on his return from a weekend shift.

Daniel has seemed hollow lately. The weather has been hard and the mine's damp clings long after he gets home. A soak in a hot tub generally sets him to rights, after which he sits in front of the TV, spooning down soup with brandy chasers, nodding and then wakening to hack up black soot.

"You're asleep, Dan." Ida prods him. "Why don't you go up to bed?"

He jerks from a half-dream. "Don't be crazy, woman. If I sleep now, I'll toss all night." For a few moments he stares at the TV without comprehension, nodding until the next round of coughing. As he predicts, the times he does go to bed early, the coughing is worse and he returns downstairs, sitting in front of the television until the last sermonette is over.

Today, seeing him waiting for her outside, Portia knows her father is hurting, hunched over the wheel, red eyes rimmed with soot. Miner's mascara, they call it. He has stopped at Whetzel's to pick up a pint for himself and a Coke for her, much of which he will use as a chaser. "Eases my coughin'," he explains, lowering the bottle. "Eases a lot of things." Daniel solemnizes the moment with another swig, and the two of them ride wrapped in their quiet world of car and weather. Worn wipers scrape companionably. Worn tires flatten the slush. Downtown the Salvation Army kettles tinkle. Christmas decorations are weighted with wet snow and the annual holiday countdown to cheer is on as shoppers duck from store to store in panic. Portia starts thinking about necessary gifts and stops when she gets to Harriet.

"What's Mr. Zanzucki like, Dad?"

"You've never met him?"

"Nope."

"No. No, I guess you haven't."

Daniel checks his rearview mirror and sneaks another nip. Home does not appear a pressing matter, so he meanders aimlessly through the holiday streets. "Well, Steve is okay, but don't go repeating that. I don't want my butt strung up. He's always treated me right."

"So why all the talk about him?"

"Just talk."

"An awful lot of talk."

"Steve Zanzucki is pretty much the man on the spot around here. We live off coal; he bosses the biggest coal mine. He's gotta get the coal or the company's on his ass and we can't cover ours. The superintendent is supposed to be in charge, but he ain't around much. Paperwork, Blanchard says. Pittsburgh business. When you need something done or have a bitch, Zanzucki's the man. But then, if he gets too rough with the men, they either slow down or strike. If he doesn't get rough enough, it's his ass. That's a fine line to toe. And God help you if the man comes looking for you. He's got a temper. That's his biggest problem. He can't handle people. Loses it. Gets arrogant. Steve knows mining, all right. He's got a real feel for the underground, more so than any man I've worked for. He knows the contract, its loopholes and how to use them, and believe me, hon, there's hells of them."

"Is he smarter than union people?"

"A good union man, and I mean a good one . . ." He hesitates. "Like your brother. He knows the contract as good as Zanzucki and maybe some better. The union has to depend on it more. But Steve has the company behind him and all we've got is some half-assed know-it-alls. The contract doesn't mean dogshit, anyways. It's just words, and words mean different things to different people. Every time a union man files a grievance and loses, the contract is rewritten against us. And we lose most of them. Can't afford the high-priced lawyers the company can. I guess Zanzucki is as fair as most. Any of them will risk a man's life for a piece of coal."

A rare mood of relaxation pervades the vehicle, binding Portia and her father in a sense of their sameness. Portia is fully aware of her status as Daniel's favorite. He cannot afford the emotional cost of expressing overt affection for her siblings. Robert and he are caught up in some macho pissing match distinct to males that she doesn't quite understand. Harriet is beyond his ken, a female of the old school, strictly programmed in womanly conventions that he can appreciate but not understand. He finds no solace in Ida, who has spurned all emotional ties. Indifference gives her control. Portia's youthful androgyny alone allows him to express the frustrated love that can find no outlet.

Daniel's mind has evidently been dwelling on his progeny. "I hope Harriet and that boy don't get serious. I'm getting enough shit from the union as it is. Most of them just think in black and white, if they think at all. They've been in the mines so long they wouldn't know daylight if it fell on them."

Daniel indicates that the conversation is over by flicking on the radio, and they listen to carols as he nips on the last of the pint. The cough has eased and his eyes have taken on a bit of the devil, a sure sign he is feeling no pain, laughing, full of himself and the season, driving over back roads unfamiliar to the girl.

"Did I tell you about Pinhead Bode? He's a crazy one. Seems he caught himself a rattler a few years back. The way he tells it, snakes freeze up in the winter, then come alive again in the summer. So Bode puts this rattler in his Deepfreeze, and every so often he takes it out, gives it something to eat, and then refreezes the critter. Says it bit his hand last year and that was why he was off two weeks. Hell, I'd bite him too if I had to put up with that kind of treatment.

"Anyways, they had a power failure over his way last week, and they forgot about the Deepfreeze. When they got to opening it, everything was thawed, including the snake. The critter got the hell out of there and they can't find him nowheres. I figured he's holed up, just waitin' to strike ol' Bode. That'll be a hell of a Christmas present."

Portia takes her opening. "I know what I want for Christmas."

"We still have to get past your birthday next week."

"I hate having a birthday that close to the holidays. You get overlooked 'cause everyone's plannin' ahead about what they're getting you for Christmas. Think you and Mum could have had a little consideration in your timing."

His raspy lungs emit a scrapy sound akin to a chuckle. "You'll be learnin' about timing soon enough.

Anyways, your mother's taken care of your birthday present."

"Yeah. I can imagine. Something 'feminine.' "

"Be nice about it, Portia. I'll see what I can come up with for Christmas. What would you like?"

"I want to go underground."

"The mines! You're crazy, woman. It's bad enough goin' down there to make a livin', let alone makin' a tourist trip. The mines, my ass."

"I want to see them."

"What the hell for?"

She frames a diplomatic reply. "I want to see where you work."

"Hon, I just can't do it. They'd fire my butt quick for takin' a kid underground."

"Jed Rinker's dad snuck him in."

"Yeah, but he wasn't a female. You're bad luck."

"Nobody believes that anymore."

"The hell they don't. Men won't work if they know there's been a woman underground."

"That's stupid."

"Maybe, but it's a fact. Miners got strange thoughts on women. A hundred years ago, up in Pennsylvania, they used women like mules pullin' coal cars up the tracks from down under. Males and females . . . they got a hard enough time livin' together. Put them together in the mines and it don't work. There's no woman can take that physical shit. The shovelin', liftin', and such. Let alone the talk, and just about everything else. If those boys want to take a piss, they just whip it out in front of you."

"How dark is it?"

"Portia, I've told you all this before."

"Is it like night?"

"Night! Girl, you ain't ever seen black till you've been in a coal mine. Out here, in the world, there's always a bit of light even when there isn't a moon. But underground, when a man turns off his cap light, he can stir the blackness with his hand.

"And the smell of it. Coal smell is like nothin' else. The sulfur gathers up your nose. Cool-like. Musty. Gets sharper at the face."

"Face?"

"That's the head of the entry, the front of the tunnel where the men are actually mining. The face moves forward as the men dig deeper.

"And then there's the rock dust . . . white limestone powder they throw around to keep the dust down. It's like walkin' through a snowstorm when they start throwin' that stuff around. Sticks to the ribs. Sticks to the miners. Their lungs. When the damp gets to it, resembles snot more than anything else."

"Why do you have to worry so much about the dust? They told us at school they don't even have it in England."

"Must be a civilized country. Here they don't care whether a man breathes or not as long as they get their pound of coal, and it's quicker just to go for it than to worry about fightin' the dust. A man says too much about breathin', they find a reason to bust him. Dust can coat a man's lungs and kill him that way or it can cause an explosion. Get too much dust in the air, hit a pocket of methane, and one spark is all it takes to blow. Bad wiring or some fool goin' for a smoke will do it. The spark hits the right mixture of gas and dust, and everything goes up in one sheet of flame—a fireball, they call it. A man would never know what hit him. Ain't none lived to talk about it."

"Can't the men do anything?"

"Government's made the companies issue what they call a self-rescuer, a metal container that fastens onto your belt. If there's gas around, you spring the face mask and wear it. What it does is change the poisonous carbon gas into harmless. The gadget might give you a little extra time to get into clear air."

"How can you tell when there's gas?"

"The foreman wears a bug light, a small lantern contraption he carries on his belt. If the crew runs into gas, the flame caps, folds over on itself. Then a man knows to run like hell. Miners move so fast they almost catch up with the rats."

"Rats?"

"Yeah. It's the damnedest thing about mine rats. They can sense an explosion or roof fall. Maybe it's vibrations we can't feel. But when you see rats goin' for the pit mouth, you'd best be right behind them."

"Aren't you ever scared?"

"Portia, a man who tells you he ain't scared in the mines is either a fool or a liar. You don't want to work with him. What with gas, the top crackin' over your head, and machinery eatin' men up, you gotta be scared to stay alive. Workin' in a hole underground ain't natural. The weird thing is you get likin' it, cravin' it. And that's when it's got you. Coal fever, they call it—havin' the dust in your lungs, your body scarred, arthritis eatin' your bones. It's goin' against the nature of things, goin' into places God never intended for man to go. Humans upset the balance of things when they go to mining, and if a man don't get a little scared thinkin' about that, he ain't much for brains."

As they head into Harlan Street, Daniel stashes his empty under the seat, slowing the car to avoid the kids sleigh-riding on the hill, where the froth of Christmas glitters on doors and windows. He comes round to open the door for Portia as she gathers her books, a subtle tribute to her evolving womanhood, and then, to reestablish the fading order of things, throws her into a snowbank. A curtain flinches inside the house, and he straightens abruptly. "Guess I'll catch it now, girl. Anyways . . ." He rubs a handful of snow into her hair. "Don't go worrying about me. The mines ain't gonna get this old body. It just ain't gonna happen that way." A cast slides over his eyes, veiling them with a caul of knowing. He blinks and the moment passes. But they are aware of knowledge shared.

6 The Crowe family makes one last floundering attempt to function as a unit at Christmas when Robert "drops by" to eat of Ida's fattened calf. The women folk bustle around the kitchen while Daniel and he closet themselves with the TV. Preening after his mother's effusive welcome, Robert cannot resist the opportunity to harangue his father.

"What'd the company give the men for Christmas this year, Dad? Heard they went all out." He knows full well workers were presented with a bag of stale hardtack candies and a shriveled orange. Most of the miners scorn the gesture.

Ida's edict for peace holds the old man at bay. "Somebody in the office must have pocketed a little on that one. Usually they're pretty decent for the holiday."

"Yeah. I remember last year. Moldy fruitcake. Christ, Dad. Don't you ever get tired of covering for those bastards?"

"You know what your trouble is, boy? You only see what you want to see, which ain't very damn much. Listen to some of those stories the pensioners tell. That hardtack was usually the only thing their kids got for Christmas."

"Shit, Dad. Every time the company pulls something, you trot out those old shits to tell us how easy we got it. Why don't you just buy stock? I keep tryin' to tell you. The only thing those boys understand is when we shut 'em down."

"Maybe you can help me there, son. There's a few things about this strikin' I don't understand. When we pull out, the coal's still in the ground. Right? Still where the company can get to it. That power plant we ship to has enough coal stockpiled for three months. So the union pulls everyone out on one of its big strikes and what happens? We wait months for a paycheck, and when we get it, it's half of what it should be. And the coal's still there, waitin' for us to dig it. We go back to work. We never catch up. We're just a little more slaves to the wage than we was before your strike. Hey, it's great, ain't it? Big union strike! Go ahead and talk it up, Robert. One thing for sure. Whatever they're feedin' you at that boardin' house, it ain't brain food."

Portia listens, understanding that at this point the two of them are more caught up in mutual abuse than argument. She tries to interrupt with a comment about the quality of the eggnog, but they aren't about to let her sidetrack them into sanity. Take a walk, she tells herself, and proceeds to do so.

As with most child-people, Portia has her "spot," a place her grandfather has taken her and which she uses as a retreat when she's restless or troubled. The cluster of black pine rises on a plateau high above the town, and today their winter aridness contrasts sharply with the house's stifling warmth. Stark trees are lushly full in dusk's half-light. The mountain self-consciously gathers weighted snowflakes into itself, their dance swollen with a grace one sees only at Christmas. She moves slowly behind the cloud of her breath, then stands motionless, willing herself part of the scene.

About fifty yards away an old buck is browsing among the drifts and misses her completely until he moves downwind. Then, catching a human scent, he snorts and stamps, scattering his harem. Five . . . six whitetails soar aloft, lost in winter's mottle. For a while she lets the quiet hold her, settling into it. A crow calls a brittle warning. Rabbit spores mark the trail.

Suddenly her name is sounded. Once, spoken clearly above her. A call not unfriendly, not threatening, but a call to some confrontation. Her fear is not knowing what. She looks to the pine trees silently shifting with the wind. Nothing. Yet the syllables still ring. Portia breaks quickly for home.

She slams the kitchen door for reassurance. Ida is comfortably ensconced over the stove.

"Don't go to banging. I've got a cake in the oven and I need some help here. All this work so's they can eat it up in five minutes, and then there's the clearing to do." Her hands move purposefully within gloves of eggs and bread crumbs, their rhythm causing her pin curls to totter at odd angles.

"Where's Harriet?"

"Don't try to sidetrack me, missy. She's in there tryin' to get the tree finished before Joey gets here. And why we can't get the tree up before Christmas like normal people, I'll never understand. Most folks . . ."

Portia is gone.

She finds Harriet in the living room immersed in dusty boxes, unwrapping ornaments from their tissue cocoons.

"I thought you said I get to decorate the tree this year?"

"You'll only make a mess of it."

"I like my mess." Portia despises the whine in her voice but can't control it.

"It was bad enough with you just helping last Christmas. Look, we'll do it this way. Let me get things started. Then you can do some."

Harriet uses questionable high-school geometry to decorate the tree: lights precisely seven inches apart; one ornament per branch, icicles regimental. She graciously extends a handful to her sister. "Now, just don't go pitching them on in clumps."

"Doesn't matter how I do it, you're gonna bitch. You can stick them . . . someplace."

Shrugging, Harriet turns to the task at hand and misses seeing Portia kick the box labeled MANGER under the couch.

The old man wanders into the room, and by the look of him, he's had enough of the holiday also.

"Grab a coat, Portia. We're outa here."

"But Mum needs me—"

"I don't give a shit. Someone may as well enjoy the day. We got our own Christmas party scheduled, the one you asked me about, and we'd best check it out. Take this slug of brandy. You'll be needin' somethin' to warm your insides."

The liquor smells foul and Harriet moves to her elbow. "Don't you dare," she hisses, immediately prompting Portia to imitate the best style of Whetzel's professionals. After a delayed two-second reaction in which she thinks the old man has given her acid, she gags her way to the surface, coughing furiously. Daniel is laughing, the first Christmas-like sound of the day. He wears an old hunting jacket with a mackintosh rolled up under one arm, lantern in hand.

"C'mon, woman. Let's move."

She is quiet during the ride to the mine site, fearing talk will sober him to reconsideration. He follows the access road, avoiding the familiar ruts, and slows up as they reach an older side road. Stopping beside a slag-covered slope, the old man reaches under the seat for the inevitable flask.

"I know I don't have to be tellin' you not to mention this little excursion, Portia. I'd get my ass fired and your mother would kill what was left of me."

"Where are we?"

"A side road leadin' to an old entrance where they cut number four too close to the surface. Here. Get these on."

She puts the mackintosh over her battered army jacket, tucking hair into a ski cap and feet into rubbers.

"I forgot gloves, but you can wash up somewheres before we get home."

Portia studies the gap in the mountain dubiously. "Doesn't look like much."

"Isn't really. Just where some fool got carried away

runnin' the miner and ran onto the surface. They told us to leave it that way. Thought it might make a good escapeway, though, praise God, we've never had to use it for such. But many's the tool been pilfered out here. It don't get much use these days, even for thievin'. Most everybody's forgot about it except a few of us old-timers. Sometimes we sneak a lunch break out here; do a little ginsangin'."

The musk leaking from the hole is the same one that clings to the old man's clothes of an evening. He kicks the blackened snow from the entrance and lowers himself feet first into the cavity, reaching up to help Portia.

"Easy now. It's fallen in."

Black dampness sucks her downward. Momentarily she is dislocated, unbalanced. Alice down the proverbial rabbit hole. Daniel flicks on the lantern and its beam dissolves into a soft aurora that merges with the blackness. One can sense "things" drifting through the crosscuts.

He surveys the void proudly. "This is it. What do you think?"

She replies with the obvious. "It's dark."

"Dark! Hell, you haven't seen nothin' yet." He shuts off the lantern.

A black hole, the minus side of oblivion.

A steady drip extends eternity.

Outside a razor wind whips.

Nothingness.

Portia gropes, finding her father's sleeve, clutching. His laughter gloats eerily, and he switches the lantern back on. The eyelid has blinked.

As her vision adjusts, Portia sees the mine's ribs aren't completely black but coated with white mucus. Daniel runs a finger through the slime, extending a blob to her. The gunk drips through his fingers.

"Old rock dust. Dry powder when we throw it on, but the moisture turns it to slime."

"Is the whole mine like this?"

"Similar. These are the old workings. Mined out. We use them for ventilation or an occasional shit. Be careful where you walk. Most men throw a rag over their leavings, so try not to step on any. We'll go down to my section where we're mining. The equipment's there."

They walk. Daniel seems to know one dark alleyway from another, but to Portia the endless black tunnels meandering right and left are the same, a labyrinth filled with discarded spools, greasy rags, and empty tins lying under a pall of dampness and rock dust. Grimy tatters of cloth whisper from the top.

"What's that?" She finds herself whispering.

"Old brattice cloth. Used for ventilation. When you run coal, you have to keep an air flow across the face to move the dust. If brattice is hung in the right places, it can send the air where you need it. Keeps gas from buildin' up when it's done right. Which ain't too damn often."

Sections become neater as they move toward the face, the brattice hanging yellow and whole. Thick cables snake along the ribs above and below. A conveyor belt languishes on rollers waiting for a load of coal to carry outside. The section itself resembles Bela Lugosi's rec room, squatting machines hovering in the gloom. Portia cannot imagine humans functioning here. The people who work these subterranean passages would have translucent skin and opaque eyes. When they speak, their voices would be as hollow and distant as their thoughts.

A faint hum from the distance transfixes the area. "What you're hearin' is the transformer, kind of a small power station that relays electric from the outside to the underground. The men sleep on it when they get the chance. A stupid thing to do because if the thing blows, they're fried eggs. But most foremen pay it no mind. When a man gets miserable enough, wet and cold, death don't look so bad in the face of a little comfort. Some of the boys set their lunches there to warm them up."

Beneath the hum a sucking sound works the blackness. "A pump chuggin' down there. Gotta keep them in the faces 'cause we're mining downhill and water tends to collect. That one doesn't sound like it's drawin' right, though. They shoulda sent someone in to check it. Mine's muddy enough without it floodin' over the holidays."

Daniel strides to the huge machine hulking at the face and strokes it with a proprietary air. "And this is my baby. The miner. She keeps the operation going." Stretching beneath his hand, the machine seems to purr, expanding teethlike bits mounted on a huge cylinder. The old man has explained to her how the bits eat into the coal, gouging the mineral from the seam and dumping into a shuttle car. These underground "Mack trucks" carry the coal to the main conveyor belt, which in turn relays it outside to the tipple and processing plant.

"Pops, you really handle that thing?"

"Child, I love it. She's part of me. I talk to her, coax her into cuttin' like she should. Nothin' else I'd rather be doin', despite my bitching."

"And you're pretty damn good at it too, Danny, though you sure can play the fool."

Portia and her father pivot as one. A man's short squat figure beneath hard hat and cap light leans casually against the shuttle car. The beam on his cap plays over the length of her mackintosh. "Christ, Crowe! You ain't got the sense God gave a jackass. Are you lookin' to get fired on Christmas? Bringin' a woman down here. A kid even. Booze eat away what little brain you did have?"

Portia's thoughts crystallize and then frantically begin to circulate, but the old man doesn't seem that perturbed. "Ah hell, Zanzucki. She's been buggin' me to see the mines, wanted to see where I worked, and I didn't see any harm in it. I know you brought that boy of yours under."

He grunts, studying the girl as she studies him. So this was Steve Zanzucki. Her preconceptions of a superman, an intimidating individual wreaking havoc, dissolve. He seems merely an oversized leprechaun, a small frame highlighted by crinkle-bright eyes beneath his hard hat.

"Your wife know about this?" He motions toward Portia.

"Hell, no, and my health depends on her not finding out. This here is my youngest. Her sister is keepin' company with your boy. Portia, this is Mr. Zanzucki."

He lightly touches his hard hat in deference. "Miss Portia, you may be the nicest bit of work your father's ever done, but you still don't belong in here."

"It's only this once, Steve, and ain't hurtin' any-body. What the hell are you doin' in here, anyways?" Portia and the man catch each other's amused eye at Daniel's attempt to sidestep the issue, and she knows suddenly things are going to be okay. The man is letting her father maneuver.

"I figured on takin' the day off, but . . . well, things at home got a little rocky. Peg and Christmas cheer aren't always compatible. You know about that. I figured this pump would need checking and it got me out of the house. Now I'm gonna have to waste another day ex-plainin' to somebody what you thought you were doin' bringin' a woman down here. I can understand you want-in' your kid to see where you work, and I'll cover your ass like you're countin' on me to, but the two of you had better keep your mouth shut. If the men hear about this and walk out, it'll be both our butts down the road and I'll be kicking yours with my steel-toe boots."

"Ah, Steve, I know it was a fool stunt, but neither me nor the girl will say anything."

"Well, since you're here, how's about takin' a look at that pump with me. Just don't expect me to turn it in for double time for you." He turns his attention to Portia. "How old's this one, Dan?"

"Just turned fifteen. Almost a Christmas baby."

"Well, she's a spirited little lady for sure. And gettin' a bit prime. Doesn't favor her sister much. Looks kinda like you but she wears it better."

Portia is getting a bit irritated at being discussed in the third person. "Joey's okay-looking. Does he favor his mother?"

"My, my. She's got your mouth sure enough. Yes, ma'am, I expect he does, seein' as how he's not cursed with my movie-star face. . . . Let's get on this pump, Dan."

The trio trudge through mud and sump holes, ducking the power cables snaking the ribs and cuts.

"I'll give you a Christmas present, Danny. Why don't you take the whole damn mine. I'm sick of all this shit."

"Givin' me the paycheck that goes with that?"

"Ha! Between what I give the old lady and the government, a man could make more jerkin' off hoboes—" He catches himself. "Sorry there, Miss Portia."

"Nothin' she ain't heard before. She don't miss much."

"That ain't necessarily a good thing in a woman."

They crawl under the belt, legs deep in black mud. Thick gunk oozes between her fingers as she scrapes it off hands and encrusted jeans. Portia tries to follow the belt with her eyes into the heavy distance, only to have Zanzucki push her down. "Careful now. That thing ain't movin', but you never know when some fool will throw the switch." His hand supports her elbow, a disconcerting gesture from a man described as the epitome of toughness. Portia watches him and her father tinker with the pump, their backs curved in the dark gloom, shoulders taut beneath overalls. When the machine comes alive, they walk back to the opening.

"Think I'll step out with you and check the weather." Zanzucki follows her through the hole, lightly landing on his feet. "Bit nippy out here."

Daniel grins at the foreman. "I got a little somethin' in the car that will warm us up."

"Hell. It's Christmas, ain't it?" Daniel hurries to the vehicle, moving quickly. A little too quickly, she thinks, angry at the both of them for his unseemly haste.

"Your old man is somethin' else." They walk toward the steaming car.

"Yeah. That's what my mom says."

"So what did you think of the mine?"

"I don't know what I think. I liked it and I was scared. It was like Pop said but it wasn't."

"Yeah. It's a world to itself, all right."

He opens the car door for her and she sits quietly in the back, studying his slouch. When he removes his hard hat, the air is shattered by a mantle of graying hair extending to the furrows on his brow. The man's face is too weathered for such excesses of hair.

"How old are you, Mr. Zanzucki?"

He laughs, turning to her. "Must be the first time you've seen this head. Well, hon, the money I have to put out on haircuts keeps me broke enough so's I don't get into trouble."

Daniel frowns at her in the rearview mirror. She gets the message, settling back to study the still-falling snow as the two men pass the pint back and forth, saying little. Her father fumbles with the radio and the occasional voices of the men drift back to her beneath Christmas carols. They finally get down to offering each other the final swig, and after extended polite bickering and on the basis of protocol, Zanzucki takes it. On its strength he turns to study Portia.

"She don't say much, Danny."

They were doing it again, talking as if she weren't there.

"Maybe Joey ought to settle back a few years and wait for this one."

"I don't know if the boy could handle her. Harriet's a bit milder."

"You may be right. Joe . . . he ain't much for a challenge." He shrugs. "Maybe Harriet can do somethin' with the boy. I never could teach him nothin'." Digging into his overalls, he pulls out a handful of stickers worn by miners on their hard hats as reflectors, visible in the dark. "Here." He extends them to Portia, watching her. "A little souvenir. Go ahead. You can use them to tattoo baby dolls or somethin'."

Knowing she is being patronized, Portia ignores the look in her father's eye that says she'd better take them. Zanzucki pitches them into her lap and fumbles with the door handle.

"You never did tell me how old you were, Mr. Zanzucki."

"You always ask old men how old they are?"

"I don't usually think about it."

"I'm between thirty and forty."

"Your head doesn't look old."

His eyebrows rise, lifting the weight of his hairline. "Danny, I don't know about this one. And I ain't got time to figure her out now. I gotta get back to walkin' those faces." He opens the car door and disappears back through the rabbit hole.

7 Despite her best intentions, Portia grows. She matures, adults say, and experiences the standard adolescent rage that surges when she is told her muddled thinking is hormonal, a teenage rite of passage. Particularly when those making this casual observation have reduced their allotted fourscore-and-ten to a time line with categorized slots for puberty, menopause, and senility. Their emotional quirks are justified. Truth is incidental. "Grown-ups" have comfortably adjusted their sights, seeing only what they want. Grown-ups cheat.

Teachers especially piss her off. They are teases, the ones supposed to know; the ones flaunting promises and possibilities they then deny. She wastes much of her legitimate schooling trying to maneuver them into giving her what she needs to know. Either they don't understand or they don't have the answers. Portia's cynicism overlooks her parents. They are victims of circumstance, of which she is one. Her peers she considers casualties. They've bought into the game. And with the special anger one reserves for successful siblings, she resents Harriet for being such a good player.

Her sister now flashes Joey's diamond chiplet across the sundries counter of the Blue Diamond Department Store, where she works after school, and autumn sends young Zanzucki off to plow through his first year of mining technology at the university. Harriet's meager salary allows her to accumulate a clutter of household gadgets that have crowded Portia from their attic room, and she begins to spend long hours in Robert's chilly cubbyhole over the porch, gradually moving in with his discards, which Ida refuses to remove.

Among them, her brother has left smoldering copies of the *Mineworker's Journal.* Portia spends many of the evenings of that dank winter studying these yellowed copies of the Gospel of Union in what little bland light filters through the sooted windows. The coal-thumbed contract pamphlet that has been thrown into a corner in frustration is still beyond her ken. Like so many miners, Robert always carries the Agreement underground, hiding it beneath his shirt to have at hand. Posted over the bureau is a newspaper clipping of the Robena widows, who watch her with glassy eyes she has yet to comprehend. Discarded leather mining boots sit in the corner, replaced by rubber steel-toes when management attempts to "correct" young Crowe's attitude by putting him to work in a mudhole. Other working conditions are reflected in the pile of thermal underwear molded with oil and sweat. The man's physical condition can be diagnosed by empty containers of aspirin, Rolaids, and Sominex.

On sleepless nights she sits at the window, studying the motor lights shuttling along supply routes, the tiny flicker as a miner grabs a quick smoke. The tipple's roar makes strange harmony with the midnight Angelus bells. The air crackles with frigid brittleness softened only by the thin plumes of smoke demarcating the town's streets.

A train's whine sears the dawn, reminding her that arteries to another world do exist and most of them because of coal. While the Earth graciously allows miners to hack a living from her, she remains an unpredictable mistress. The women understand her female temperament better than their men and consequently are more wary of her power. Portia's lesson comes hard.

The cold February evening is as usual. A reluctant Harriet complains as Ida drags her to a sodality meeting, leaving Portia to pack her father's bucket. Feeling morosely adult, she stretches the bologna and bread for the extra sandwich routinely packed by miners' wives to help their man's chances if he is trapped underground. She reads no meaning beyond tradition into the chore. Obviously the unthinkable will never happen.

Daniel is on night shift that week and he is predictably in an unpredictable mood. "Man don't know when to eat, when to sleep, when to shit." The family carefully works its life around him, keeping the silence, ignoring mealtimes. Now he moves through a groggy haze, taking his bucket, kissing his daughter absently before leaving. Portia sleeps soundly that night, bored by a grisly book of Robert's, and when she is roused by Ida's groping hand, thinks the plot is continuing.

A stark dawn has stripped her mother's face of flesh, pooled her eyes into cold agates of shock. She claws her dream-wrapped daughter into wakefulness, pushing her toward the steps. Portia watches the woman plod aimlessly around the kitchen before finally turning the flame on under the coffeepot. Then she slumps onto a chair, suddenly stilled except for the fingers worrying her rosary.

"What's the matter, Mum? A nightmare?"

"An old one, child." Ida leans her forehead against the cool window, studying the lights below, her fingers pacing her beads. "The dispatcher's wife called. Somethin's happened on your daddie's section. I hate puttin' it on you, but Harriet gets so worked up and I need someone to sit this out with me."

"Dad! It got daddie."

"No . . . we don't know that. But she said it got two men."

Portia studies her hands, a translucent white. Touching one, she wonders at the blotch of red that rises to its surface and rigidly moves to her mother, seeking the wound.

"Remember, girl, there were eight men on that section. The odds are with him." Walking to the table, she lowers her scarred head. "Dear God! Just listen to me wishing this on some other woman."

Ida's fingers return to her rosary, the words empty mantras, soothing in repetition. "Holy Mary . . . now and at the hour of our death." His death? Portia wonders what a man looks like after he has been crushed by tons of rock, and can only relate to a dog she once saw after it was hit by a car, a twitching mass of flesh. She turns her head into her mother's prayer. "Holy Mary, mother of God . . ."

Then she hears the door open and her mother's cry, "Oh, my God!" as it slams.

Robert enters the room, looks briefly at them, and stares at his splayed hands.

Later Portia will regret her instant resentment of her brother for being alive, but not then. He leans against the refrigerator, his body leaving a sooty imprint.

"Daniel?" Ida rasps the words and her son nods, tears tracking his coal-grimed face. The woman slips to the floor, Portia's arms around her, and a high keening tears the fabric of the house. Moving to pick up the fallen standard, Robert lifts his mother from her fetal position and places her on the couch, where she slips into the imprint the old man's restless evenings have made. Glancing at Portia, he nods and she understands. Her own grief must keep for later.

"Lock the door and don't answer the phone. We need to calm her before everybody starts coming down on us." He forces a shot of Daniel's brandy between Ida's clinched lips and then tosses a tumblerful into himself. "I'll have to tell Harriet. You call Tom . . . if he hasn't already heard."

As the first searing pain of death dilutes into unreality and word of the accident spreads with daylight, the driveway becomes packed, cars overflowing down the hill. Jabbering mourners surround Ida and her spawn, instant celebrities in their tragedy. Portia is amazed at how fast they gather, like crows spotting something shiny. Death must have some brightness about it, she reasons; some unique quality that can be detected at a great distance by a mourner circling aimlessly. The house expands with friends, half-friends, and friends of friends, all making inanely appropriate comments. Neighbors begin sending in food, heeding the Evangelist John's admonishment to pass from death into life, ensuring their survival by ingesting ham sandwiches and Jell-O salad. People push life into their mouths with both hands. Pleasantries are exchanged. Men discreetly pass their pints. Potato salad runneth over.

With night's lowering, the well-meaning finally depart and Portia again sits with her family around the kitchen table. Pansy alternately dozes and says her beads as Robert and Tom refill their tumblers silently. Harriet is curled in Joey's lap, crying. Ida, wired with coffee, finally manages the questions.

"I want to know, Robert."

"Ma . . ."

"I want to know what happened."

"Joe Yarnell was workin' the section. I'll tell you what he told me. Dad was workin' as miner helper and Sootball runnin' the machine because they were training him to operate it. Mum, it wasn't that bad. Not for Dad, anyways. I mean, the whole thing is hell, but at least he went out easy, like goin' to sleep."

Ida's look is skeptical.

"They'd just had shift change and Yarnell said for some reason he wanted to hang back, like he could feel something. He said Dad seemed uptight, too. Anyways, Sootball and him were at the face and Dad must've heard the top crackin' 'cause he yelled to Joe, and him and Soot both took off runnin'. Soot got covered but Dad, bein' ahead of him, only got a slab in the back. Just a bruise, they figured. He wanted to walk out, but Joe said they made him get on the stretcher. Said he seemed a little shook but okay. When they got to the tracks, Dad gave a little gurgle and that was it. According to the doc, he drowned in his blood. Said he never knew what hit him."

Sobbing, Robert becomes Ida's child again as she soothes him. Harriet sinks deeper into Joey's being while Tom's stooped form grasps Pansy's elbow, propelling her to the master bedroom, where they will sleep tonight. Ida cannot face the soiled, accusing sheets. As her family turns each to another for comfort, Portia finds herself alone and turns to Daniel's time-honored cure for loneliness. She pours a heavy slug of brandy into Robert's tumbler, noting abstractedly that her hands are shaking. The drink burns her throat but another one stifles that. Climbing the dark stairs, she stumbles over the old man's slippers and, holding them, moves to the bed and collapses. He promised. He said it wouldn't happen that way. The brandy burning in her stomach transfers itself to her head, and she shifts into unconsciousness with the vague realization that part of her sorrow is for herself, her aloneness.

In the morning Robert approaches the decisions that must be made and his mother will not face. Should they buy a new plot or use the one where generations of Crowes have been buried? After Daniel's interment, there will still be space for Ida, but then she never had much use for Tom and Pansy, outside of a few forced loans that were never repaid. She will not lie easy there. They purchase a new lot, high on the lip of the graveyard. And which funeral home? The Wyzanskis are Catholic but Byrnes does a better job of things. Either way, someone will be miffed. Business is business.

The funeral home (the Wyzanskis') requests clothing for the corpse. They fold Daniel's seldom-used black suit into a Piggley Wiggley shopping bag. Do they send shoes? In the end they send them. A friend offers to buy a boutonniere and it seems this is the custom. The carnation's wilting on the third day will coincide with the funeral. Choosing the coffin is the worst of it. The undertaker changes hats to become salesman. Indicating a bronze monstrosity lined with satin ruching, he intones, "This is a favorite for men. Notice the detail, the quality. We snapped up all of these we could get at the time. You don't get craftsmanship like this often." Their final choice is military in its simplicity and they leave with the impression that they are somehow begrudging Daniel his due.

The first viewing is scheduled for that night and the family is requested to arrive fifteen minutes early. If there are to be any histrionics, the Crowes have a quarter of an hour to get them over with before confronting the mourners. Curtains facing the street on the hill are conspicuously still as the family files into the waiting car. Black mourning chic is mandatory and clothes are a problem. Portia's outfit is a grab bag assortment of relatives' garb, including Harriet's panty hose. They are too short for her and she will spend the evening groping at their elastic.

Outside the funeral home the family forms its ranks. The edifice is a Victorian has-been, once the home of the meanest son-of-a-bitch coal operator since Rockefeller (Daniel has told her he choked to death on a lobster shell). The director's greeting is solicitous, hands folded across a slight paunch draped in expensive broadcloth. "Side chapel," he says, indicating with a graceful movement. Undertaker training must offer a course that includes that gesture. Navigating the carpet, the family moves into an aura of gladiolus. The banked flowers soften the edges of the raised coffin lid, white satin gleaming, as the familiar profile rises slowly from its depth.

They move closer. Daniel's face has a translucent alabaster sheen reflecting the surrounding candles. Ida wilts but Portia merely feels relief. So. He is only a corpse. She studies him, feeling spitefully alive, willing herself to accept this used-to-be thing as her father. Death, as rumored, is absolute.

The man's facial muscles have relaxed, releasing the tension gathered over years. His coal-clogged pores are unnaturally clean. "He looks so good," mourners exclaim. But the expression on the old man's face is not young, merely satisfied. Portia wonders if he is pleased to be out of it all.

The second night's vigil is less tense. Company executives have paid their respects to the bereaved under the costly embankments of flowers they have sent, hoping the widow will not give them trouble over a settlement. Closest friends and relatives have exercised their privileges and already viewed the body. This is the time for duty calls, and it no longer seems necessary to barricade the coffin with the bodies of the immediate family. Ida sits in a corner where she can study Daniel's face. Tom and Pansy are slouched in the back of the room, obviously befuddled at death's misplaced choosing. A blue bruise appears on the corpse's face. Robert points it out to the mortician, who corrects the blemish with a bit of makeup, clicking the compact lid closed with an air of finality when finished, sliding it into his pocket and gliding away. The bruise slowly resurfaces.

The mourners persist in touching the body, as if reassuring themselves of death. They evolve a chant.

"Still such a young man."

"Seen it happen so many times."

"They certainly did a nice job with him."

The family quickly learn their responses:

"Yes, he does look good."

"Well, there's always that chance in the mines."

Turning as people approach, Portia automatically extends her hand to Steve and Peg Zanzucki. Both ignore the gesture, Peg advancing to the coffin while he briefly cups the girl's face with his palms. They are cool.

"You okay, kid?"

"I think so."

He shuffles uneasily from one black-patten-shod foot to the other, and they both watch his wife, who seems to be attempting to climb in with the corpse. Portia knows her only at a distance in the vague way everyone knows everyone else in coal towns. Close up she is a scarred simile of Joey, eyes moving erratically, body coarsely thickened.

"Why, Steve," her staged whisper carries, "he makes dying look almost pleasant." Nauseated, Portia turns to see Harriet and Joey coming in the door. They are late. Why they are late is written on their faces, and that is too much. Ignoring Steve's handkerchief, she moves into the shadowed vestibule, bracing against the wall behind a palm sheaf. A head leans into her back and she turns into Ida's arms. They had fought for the love of the same man, each for a varying security, and he has called the game off.

8 Ida makes for a surprisingly complacent widow, Portia thinks, regarding
her mother curiously. The woman sits
animatedly in a lawn chair at the ballpark's edge, Coke in
hand, chatting with the other ladies, none of whom has
the least idea what the game is about. She is demure in
head scarf and pedal pushers, almost just flirting with the
male spectators sitting nearby. Wives acknowledge her
subtle appeal, secure that she will never use it and aware
of the need to find "someone for poor Ida." Daniel's
death has made her a person of some consequence, assured of the respectability his alcoholic habits had
thwarted. Now she flourishes.

Portia lies flat on the grass fringe next to the playing
field, its snowy sand diamond somehow having escaped
coal's taint. Against a Saturday blue sky the crack of a bat
echoes; a ball is pushed higher by tears and jeers. She has
no particular passion for the game, but it is one way to fill
up the supposed solemnity of Memorial Day and kick off
the supposedly mythical summer of her sixteenth year.
Harriet sits complacently on the bleachers, seemingly en-
tranced as Joey snags fly balls. Despite apparent concentration, Portia knows her mind is elsewhere, centered on
the logistics of the impending midsummer nuptials. After
confronting shortsighted teachers who do not recognize
his innate brilliance, young Zanzucki has strategically

withdrawn from the university, forsaking mining technology to explore the ever-titillating field of life insurance. Harriet is not one to let her intended flounder in the shallows of bachelorhood and consequently has moved up the designated matrimonial time slot from three years hence to this July, a ploy that gives her the undiluted attention June's horde of brides cannot commandeer. Portia herself dozes as the sunlight backs off into shredded rain clouds, half-listening to the oldsters behind her emitting tobacco juice and comments.

"They got to do somethin' about that third baseman before this team amounts to a damn. That's where the other boy's got 'em. Now, that O'Brian kid . . . he's good. A solid man in the field, and look at his swing. Moves up that plate like a pig to shit."

The simile causes Portia to rouse herself somewhat, and she regards the O'Brian in question. In that moment, all complacency passes. For the rest of her life she will be able to recall the precise tautness of Saul O'Brian as he stretches his length across home plate, graceful and easy in his skin, unfolding into a lingering swing connecting easily with the pitch. He rounds first, sliding into second under his gaping opponent, and straightens. The moment shatters. Yet when she is as old as her grandfather, when memory is a living extension of herself, she will recall this instant of recognition, the moment it all made sense.

Dimming sunlight silhouettes his figure against the approaching cloud bank, and that is also as it should be, measuring this not uncommonly tall individual whose height encompasses the day. She lies back on the grass stunned, physically sick that such emotional extremes can be experienced.

He has been there all the time, this satisfaction of every unknown desire and hormonal rush. Why hasn't she noticed? Oh, she remembers well enough seeing him around, usually with his widowed mother. Frequently they have driven past the duo on Sunday mornings and Portia has observed him, an intense, chubby man-boy about a year older than herself, prayer book under arm, escorting his mother to the Pentecostal rites. Sarah O'Brian has preened herself with the superiority of the religious pecking order. Methodists and Baptists were expected to condescend to Catholics, and they in turn snubbed Pentecostals, who, as everyone knew, were slightly nuts with their frenzied singing and carryings-on. Ida has fed her superiority with the invariable comment that, despite Sarah O'Brian's stern carriage, she is no better than she should be. "That woman chased Rubert O'Brian into the ground, and let me tell you, there was little enough time between when she got him and when that boy was born. But she never managed another one. Probably because she got religion after they was married and that's when she went straight for his soul, pushin' him into them Holy Roller ways. Next thing you know, Rubert leaves St. Bernadette's and is preachin' that heresy. He was drivin' to one of them tent revivals on the mountain when he was killed. Man didn't have no business goin' anywheres in that fog, but she said he heard God's call. Had to go. Strange God that calls a man to his death.

Now she's got the boy all wrapped up in that Pentecostal stuff."

All these years Portia knew she had been set apart for something; she knew her life's ways must trickle from this valley, somehow coloring the beyond. And here is the path, the way of it. I will have him, is her thought. I will have him if I go to hell for it. Just so he doesn't.

Harriet is tugging at her. "C'mon, Portia. Those clouds are moving in fast. It's going to storm bad in a few minutes and we'd better get Mother home. Grab her chair." She looks at her sister's pulsating aura. "You okay?"

Portia is still studying O'Brian, his form edged with the sun's remnants, shirt expanding with the wind.

"C'mon. Get Mum movin' before she gets wet. Spoil her hair and she's liable to piss up a rope. Joeeeey . . ." Her voice screeches into the wind. "Come and help." The rain approaches, a visible wall draping the Appalachians, pushing waves of dust-sodden air to the ground. The players jog off the field, O'Brian passing near her. The hunger for contact pushes her to catch at his sleeve.

"You played real good out there."

He regards her quizzically. "Yeah? Well, it won't count for nothin' now that we're rained out." He keeps moving and she stalks his retreating figure.

"It always counts for something." Saul turns to regard her at this strange statement. She fumbles for firm ground. "So there'll be a makeup game?"

"Probably next week." The remark flies from his

shoulder as he runs to . . . somewhere. Momentarily she stands, rain saturating her, then takes off in a wild sprint. The storm catches her full as she reaches Harlan Street, sheltering in the Crowe shed, knowing she must consider what she has found before entering life again.

The alley spews trash and soot into gutters where it will lie indefinitely. Pellets bombard the shanty's tin roof; her core shatters into sparks, recalling his face, the leanness gentled by skin with the cast of cream, blending dark hair and eyes. She remembers how he leveled the bat, his fingers moving along the narrow base, curving as he gripped, caressing.

It will take years for her to understand the burden of perfection she placed on him.

The storm quickly resolves itself into prism slashes and Portia follows the surge of her spirit. She becomes a phenomenon in motion, sprinting from the shed, flying along newly polished streets, ducking pedestrians, and running hell bound for the mountain.

The hollow above the town is fresh, newly washed. Foliage glitters; dust and cinders congeal into crevices beneath the pines. Sitting in the cleanliness, she laughs. Her laugh brushes hysteria as she unties her sneakers, unrolling socks. Nakedness would better express her mood but being barefooted will suffice. The incredible capability of her emotions can only be expressed using the adrenaline that moves her legs. She is amazed at her power to feel so, transferring it into a wild running motion that is aimless, having purpose only in its expression. Running through the long meadow grass, twirling its freshness around her, she allows the moisture fragments to soak her cutoffs until their weight approximates that of her happiness. She runs above the sodden Earth, above existence. She runs the length of the plateau, then back. Trees reach futilely. Grasses swipe at her passing. She runs with the newness; she runs with the intensity of being predestined to happiness. So. This is it. This would have to be it. No feeling could exceed this overrun of emotion, this soaring. So this is what she has been looking for in the smooth men in her books, the gangling posturing of the local boys. And to have stumbled onto it so easily.

The enormity of her luck stops her before giving way to another exultant surge that shatters grass and brittle greenery. Finally spent, Portia allows herself to slow, considering what has happened.

Everything is beginning; everything is on the cusp. And she has to make it happen. Somehow she will manage. The primary obstacle, finding him, is over. How could he not respond to her? No one can ignore love.

Righting herself, somewhat diminished by exertion, she heads home. But with the knowing.

9 Portia has little chance to study the gospel of Saul O'Brian during the next few weeks. The rituals and demands of Harriet's impending nuptials limit her to sandlot sightings, where she spins her web to no avail. There is no avoiding The Wedding, which has been dangled before the family for so long it has become a major reference point. Subsequent happenings will be dated before or after the event. Portia has ceased to expect it to ever really occur; rather to be suspended in an eternal freefall. But the designated July morning has come and she wakes to it slowly, reaching. Her fingertips stretch, gathering up sleep's loose bunting, reaching widely for dreams. She stretches a bit further, sufficiently awake to consider possibilities, and her hands collide with the headboard. Something is to happen today. The Wedding.

From below, voices rise and fall, followed by nervous laughter. Instead of breakfast smells the house is saturated with cloying carnations, the odor of spicy breath mints, and coffee, the only sustenance available. On this morning of mornings no food will sully the Crowes' starched and slip-covered home. Later, much later, this military regimentation will dissipate with returning revelers who will hold forth on the bride's beauty and the groom's luck.

Raising herself to the window, Portia is amazed that

the weather, the one variable in Harriet's long-range plan, has cooperated. Air and sky are shot with summer. The day's glow vibrates, waiting to be struck. Looking down Harlan Street, she can see curtains opening, doors nudged ajar, shades being rolled up. The street is up early for a coal town on Saturday, but this is their day too, the coronation of one of their own. All the neighbors, of course, are invited. And the Sodality of Mary. Ida's bingo chums. The old man's mine crew with their families. Harriet's school friends. Joey's fraternity brothers. Zanzucki relatives within striking distance from Baltimore and Pittsburgh, a maneuver bringing in legions of people whose last names end in vowels. If indeed they do come. There is some question about how hard Peg Zanzucki has worked at following up on invitations.

From her window Portia watches sleep filter off the houses, a visible vapor drawn by the sun. The familiar rituals of the hill begin.

Mr. Sims, a smug Buddha of a man, lets out his cat. Immediately all the dogs in the neighborhood converge. Sims slams the door on the arching, snarling feline. The cat is on its own. It will do fine.

Mrs. Pratt is sweeping the night's accumulated coal dust from her porch, her back bent from fifty years of such toil. She has masterfully fought a losing battle against a valley full of furnaces that persist in pumping out grit during her restless sleep. Mrs. Pratt has become resigned but not defeated. Her lace curtains gleam defiantly.

Nina Petruski, the street's resident crone, cautiously pokes her head out the door. She looks both ways and then both ways again. Clutching her housecoat in a desperate grip, the woman makes a dead run for the milk bottle, crossing the treacherous five yards to the porch steps. Throttling the bottle by its slim neck, she sprints back inside, iron-gray hair on end. God forbid any man on the hill should be tempted by the charms Nina Petruski has hoarded for sixty-five years.

Looking into the backyard of the neighboring house, Portia watches as a slamming screen door ejects a half-dozen kids, none of them over the age of eight. They attract the neighborhood dogs, already bored with the Simses' cat. Settling for the next best, the mongrels begin a free-for-all with the children, churning the yard into a howling mass of cartooned pajamas, thrashing arms, and snarling animals. A woman of Rubenesque proportions appears, hands on hips.

"Okay. Enough is enough. We have a weddin' to be gettin' ready for and I don't need this. Harry McDonald! Get your butt over here. Harold, move away from that dog. Don't let it lick you. God knows where that tongue has been. Helen, just look at you." The child has fallen into the compost and is littered with tomatoes. She has the look of a very young soldier with a head wound. "And you were goin' to be so pretty today. Even wound your hair up in rags, and now we'll just have to wash it again."

One of the boys is using what could be a pajama top in a tug-of-war with a dog that could have been a German shepherd if its mother had been more selective. Mrs. McDonald swoops, booting the dog and marching the boy toward the house by the scruff of his neck.

"Inside, Homer. You get inside that house, and you too, Henry. I'm going to leave the lot of you with your grandmother today. I swear I am." At this point, Harold McDonald III, age eight or thereabouts, emerges from under the porch and throws himself wailing into the gritty sandbox. Astronauts grin from the seat of his pajamas. Mrs. McDonald glances up toward Portia's window, a half-smile belying her dire threats. The young woman marvels at her ability to be perpetually amused by her brood.

"Feared they'd wake you up, honey. Lord knows, they're hellions at any time, but with this wedding today . . . Now, that one"—she jerks a thumb upward toward the McDonalds' master bedroom—"a slag heap could dump on him and he'd not rouse till he got his ten hours in." Laughing, she rounds up the kids, a process never likely to end, since in his waking hours at home, Mr. McDonald seems set on complicating the situation. Complications arrive every year.

The sun catches at rain spouts and chimneys, gilding each in turn. Momentarily it catches in the tangle of Portia's hair, flashing copper tints. She stretches, feeling her nerve ends respond, remembering how as a child she would study the world through amber beer bottles to assess its possibilities. Maybe today has possibilities but there is a dead fly on her windowsill. She is sixteen and occupies a world of dead flies and soot. Her personality is porous and she has no handle on herself beyond the certain knowledge of a boy she cannot reach. Her bridesmaid dress, glowing in a strand of sun, gives no answers.

Harriet and she have wrassled long and hard over that dress, scuttling princess lines, sweetheart necks, and Necco-wafer colors before compromising on an orange pastel. Apricot, Harriet calls it in the item she has prepared for the paper's society page. "Miss Portia Crowe was strikingly attired in a simple apricot gown with caplet sleeves."

Clothed in oversized T-shirt and illusions, the woman maneuvers her way through the hall and down steps littered with discarded gift wrap, extra invitations, napkin samples, and Harriet's accumulated household excess. It is assumed visitors will not trespass into these upper regions, so anything goes. Harriet's bridal gown is encased in plastic against the far wall, an elaborate piece of meringue that has set the family back five hundred dollars. The bride has rationalized this expense by assuring Ida that Portia will undoubtedly wear it someday and then it will be passed on to her own daughter, a family heirloom. Portia knows there is no way she will ever wear that dress, and her snooping through her sister's drawers has made it plain that Harriet plans very un-Catholic precautions to assure she will produce no offspring.

Harriet's six-month, prewedding checklist has been intimidating: choosing wedding rings, enduring medical examinations and blood test, selecting photographers, perusing catalogs, picking attendants, color-coding the flowers. They don't go with . . . talk to the florist. Rent the tuxes. They don't fit. Return the tuxes. Bachelor dinner. Rehearsal dinner. Catalogs. Invitations. Reception. Cake. Catalogs. Honeymoon. Coffee.

She follows a barely negotiable path through what resembles a display room for the Name Brands Foundation: Fosteria, Corning Ware, Tupperware, Toastmaster, and Waring. A sea of blenders, peelers, toasters, and linens are arranged on tables and stands. Against the window, blocking most of the light, leans the ever-practical gift of her ever-practical mother, a Sealy Posturepedic mattress. Ida has mentally blocked the gift's more exotic possibilities. Portia's personal favorite is the pink toilet-paper dispenser with a built-in radio. It was sent by a distant uncle, and the general feeling is that he isn't distant enough. She can't wait to meet him.

Perfumed steam tells her Harriet has the bathroom cornered, so she goes seeking the coffee. While waiting for the brew to perk, Portia speculates on how soon she is liable to get to her toilet. Harriet's six-month beauty schedule began with an agonizing diet she didn't need and a succession of experimental hairdos culminating yesterday in a final styling accompanied by facial and manicure. Sniffing the steam, Portia figures on being barred from the bathroom for another half hour and considers the possibility of attending her sister's wedding unwashed, unclean, and unshaven. Carrying her coffee to the porch, she stretches in the sun, sipping.

Ida flutters out, extremities in motion, "pretty as a picture" in dusky brocade. Portia has been forewarned not to stand close to her, as their colors would clash. Ida too has been dieting and dying, and the results have unleashed a semblance of the girl in her wedding photo. But as she settles on the porch swing with shuttered face, the effect dissipates. Hazel eyes are ringed with fatigue and she exudes an indefinable muskiness. Yet she looks better than her son, just then stumbling out. Although the tux gives him a roguish appeal, Robert looks ragged, eyes bloodshot and yellow; he alternates swigs of tomato juice laced with beer and Alka-Seltzer.

"Robert, you look like hell."

A grunt and a burp. "Watch your mouth, girl." Coughing, he pulls a handkerchief from his pocket. "That son of a bitch Zanzucki tried to drink me under the table, and damn if he didn't do it. Son of a bitch."

"Well, you didn't have to go along with the son of a bitch."

"I'm tellin' you, Portia, just 'cause you're a smart-ass senior doesn't mean you don't have to watch that mouth."

Resentful that her mother says nothing to undermine Robert's assumed authority, Portia regards her quickly aging brother, his hands trembling as he sticks the kerchief back into his inner pocket. Already his liquor consumption is growing and his resistance is lower. Ida regards him with the look of a mother both seeing and hearing more than she chooses. "Portia, your brother is right. Try to watch your language. Today, anyways. The Zanzuckis, you know."

Bunny slippers bouncing over the floorboards announce Harriet. The slippers, like so many of yesterday's props, will be discarded today, replaced by the satin thongs chosen for the honeymoon. Erotica, Joey's favorite perfume, encases her. She is on the runway, motors revving, awaiting the final glory of her mate. Portia considers telling her she looks good.

"For Christ's sake, Portia, you're late. Do you have any idea what time it is, and you not even started?"

As it is her sister's wedding day, the younger woman decides against raising the issue of the bathroom, the trade-off being that she withholds the compliment.

"And Portia, I heard what Mum just said. I would appreciate it if you would just try. . . ."

"Try what?"

"You know what I mean. Don't embarrass me. Just try to watch your language and manners. I'm not worried about people that know you, but there's a lot of out-of-town folks here that aren't used to that sort of thing." Dismissing her sister, she turns to Ida. "Mum, would you help me with my gown?" Portia watches her sister leave, feeling the old tightness rise.

Ida tries to dispel the impending storm. "She doesn't mean anything . . . just being the nervous bride, wanting everything to be perfect. Go along with her. And it will help things with Peg. You know how particular she can be."

"Mrs. Zanzucki is particular over everything but her—" Robert's glance shuts Portia up. She watches something register on his face as he scrutinizes the porch boards.

"Reminds me, Mum. Steve asked me to tell you. Peg's not going to be able to make it."

Ida freezes at the unspeakable. "What! What's wrong? I know she has her dress and Maude did her hair yesterday."

"Steve says she's been pretty sick. Said to give you her regrets."

"She can't be that sick. Her only child's wedding!"

"It's some kind of female trouble he didn't want to talk about. Said she's had it for years. Acts up when she gets excited."

Excited is one word for it, Portia thinks.

"I didn't realize she had a problem like that."

The hell you didn't.

"Is she hospitalized?"

Institutionalized?

"Well, it was certainly thoughtful of him to attend Joey's bachelor party with that on his mind." Her lack of sarcasm is commendable. "We'll have to keep an eye on Steve today. He must be upset, especially if she has to be hospitalized." Which Ida firmly hopes, that being the best alibi possible. She rises to help Harriet with her dress, pleasure in her own diminished now that Peg Zanzucki has robbed her of the chance for comparison.

Portia makes a vague effort to confront the situation. "Robert?"

"Forget it, Sis. Now go get dressed before Harriet starts a fit. I'm more than ready to give her away right now."

Portia showers in the steam-sodden bathroom amidst wilted toilet paper, smudged tissues, and scattered lingerie. The shower is short, as the hot water has expired.

She jogs for a few minutes to dry, towels also being in shortage, and takes deep breaths from the open window trying to purge any lingering Erotica from her body. The vague shadowy figure she can see across the alley is probably the adult McDonald priming himself for the next family addition, but she doesn't really give a damn. Somebody may as well be having fun.

The old forbidden recklessness is coming on her. She starts out trying so hard to please, gets nowhere, and ends up not giving a shit. Without moving from the window, she dresses slowly. If McDonald is enjoying the show, he must have a highly developed imagination. Upstairs she dons the gown and confronts truth in the warped vanity mirror. The apricot dress is baggy despite careful fittings, and the old ploy of strategically stuffed hose in the bodice throws her body completely out of sync. Steam-cleaned hair rises round her head in a fuzzy aura, and what the sun has done to her complexion is not to be salvaged by the heaviest weapons in Harriet's beauty arsenal. Her elbows are misplaced, and knees protrude awkwardly. She mentally flashes on Saul's physical beauty and groans.

Downstairs her inadequacy is fueled by the sight of Harriet, who is gorgeous. One doesn't expect that of one's sister. The bride manages her draped satin billows with innate grace. Ida tucks her into the waiting Cadillac as Harriet offers her one flawless cheekbone to kiss. Why hasn't God played fair?

Portia and Robert ride to the church in silence, both conscious of some sense of passing akin to Daniel's funeral. The woman wonders whether the moment begets the ritual or the ritual the moment. Robert contemplates the amount of overtime required to replace the money forfeited for this ceremony. A few curious bystanders who make a career out of observing weddings hang quietly outside St. Bernadette's. Harriet waves graciously to them as the party disembarks at the church.

The sanctuary is hushed beneath feathery voices and the poignant notes of the organ as the bridal party forms stylized ranks, self-conscious in their momentary importance. The wedding march begins. Joey and his attendant step to the altar, expectantly watching the void where the bridal party is to appear. Portia concentrates on sorting out her feet, trying to find the orderly sequence she has rehearsed, hoping her toes can maneuver the dress. "In her simple apricot dress with caplet sleeves, Miss Portia Crowe demonstrated her unique version of a half-gainer into the floral arrangements."

People smile encouragingly as she moves to the rhythm of the event. Swing and pause, one step at a time, steadily, slowly, leading the pack of attendants down the aisle. Dear God, why did she let them talk her into this? Swing and pause. Damn those shoes. In the front pew Ida cries copiously, mascara blending into the smudges beneath her eyes. The altar is imminent. Home base! Portia pivots to the groom's side and confronts Steve Zanzucki alone in the first pew. He looks good in his tux and he knows it. He is pleased with everything. Himself. His son. Her. Probably even his wife's absence. Catching Portia's eye, he grins, and in spite of the occasion, she grins back.

The ceremony is a blur. Harriet and Joey are blessedly joined in a long service replete with nuptial Mass, impressive but baffling. Somewhere Portia recognizes that the ceremony is a deception, having no roots in reality or commitment. Time to work that out later.

"Do you, Joey?"

"Harriet?"

The organ peals triumphantly and everyone exchanges hugs and kisses. Joey is enthusiastically pummeled for having survived some test of manhood, and Ida wipes the last of her mascara off upon his shirt.

Flashbulbs.

A little to the left.

One more, please.

Joey and Harriet pose artfully. And Steve Zanzucki is shaking hands all around, smiling, saying the right thing. Stopping in front of Portia, he stoops to kiss her cheek. His lips are pleasantly dry.

"So, girl, let me look at you. You cleaned up nicely. Your daddie would be proud."

Her eyes have a sudden ache and she turns away.

"What's the matter, hon?"

"Oh, I don't know, Mr. Zanzucki, it's just . . ."

"Steve. We're family now."

"Steve." The name edges stiffly from her tongue. "All this fuss. I miss Pops. People are laughing at me."

"Who would be laughing at you?"

"You, for one."

"Well, when did that start botherin' you? You never seem to give a damn for anyone's opinion, including my own, which I might say is high. There's a lot of Daniel in you."

Portia's eyes fill as he puts a name on the day's void. She turns abruptly to the limos pulling up in front of the church. An usher, one of the groom's fraternity brothers, waits to escort her to the limo, but Steve takes her elbow, moving her purposefully toward the vehicle. "You're doin' fine," he whispers. "You got class. Remember that."

The sun glints in his eyes, silhouetting the disturbing bush of hair that will not be groomed. Shutting the door, he gives her arm a reassuring pat before stepping back as the limo pulls out.

The American Legion parking lot is jammed with cars. Portia does some quick mental calculations. Figuring four people per car and more if you count kids, with sixty vehicles here and more coming, that makes over three hundred babbling individuals. And she is under strict orders to be "nice," which means she will have to remember names, family connections, and the fate of distant cousins. The reception line forms and they come. Portia's gloves are mangled before the fiftieth hand. Friends gush as if they've never met her before, and she is kissed by total strangers who remember her from back when.

Joey and Harriet cut the cake and the line regroups for the assault on food. Camouflaged by the confusion, she grabs a glass of champagne and slips into a corner. The liquid is tepid but still capable of emitting a fizz. Not bad. Not bad at all. Portia flinches another from a passing tray and the third is surely rewarding. She is beginning to feel the sought-after detachment. No one has missed her. The bridal couple are accepting congratulations for having done the world some kind of favor. Robert is at the punch bowl, trying to incite union violence. Portia has seen this film before. She is not keen on seeing it again, and she sure as hell doesn't want to be part of it. But you have to be part of something; you have to hook in somewheres.

Lights dim as the band relaxes into something that may be a waltz. She has heard it somewhere; maybe at the dentist's office. Applause sweeps Harriet and Joey onto the floor. Ida and an awkward Robert follow them. She thinks of the flourish Daniel would have given the moment. The beat comes for the groom's parents to join the swaying couples. Too bad about that, she reflects.

Portia is suddenly whirled onto the hardwood floor, knees buckling, but is held firmly by Steve Zanzucki. He authoritatively moves her body while she clutches at him, trying to monitor her feet, realizing if his grip is released her fate will be similar to the one she faced at the altar. Applause rises approvingly. Old Man Zanzucki has done the proper thing for once. Musta felt sorry for the kid. He grins at her as they manage the treacherous dips and with a flourish hands her into the arms of a startled Saul O'Brian.

"Here, son. I've other things to tend to."

Taking the boy's hand, he secures it around Portia's waist. The dance is briefly formal and the concluding ripple of applause deposits them at the sidelines.

He eyes her confusion. "You okay?"

"How'd you get here?"

"How did I get invited? My mom plays bingo with yours every Thursday." His face melts into the shadows, each angle complementing the other. My God, he is beautiful. "That's as close as she'll come to conceding Catholics space on the planet. Obviously, she wouldn't and couldn't come without an escort. She's the lady guarding the punch bowl lest contaminants find their way into it." Looking to the refreshment table, Portia meets the shrewish scrutiny of the polyester waterfall of Sarah O'Brian, flaunting chunky plastic jewelry. Beneath harlequin glasses, the red slash of the woman's mouth is tightened in angry ownership. Locking eyes, they acknowledge each other's instant dislike.

"I didn't think you knew who I was the other week."

"Everybody knows everyone else in this town."

"And then Steve . . . Mr. Zanzucki . . . grabbed me so quick. Next thing I ended up with you. It was crazy."

He shrugs. "Who knows what that man is thinking?"

Stunned by disbelief that the Fates are allowing her this proximity to this deity, Portia does not want to tempt them by doing the wrong thing and opts for a silence that might pass for maturity. Standing nervously beside him, she nibbles on nuts and mints, avoiding champagne's demons, and wonders how to hold the moment. Saul shuffles from foot to foot. Is it possible he is as uncomfortable as she? Is it because of her? Maybe it is just the setting? Since the newlyweds have left, seduction and gluttony have become rampant among adults, leaving children on their own to run amok beneath paper-strewn tables. Older guests doze in blissful oblivion. Portia would suggest leaving to him if there were someplace to go but knows the occasion's remnants will soon gather at the Crowe house. And she can hardly go strolling the streets in her apricot caplet.

A snare drum whisks into life; a trombone sobs. Saul acknowledges the music with a half-smile and, ignoring his mother with whatever dignity a seventeen-year-old can muster, turns Portia onto the dance floor. They move unsurely, partially because of technique, partially because he must constantly kick paper cups from beneath his feet. Screaming kids fade. The spot between her shoulder blades that his mother has fixated on ceases to burn. Portia breathes in his odor; indefinable, but his. Chancing a glance up, she meets his own study. Uncharacteristically they hold the gaze until he looks over her shoulder and runs against his mother's presence.

"Let's get out of here."

Outside in the parking lot, they confront each other and the situation. "Where do we go now?" Portia asks.

"Damn if I know. Leaving seemed like a good idea at the time. Didn't think about what's next."

The Fates flash her a thought. "We can follow this alley to a trail up the hollow. My granddad took me there when I was a kid. You'll like it."

He chews his lower lip, seeming to throw his thoughts elsewhere, then shrugs. She feels threatened. His regret is obvious.

They walk, subdued, aware of some lingering responsibility to the adult world that will want an accounting. "Your mother . . . she's pretty strict with you?"

"My dad passed when I was six, and she's confused about what to expect of me. One minute she wants a kid; the next I'm 'immature.' "

"Mine's dead too. Last February."

"Yeah. His passin' had a lot of people upset about conditions at the mine. They didn't much like the way of it." She looks at him quickly. He is the first of the community to openly question the fatality in her hearing. In doing so, he vindicates Daniel of an unspoken accusation that his negligence precipitated his own passing and further binds her to him.

They talk no more, using their breath for the steep climb. The plateau's black pines are verbal in a high wind. Portia twirls in the grasses, mindful of the last time she did so, and turns to him. "Nice?"

"It is nice."

She wanted him to be stunned by the field's rich possibilities.

"I spent a lot of time here when Pops died."

"Least you got to know him. I was so young when mine passed. He was hurt in an auto crash on Pine Ridge Mountain. Been better if he'd died straight out."

"You don't remember him at all?"

"Sometimes I think I do and sometimes I think it's

just what Mother's put in my head. He was a minister, you know. Had been at a revival in some backwater hollow that night. Mum said he oughta go despite the fog. God protects his own, and that stuff. Anyways, another car hit him head-on. He was in a body cast for months. That's mostly what I remember: him spread out over a jungle gym set in the front room. People would come in to visit and stare and yap. He finally died of a heart attack. Scar tissue had built up around his valves. Sometimes I think he willed himself to die."

"I believe that can happen."

He shrugs. "I wish I could remember more, but it seems I can't ever get past all the mess at the end. Well, a mine accident can't have been fun. You got good thoughts about your ol' man?"

Burying Ida's deriding monologues, Portia dares herself to think on this, to confront the sins of her father, and finds so few. Daniel's failures were those of love. She speaks with new precision.

"Pop was the nicest drunk you'd ever meet. He fought some hurt inside himself that he couldn't cope with. Of course, Mum's rewrote all that since he was killed."

"You notice you said 'killed.' Not 'died.' Do you feel like the mines killed him?"

"I just don't think about it. I get too mad. But yeah. They killed him. All the guys on section said the top wasn't supported. The company hushed that one up quick, probably paid off some inspector. Robert wanted to fight it, have an investigation, but Mum was scared he'd lose his job. She got a small settlement and Robert helps her out. I think she just didn't want the ugliness, that maybe they'd say he was drunk at work. Mostly she's relieved he's passed, and then she feels guilty about that."

"Death can screw up your head. My mother's decided that since the Lord has taken away, he's due for a little giving and she wants another preacher. So I'm to be the next Billy Sunday."

Visions of writhing, screaming individuals lost in an ecstasy of religious fervor flash across her mind. "God! That's creepy."

"I don't know. It might not be too bad if I knew I had the call. I've accepted Jesus as my personal savior, but the Holy Spirit hasn't come upon me yet."

"How do you know that?"

"I haven't been given the gift of voices. Most everyone else in the Church speaks in tongues. But Jesus hasn't gifted me with the Spirit yet. I'm still, as the Bible says, 'a sounding cymbal.' I can't speak for the Lord until He gives me a voice to use."

Portia has always figured that speaking in tongues was one of the anti-Pentecostal folktales akin to Catholics' worshiping statues. She quickly glances at his face. Christ! He is serious. Perusing her private views on religion, she finds she cannot relate to this intensity. Her personal idea of immortality is seeing her name on the binding of a library book. Regrouping is necessary. "Catholics aren't much for the Bible."

"You should study it, Portia. Look to the New Testament. That's where Jesus gives His answers."

His easy familiarity with the name "Jesus" embarrasses her technical Catholicism. She has been taught never to "take the Lord's name in vain," and when using it, even in prayer, to bow her head. His solemnity prompts her to busily rearrange her turf. "Did you ever think maybe it would be good if there weren't any God? People would be more responsible if they didn't believe someone was there to bail them out."

He disengages his tie from around his neck. "How could anyone not believe? Why would they want to live?"

His finality is not to be debated. She does not say she would live for him, even believing there is no God.

"What if you put the time into divinity school and then found you didn't have a calling?"

"Fundamentalists don't require a lot of education in their preachers, just Bible knowledge. At least it'll get me away from this." He indicates the coal-scarred hollow below. "Maybe Jesus will speak to me elsewhere."

She nods mutely, wondering how anyone could bear to leave these mountains, intent on her hand, which he is bouncing lightly on the palm of his own before firming his grip and pulling her into a kiss; a soft mute passing, easing around her, onto her, hands not touching so much as lingering. The color in her face clashes with the drooping apricot caplet sleeves. Freckles rise to the sun.

She kisses him in turn, moving from his mouth to

the top of his head as he lowers himself onto her breast. Her touch is more wonderment at his existence than sexual. Saul pushes his loins against their clothing, grinding against her as if to melt, then groans. Portia is confused but senses his tension has passed. She has won at something even if she does not understand it.

10 Portia plays her hand against God and a stacked deck, insidiously working herself into Saul's orb, subduing herself into a fragile presence that will not disturb his life's strategy. Their formal dates are tokens: encounters bracketed by the clock, observed by parents and peers. But on easy summer evenings, she stretches out along the infield grass and watches him at his game, aching at the graceful arc of body, finding subtle eye contact to be a sensual thing when subtly exchanged before so many.

When possible, they meet at the plateau, passing days of shimmering sequined haze. If her face is tense and eager awaiting him, and Portia is always the one to wait, she is quiet as he flings himself down on the grass beside her. They speak or not, as they please, though she deftly talks him around to himself, trying to catch up on the strange possibility that he had a life before this summer. Portia speaks carefully of herself, giving dusty answers framed to suit. The town below moves unaware. Evenings, Cogan's Bluff compresses itself into a scattered tracing of lights while their world on the ledge merges with arching frenzied insects that echo some insistence within her. They burrow together into the thick meadow, faces imprinted with field bloom. She is never insistent, quieting his brown eyes, falling into their simmering warmth. Physical encounters are limited, a curious probing, an exchange of moisture on the upper lip, a discreet touching of flesh, but as they approach the core, always Saul backs off, leaving the both of them with bruised mouths and burnished skin. Many evenings she follows the Coleman lantern down the trail, limbs distorted, crotch aching, anger flaying her at his stupidity, his God's stupidity. Such a cocktease! A sterile "Good night" is given beneath the yellow porch light, neighbors and insects rampant, and she drifts upstairs ignoring her mother's curiosity. Sprawling on the bed, Portia chews a corner of the chenille spread, fibers flaking her mouth, and admits to herself that sometimes failure is possible.

It would be nice to say the predictable does not happen, but Saul leaves for college and moves beyond her wooing. She curses this new void. She curses with the talent bred by miner forebears and polished at Whetzel's. The furies that entered her on finding him do not become latent, but strangely, she does, participating disinterestedly in the mini-dramas of her senior year.

Snow is heavy that winter, folding her in a cocoon of immobility. Waiting and weather are both white. The urine patches of dogs become a personal affront. Sometimes things are okay. Sometimes she can trail her fingers across faceless library bindings and a title rises to them. Sometimes Portia even forgets Saul, although she denies this to herself afterward. She feels strengthened, rested, and strangely content. At those times she becomes careless about centering her emotions on him and feels him slipping away. Then with the end of her senior year, Portia must confront her own distancing from the coal town.

A scholarship to West Virginia University thrusts Portia into higher education despite herself. She threatens to boycott Morgantown, but knows full well her alternatives are a stint in the local sewing factory or an army career. Everyone has reasons for wanting her to go to college: "Pass up a scholarship!" "You're too smart to stick around here." "Boy, if I had your chance . . ." "Be the first college graduate in your family, girl." And again, "If I had your chance." The latter is invariably voiced by some classmate getting off work at the Piggley Wiggley and waiting for her date and making conversation while smugly content in the set of her life.

The scholarship allows the family to feel supportive without entailing a real sacrifice, and Portia figures if nothing else, she will come away with some idea of how "they" think. Measured in miles, the distance to Morgantown is not that great, but it is a different world and not one she is sure she wants to be part of. Cogan's Bluff rarely receives the breezes from the university. Portia thinks of the institution as a learning center, never visualizing a lifestyle so drastically deviant from that of the sleepy coal town in which she was raised. Contrasted against the rough life of the miners and survival tactics of their women, this improbable society of easy virtue and loose money swells with licentious excess. In the Eighties they evolved a name for her encounter with urban values: culture shock. But in the mid-Sixties, this term had no meaning. Morgantown isn't culture any more than Cogan's Bluff is a void. Morgantown is warped values and intellectual regimentation.

After deciding she loathes the place, an emotion too intense to sustain for any length of time, Portia settles into concentrated misery. As part of her survival strategy she chooses journalism as a major, idealizing it as a field that sanctifies shoddiness and bleak corners. The scope of her training is defined by deadlines, lead lines, crop lines and cutlines. The university largely ignores the writing aspect of such a career, but much related learning is done in seedy bars over draught beer and in scuzzy corners with lots of talk, most of it superfluous. She finally gets around to sex, most of it pretty gritty. The novelty of waking up in the morning next to a male body quickly fades in the process of persuading him to leave.

Portia sticks out Morgantown until she gets her degree, mostly because of the hell that will be raised if she doesn't. Also she feels she owes it to Edith, her old librarian and mentor. Someday the books in the library will run out. Edith at least had the foresight to warn her of the need to replace them.

At the conclusion of her last final, Portia purchases a one-way ticket to Cogan's Bluff, a statement of intent. She sits near the front of the bus, where she has a good view of the roadway as the highway snakes its pitted length through the hollows. Boxcars and tipples evolve, marking the unpatrolled boundaries of coal country. Trailers totter on shaky ridges. An oversized truck nudges the bus onto the grime-scarred berm. Litter beckons her home. She walks from the depot, hoping no one is looking. No one is.

Ida reinstalls her with some little flurry. She is being courted by one Mr. Tandy of Tandy's Pharmaceutical and has little time for leftover children. Portia's diploma is received in the mail, duly framed and hung in the front room to be commented upon when front-room occasions arise. The graduate submits an application to the local newspaper, which puts it "on file"; the paper's staff quota is filled by two antiquarians, one of whom snaps photos with his Brownie. She would have liked to work at the library, but there is no money for assistant librarians and no need for one, anyways. Edith is blunt about that. Sentiment notwithstanding, she is not about to have her turf invaded, especially by anyone demonstrating enthusiasm. Portia ends up at the Chamber of Commerce, sorting dusty files for sixty-three dollars a week.

The organization is tucked into the rear of the Farmers and Miners Bank, with which it shares many things, including an attitude of self-righteousness and the boredom of its employees. Like the library, this bank was built in anticipation of the boom that never came. While the Chamber of Commerce rented some of the excess space, the Chamber never paid the rent and the bank never tried to collect since the officers of one are the officers of the other. The Chamber's main achievement is a brochure extolling the glories of Cogan's Bluff. Its cover shows a steam locomotive pulling a coal train past a crossing where a 1948 Ford sits patiently. Portia's duties are to send out endless numbers of these pamphlets to remote companies that never respond. Occasionally she sorts through the files for the correspondence of men long since dead. Men not literally dead try awkward come-ons. The vice president suggests she might accompany him to a meeting in Charleston detailing the quirks of interest rates. Miners' sons who have invaded banking by becoming tellers offer to share her lunch hour and any other available goodies. All are the sort who cannot handle rejection and salve their pride by ignoring her. In a coal town where status is defined by marital standing, Portia remains a curiosity.

The heavy summer heat forces her to spend most evenings on the porch with Ida and the smitten Mr. Tandy, sitting on the front steps reading against dimming light. The courting couple gentle the porch swing and watch the neighbors watching them, until Portia's silent intrusion moves them to take a drive or watch TV. The day's bracelet of light fades rose and navy; her life fades with no such color. The first summer home passes thus.

She avoids confrontation with people and with herself. Fall begins to crackle. Heavy insects beat against the cooling mountains, protesting the coming dormancy. And Portia feels herself clamor with them. One evening she follows the crevices of her father's footsteps to Whetzel's. After that, everything just kind of happens.

11 Ida's cultivated cheerfulness can be gagging, Portia thinks, especially in the morning. "Imagine that," she chirps over the newspaper, with much stirring of prunes and flakes. "I never would've thought it. Reverend Moody is retiring and that boy is taking over his ministry."

"That boy?" Portia spits on a snag in her hose, rubbing in the phlegm.

"Saul O'Brian. Your old beau."

"That so." Portia strokes furiously. Colorless nail polish is needed. "Wasn't aware he was back around."

"He left a good job in Newport, they say."

"I wouldn't know. We haven't kept in touch."

"Can't blame him, the way you're carryin' on."

"What's that crack supposed to mean?"

"This hangin' out at Whetzel's. You runnin' around. It's makin' a lot of talk. I'm sure Sarah's heard about it."

"Talk's all people got to do around here, and all they got to talk about is people who have something else to do. Well, maybe O'Brian will take the heat off me for a time. Hot young blood in the Fundamentalist pulpit. Have the town in a revival frenzy."

"I'm just surprised he'd come back here, with his education." She regards her daughter meaningfully.

109

"Guess everybody's got something brings them back. Probably his mama. That sure wasn't my reason."

Ida snorts. She is past insults. "I just figured he'd stay in some city. That's what sensible people do with their college degrees."

"Saul always wanted a hands-on ministry, and for sure that's this town."

"Don't be gettin' uppity, missy. I hear there's a lot of hands-on at that bar. I don't expect we'll see much of him now, anyways."

"Not unless you convert. Saul isn't going to taint his soul with no Catholic."

"It ain't religion that's gonna be puttin' him off. Not yours, anyways."

"Speaking of me, I'll be late tonight."

"So? Jerry and I are goin' out and you know your way home, Portia, you're twenty-two and educated. We are likely goin' to get married. Now, I'm not trying to run either you or your brother out. It just seems to me the both of you—"

"I'm gone, Mum." Slamming the door, she finds herself already thinking that maybe she should stay home tonight. What if he did try to call? No. This is bad. This is very, very bad. She will not program herself. She will not have expectations. She will have a life. Hell, even in Cogan's Bluff there have to be possibilities.

That next week Portia registers for teacher certification courses at the community college, having faced the fact that while Cogan's Bluff will not require another journalist in her lifetime, the local high school regularly chews up and spits out instructors on a spindle of abuse. She shares her evenings with other jaded adults, worn out from underpaid jobs, trying to find a way out. On weekends she brackets herself with books in the attic room. Fall and winter pass on a wave of uninspired educational pursuits. Portia is rotting. She thinks of her grandfather's "law of holes": When you're in a hole, quit digging.

Following the rules works for a while, then one Saturday too many, she regards her mother and beau Tandy nursing iced tea and watching game shows. Restless, she goes to her room, tames the frizz, applies heavy eyeliner, and allows her leather Dingos to stomp satisfyingly down the stairs.

Ida eyes this outfit, delicately picking a bit of lemon from under a tooth cap. "Thought you had studyin' to do." Beau Tandy's face remains bland. Portia's departure will allow them to do some mature necking, but one must exhibit token concern over the activities of a young single woman. Once he is the man of the family . . .

"I've got all weekend for that."

"Whetzel's?"

"You got any other ideas?"

Tandy spreads his palms upward. "It don't look good, Portia. All them ol' winos and drunks."

"They don't serve wine, Jerry."

"Well, there's a lot of talk goin' round."

"Talk is all it is. Mum knows I messed around some at the university. She didn't like it, but as long as she didn't have to hear about it from the neighbors, she could live with it. Right, Mum?" Ida remains determinedly engrossed in the newspaper. "I come home and the worse I do is hang out a bit. So Cogan's Mill has me screwin' all of Mine Number Two. I am expected to molder in this house waiting for Mr. Right. Frankly, I don't think God makes Mr. Rights. I think they're created by frustrated housewives who won't admit to their own lives and get their kicks spreading smut on people who still have some kind of chance." She glances again at Ida's determinedly bland face. "Enough said." Portia hits her stride and is out the door but turns once, seeing that the TV's lights have already dimmed.

Whetzel's is jammed with sweaty men, particularly young single miners with loose money, many having come directly from work and still in semi-blackface. They lounge outside the building, draped over crates and empty kegs, beers in hand, savoring the evening air. A few women of sandpaper consistency loll about. Portia is eyed briefly, then dismissed. When she first got back from Morgantown and began hanging around Whetzel's, she was a new face. Guys lined up to score and the women sourly eyed her freshness. Now the word is out: She talks good but won't play. Men have no time to waste on women who tease, and consequently, she has ceased to exist for the females.

The jukebox blaring against the clamor is new, but the rest of the bar defies the early Seventies, remaining as it was in Daniel's day. Noticing Robert leaning against the bar, she starts to move in another direction, but he has seen her. Giving her a dirty look, he grabs two beers and then her arm, and steers her toward a table. "Why don't you keep your butt home? Sit here and keep away from me."

She grins. "I didn't come here lookin' for your company."

He positions the beer and glass in front of Portia and, having established himself as fraternal protector, moves on. She looks around. Most of the men avoid her eyes. Sweaty discomfort finally moves her to a bar stool, forsaking the table with its surrounding chairs that emphasizes her aloneness. She solemnly dumps salt into her beer, reactivating its fuzz, and broods on her situation. Only a few old miners, flattered by her attention, will pass the time, idly patting her hand as they unwind their stories. Whetzel's is no longer a lodestar for her loneliness. Finished nursing the beer, Portia decides to stretch the moment by using the ladies' room.

The facility is an infrequently used closet. She closes the door behind her knowing that some miners, moved by their need, cross gender lines to relieve themselves. The toilet is piss yellow and clogged, reeking of urine. Relief in the back alley would be healthier than whatever obscenities crawl on the toilet seat. A further reminder of crossover use is a rubber machine advertising wares in a variety of colors. Feeling optimistic, she gambles a quarter and receives a sky-blue specimen and tucks it in her back pocket . . . for whatever. Trying a smile on the grisly image in the mirror, she grimaces and edges back into the sweltering room.

Needing a connection, someone to talk to, Portia moves quickly among backs and faces, her awkwardness tangible. If male, she could have stood quietly, nursing a beer. Her female status prohibits such casualness. Words melt around her: mother-fuckin'-son-of-a-bitchin' fucker. She sees Randy Miller, a fellow high-school student until the age of sixteen, when, daunted by the powers of education, he dropped out of school to go underground. Moving toward him, she sees a more interesting possibility. Beneath twirling Stroh's signs, in a union bar, the unlikely aura of Zanzucki gleams. She passes Randy with a brief nod and purposefully bumps into the foreman's bar stool.

"Excuse me . . . I . . ."

The hand cupping the forehead drops; eyebrows rise, furrowing the skin on the forehead. He swings around to face her.

"So. Miss Portia. Put on a few years and a few pounds. Does your ma know you're hangin' out at bars?"

"According to my mum, I've already gone to hell. This is just killing time."

He grins approvingly. "In that case, I'll buy you and your brother a beer. Get a little family thing goin' here. Give me a chance to catch up on what that boy of mine and your sister are doin' in the big city."

She studies him as he pays the bartender. The creases are deeper, his face a little more brittle. The belt buckle, a brass Peterbilt, supports a three-inch overhang. The man is wearing out from the inside.

They approach Robert's table. The several union men sitting there nod, then rise to leave. Zanzucki elevates his brows. "Thought I'd buy you a drink, Crowe, us bein' kin. Hope I ain't makin' trouble."

Robert must confront the fact of family ties. "Naw. They was just leavin'. Sit down. That boy of yours takin' care of my sister?"

"That's what I come to find out." Steve sits, knowing full well that every averted eye is scrutinizing him, knowing that the right man in the wrong mood could start a hell of a brawl. Robert's face reflects these thoughts in a two-second flash as Zanzucki watches him amusedly. Angered by the scenario, Portia ignores the proffered chair and moves on to Randy Miller.

"Portia." The boy-man lurches forward, dumping most of his weight on her shoulder and some of his beer. Randy has been underground only a few years, but already his baby-faced freshness is scarred by narrowed eyes and tobacco-stained teeth. "Yes, ma'am, Portia, you've grown up a bit since I left school. Not so high and mighty anymores either. And you're a damn sight prettier than your brother."

"Least I got all my fingers."

"Well, them roof-bolters is hard on a man. And ol' Robert don't have an easy time of it with his union leanings. Me, I've been workin' steady. Been holdin' on to most of it. But come Saturdays, a man gets restless." He laughs and beer vapor condenses on her eyebrows. She glances toward Robert's table. Her grandfather has joined the other two in talking, but Zanzucki catches her eye. He is aware of her predicament and enjoying it.

"Let me buy you a beer, girly-girl." Portia still has a brew in hand, but he is holding up two fingers. She sips slowly, remembering the restroom, her eye wandering.

Randy sees her lack of interest and drapes a detaining arm across her shoulders, one hand just almost skimming a breast. He's not going to give her any chance to pull her smart-ass shit and brush him off after he's sprung for a beer. His enthralling dialogue continues.

"Yep, a man's pretty much gotta have a CB. Use them for everything. Cops. Shootin' the shit. Pass the time. Line up some puss— Oops, sorry about that. Course, I've never had to buy me any. If it ever gets to that, I'll cut the damn thing off. But you oughta hear them ol' broads when you get on the interstate, especially comin' into Charleston. Hot Box Bertha and Pussy Wet. They sure talk a line. . . . Man can't help gettin' a bit hot. But I like to see what I'm gettin'." He looks at her speculatively. She wills her beer to its destiny.

"Ahhh, Randy. Think I need to take a walk."

"Hey, now. Here I am, knockin' myself out to be nice to you, and you up and take off."

"Randy, I'm just kinda feelin' my beer."

"Oh. You gotta take a piss. Why didn't you just say so? I'll watch the door for you. Some of these boys get feelin' good, they lose their sense of decency."

"Not you, though."

"My mama taught me right."

Randy's chivalry has ruled out the alley, so she squeezes back into the smelly cubicle, squatting uneasily over the toilet, wishing for a can of Lysol. The door's flimsy lock jiggles and Portia places one foot square against it while trying to hold her aim over the toilet. With a contortionist's agility, she pulls up her jeans and rinses her hands in the yellow water, making shadow pictures and obscene gestures to the wall to dry them. There are no paper towels and the cloth towel on the roller bears the imprint of years of usage. Exiting through the now-quiet door, she finds Randy gone, probably for a refill. She mourns for the bygone bar days of Daniel and ol' Tom. Things aren't fun anymore.

Zanzucki sits solitary at the table, moving his chair to make room. "You back? I thought you and young Miller was comin' to some kind of understanding."

Some of Ida's training keeps her from answering. After all, he is an old man, all of fifty.

Zanzucki holds up a beer bottle, studying her through its amber softness. "You look kinda good like this, Portia. Hides the flaws. Makes you look less like a bitch."

He watches sardonically as her face flushes, matching her hair, hot color emphasized by the beer bottle. She curses herself for reacting to his goading and fights to stifle her anger. Robert returns to the table, having found old Tom in his wanderings around the bar and bringing him back in tow. Seeing her grandfather is tense, Portia fights for control. Behind him, young Miller's face falls into focus.

"Howdy there, Zanzucki. Robert." He pulls up a chair next to Portia and squeezes her shoulder, abeit somewhat higher than before. Robert stiffens but ol' Tom drops a restraining hand on his arm. Randy pushes his luck. "Portia, how's about I show you my car. New Monte Carlo. Your brother won't mind and old Zanzucki here can busy himself with your granddaddie. They're both about beyond botherin'.''

Zanzucki brushes his hair back as if exploring strange territory. "Kid, it seems to me you should have a little more reverence for your elders. Or maybe you're trying a poor joke. I can understand your sense of humor being a bit off, what with the amount of beer you've got in your gut."

Portia willfully agitates the situation. "Don't know why you'd object to being called old, Zanzucki. You're quick enough to call women bitches. And Randy, I make my own decisions. I'm not goin' nowheres with you."

Rising, the boy braces himself against a chair. "Have it your way, girly-girl. I should have expected as much, you hangin' round bars like you do. My mama's heard all the dirt. You must be as much a whore as—" Robert, Zanzucki, and old Tom are all on their feet. Randy backs off. "No offense, just thought you might be wantin' to hear what's bein' said. And Zanzucki, from what else I hear, you might be losin' that hotshot job you got if you don't lay off the rotgut a bit."

"Could be, boy. A man gets a big thirst tryin' to get work out of fools like you. But anybody who gets my job gets it to lose it. And frankly, I don't give a shit. Sure, I'm gonna lose this job. I got the smarts to know that. I also got the smarts to get drunk without makin' a jackass out of myself."

Somewhere in this monologue, Miller has lost control of his chair and his head slumps onto Portia's shoulder, and from there, to the table. Zanzucki props him back into his seat and looks to Robert with a silent question, then nods.

"Miller, why don't we ride you home, boy. You can pick up that jalopy of yours tomorrow."

"Jawhanna put ya any trouble."

"Hell, boy, Robert and me been wantin' to drop in on your old man anyways. This'll give us the chance." Further objections are stilled by a thin dribble of spit coming from Miller's mouth.

Robert consults Zanzucki. "Okay with me, but can we use your vehicle? I don't have mine and I'd druther not fool with that contraption of his."

"Let's get him out of here."

Robert turns to his sister. "Portia, you comin'." It is not a question.

They maneuver the flaccid body from behind the table. Randy occasionally mutters something that could be anything. Unsteady on his feet, he roughly pushes Zanzucki to one side, sending the trio crashing to the floor. A group of union men instantly encircle them, antagonism heavy in their scowls. Zanzucki rights himself and faces them.

"Easy, now. We was just tryin' to get Randy here home without him killin' hisself. But if any of you want the job . . . ?"

The miners study the situation, mutter a few choice words about management drinkin' where the fuck it belongs, and part for their passing. To reach Zanzucki's car, they must maneuver Randy over upturned trash cans, beer bottles, and discarded pizza. The odor of urine overrides the garbage. Despite the two men, Randy falls and they fish him up, rank with anchovies and flat beer, depositing his body with rough ease into the back of Zanzucki's glowering Pontiac. The men climb into the front seat, leaving little doubt as to where Portia is to sit. She positions herself as near to the window as possible, leaving Randy slumping midway on the seat, alternately snarling or drooling. Suddenly he is against her, bloodshot eyes intent.

"You do kinda like me, doncha, girl?"

"I like you fine, Randy."

"I know you're smarter than me. Hell, about everybody's smarter than me. But we get along."

"Yep." She hung closer to the door. "Robert . . ."

Portia's voice is stilled by a wet mouth, tongue probing sloppily, tasting of sour beer. She pushes against his deadweight, aware that Zanzucki is laughing from some faraway point as Robert stops the car to extract her. He isn't that concerned over a kiss, but the follow-up might be a bit messy. Portia surfaces, sputtering.

"You ignorant sons of bitches. Sitting me back here with that drunk. You try it, Zanzucki. Let him slobber over you. He'll probably never notice the difference."

Robert moves to exchange places, but already Miller's stomach has begun its protest. Foul liquid spews from his mouth, clogged mucus landing on Portia before she can maneuver to open the door and push him toward it. Head hanging downward, he relieves himself of a dinner that seems to have been sauerkraut and hot dogs.

"Your kissin' upset the boy that much?" Zanzucki

shakes his head in wonderment as Randy continues to puke.

"Just drive. Get rid of him and get me home." She strips off her sweatshirt, sodden with half-digested food.

"Can't play with the big boys?" Zanzucki says, laughing. And she hates him. She hates the male sex universally and completely. Men can go to hell. Straight and directly to hell.

Randy is deposited at his father's with a minimum of good-ol'-boy talk as they steer him through a growing rain. The ride back to town is rigidly quiet and Steve stops behind Whetzel's. His words are to the trio as a whole but somehow directed to Portia. "You want to go back in or are you finished partying for tonight?"

Robert wraps it. "I think we'd better head home."

"And I'll have to hear Ida's mouth go on. Not likely."

"Portia . . ."

"I've had enough of all of you." She gets out, slamming the car door and throwing the offending sweatshirt amidst the other debris in the alley.

Robert snarls, "Then keep your little ass home."

Zanzucki regards her shivering frame. He appears to have something to say but instead merely hands her an old sweater from the seat of the car. It smells of coal. She reaches to grab it and he takes her arm firmly, pulling her face down to meet his. She is aware of the awkward clack of their teeth before her mouth involuntarily relaxes into his hard kiss. A hand firmly cups her breast, lightly brushes the nipple. Then he releases her, laughing at her dazed expression. "You've been playing with the little boys too long, Portia. Quit the tease and try something with a man."

She stumbles backward, almost falling over a cat, and finds she is crying. The tears are camouflaged by an increasingly steady drizzle. Zanzucki's Pontiac moves on, leaving her to trudge toward home.

12 Cogan's Bluff's streets are muffled with the accusing silence of a religious community on Saturday night. The rain is ironically comforting, a warm May drizzle that matches her mood and discourages evening traffic. At the base of Harlan Street a battered Volkswagen with Virginia tags moves past her, then stops. Portia quickens her pace. She does not feel like any encounter, even with a stranger needing directions. A familiar voice thickened with manhood calls to her.

"Where are you off to this time of night?"

Saul leans from the car.

Pausing under a streetlight, she absorbs him, knowing even in her present disposition she has no resistance.

"Mum said you were back in town."

"Yep. I took Cogan's Bluff for my first ministry. Can't believe it myself, but there was Mother to consider. Get in. I'll give you a lift home. You are going home?"

She ignores the remark and gets in the car, its interior aridly tidy except for a box of hymnals in the back and the case of inspirational tapes he moves to make room for her to sit. She is very aware that the odor of vomit still clings to her, mingling with cigarettes, alcohol, and coal, all intensified within the vehicle's compact interior.

He ignores the smell with aplomb. "So, what's been happening?"

"Nothin' much. Working at the Chamber. Taking a few night courses for teacher accreditation. I'm sure your mother has filled you in on any of my more exotic escapades."

"Where you comin' from? Whetzel's?"

"Yep. I'm not exactly bearing the odor of sanctity."

He moves quietly through the streets, obviously in command of this situation, of any situation. "None of my business. Right?"

"Yep."

"Aren't you dating anyone?"

"Nope. Just hanging round."

The Crowe house is blessedly near. As the VW chugs to a stop, the front-window curtain flinches and an interior light flashes on, quickly followed by one on the porch.

"You have a suntan," Saul observes.

"I've been doing a little gardening now that the weather's warming. Study some outside. Once in a while I go up to the old plateau." She mentions the latter pointedly.

His hand traces the sun lines on her collarbone. "I missed you."

She studies him, wanting to believe. How all of a one-of-a-piece thing he is, she marvels, knowing she will never get tired of looking at him.

"You're just bored, Saul."

"No, I did miss you. You were an experience. I just wasn't ready to handle it at the time."

"I'm still the same."

"You shouldn't be. I worry about you, Portia. You need to be making a life for yourself."

"Christ, Saul. You sound like my mother. I'm probably destined to be the family's cranky spinster aunt, but I am sure as hell going to make some interesting memories."

Moving his hand from her collarbone to the nape of her neck, he kneads the flesh there. Portia studies the crying windshield as if transfixed, afraid to lose his touch. Finally lulled by the play of his hand, she stretches and loosens.

"There haven't really been that many guys that interest me. Just a couple at college." Why is she telling him this?

"I heard you'd moved in with a guy."

"I lived with a student for a while. He was okay, but it got old, picking hairs from the sink and flushing buttsies down the john. I don't mess with anybody around here; just hang out a bit."

His hand rises to the damp frizz of her hair, which springs to his touch, and she turns and scrubs her face into his wool shirt so he won't see the pleasure there. Turning her mouth to him, she feels cool lips with new knowledge and closes her eyes at the taste of his breath. Her voice surprises herself.

"Oh, shit."

"What!"

"All this means is that you will get around to missing me again."

"Portia, just shut up. Shut down your mind and your mouth. For once."

His follow-up is openmouthed, moist, and lingering, then he shakes her off.

"This isn't the place for this."

"Yep. The new minister can't hardly be seen necking in a parked car. And under a streetlight."

"Cut it, Portia. We need to talk. Your house?"

"Mum is at this moment being seduced by Mr. Tandy. Or vice versa. I don't think they'd take kindly to losing momentum."

"Well, you know there's no considering my house."

"Saul, how about the mountain?"

"C'mon, Portia, we're not kids anymore. Besides, it's raining."

"The Coleman's in the shanty. And an army blanket."

He grins at her. "To sit on, of course."

"Well, of course."

"Okay. Let's go."

The path to the hollow is overgrown. Water drips from sprawling brambles, soaking them before they reach the high ledge. The smell of early honeysuckle is tangible on her face. He motions toward the pine cathedral, where heavy greenery somewhat shields the ground, and they spread the blanket on the browning needles.

"We gotta be crazy to be doing this," he says in passing and reaches for her. She is lost even as she lies quietly under his weight, feeling a pine cone pierce some vague extremity, the lull of tepid rain misting her hair. She was lost when she first saw him under the dim streetlight. His hands slide down her body and the moist never-reaches between her legs arch to meet him. Saul presses deeper into her, burying his head in her neck, and she allows her hands their way, moving restlessly over him, ensuring his presence.

"Portia, we're not talking."

She smiles, pressing her leg between his, feeling the stiffness expand. His hands cover her breasts, purging them of Zanzucki's touch. She flips half the blanket over their bodies against the rain and relaxes to his movements, biting her lip as he slips his hands up her T-shirt. He pauses momentarily, startled at finding no bra, and she moves her body up against his open palms, teasing them with her nipples.

He murmurs something and she stifles a flash of hope. "What?"

"You're so beautiful."

"Hardly that."

"Your body has no straight lines."

"Would you like to see me?"

"Portia . . ."

She stills him, pulling off the shirt, and the small cones of her breasts rise in the lantern's light, nipples high.

"You're seducing me."

"I can stop."

He watches as she loosens the catch of her jeans, letting them drape about her hips. His hand pushes them lower and she brushes his crotch with her palm, watching his face as she strokes him. He pushes her back into the blanket and she opens his shirt, allowing their flesh to rub damply. A clap of thunder splits the pines as the drizzle hardens with him and they merge in the blanket's cocoon.

"Oh God, Portia."

"Just once, just this once, leave him out of it." She takes her pleasure from his, holding off to control the moment, and soon he releases himself into her. Momentarily they still, then she feels his tears against her face. His pain elates her.

"You wanted this, didn't you, Saul?"

"Yeah. But that don't make it right."

"It is all right. Really it is."

They say little dressing, but she sees a thought cross his face. "We are okay, then, aren't we?"

"Sure. We're okay."

"Good. I didn't think about using anything, but I guess you would know."

"About what?" And realization dawns. "No. I don't like pills or wires in my body. And I don't do this on a regular basis."

"You sure seemed to know what you were doing." He clinically and coldly slams his belt buckle into place.

"Yeah, and I guess you'll be telling me this was your first?" He turns from her. "Jesus, Saul. It was, wasn't it? I'm sorry. No, why should I be sorry. You wanted it. You're not worried about me, anyways. I don't even think you're worried about God. Just afraid you've screwed your image as a man of God by screwing me."

"But you think we'll be okay?" He is pleading.

"We should be. Just from now on, why don't you carry rubbers like other guys?" She tucks in her shirt, fury mounting. "With that advice, I'll leave you to think about things. Drop off the lantern at the shanty when you get a chance. You'll need it. You seem to be the one who can't see clearly." Portia tears down the dark path, face and clothes sodden, turning once to see the lantern plodding behind her. The bastard. Remembering his car is in front of the house, she lets herself in through the alley, quietly taking the back steps to Robert's room. Ida answers the knock at the front door. She hears a blurred exchange; her name is called and then feet shuffle and a car pulls away. Portia stares at her trembling hands, feels the moist soreness between her legs before moving to the window. Below the constancy of the mines, the dance of the coal continues. Shifts move in ever-changing patterns. Somehow she is reassured.

A time of nothingness follows. Spring flexes itself into summer, a simmering cauldron of melting green. Most of the town's citizens settle into evening barbecues or a cold supper and an evening of porch-sitting. Streets are empty in the arid afternoons, hammocks of humidity strung between evening's coolness. Many of the populace have evacuated to summer cabins along the West Fork River; others take vacations to Kennywood or the Virginia shore areas. Town-cloistered adults slumber during off-work hours while kids bicycle over gummy streets to the chlorine-polluted pool. Sweaty infants plague mothers busy diagramming afternoon soaps. Flies cluster onto the sticky papers churning over TVs. And Portia guards her private hell. The "flux," as Ida calls it, has not followed the moon and she knows. Her mother watches her curiously, noting the new calm, the disinclination to leave the house despite school's summer break, the abandoning of Whetzel's and the library. Something is happening. She is alternately worried and hopeful about her daughter's moodiness.

Portia spends most of her free time in the attic bedroom, hand cupping her stomach, where in six weeks fluids have collected, cells accumulated. Studying the jigsaw of her life, she figures the child is none of Saul's business and proceeds to jimmy the pieces to where they can fit. Living at home has allowed her the margin of some small savings. Morgantown is familiar territory and she knows she can find an obscure job at the college library for a while, maybe transcribing. Pride is not an option. Let welfare pay for the baby. Once the child is born, she can point to some anonymous and irresponsible Morgantown male as the father. The family will accept the tangible fact of a baby and not try to figure where she was living when it was conceived. Ignorant of the reason for this new spurt of independence, Ida watches suspiciously as Portia arranges to rent a room at the university beginning in August.

Summer smolders, hot dust sucking out time. Tossing restlessly in pregnancy's fatigue, weary of days and sleepless at night, she wakes sweat-soaked and finds Saul sitting at the edge of her bed.

"Saul! Does Ida know you're up here?"

"She sent me. She's been worried about you. Says you've been moping around a lot and talking about moving to Morgantown."

"Yeah."

"Bit sudden, isn't it?"

"Not really. I decided over a month ago."

"I should have come around. Things have been hectic, getting settled at the church and all."

"Sure."

The quiet stretches. She lets him break it. "Do you regret that night?"

"No. It wasn't shabby."

"Wasn't it? Sex is supposed to be a key spiritual experience. I messed it up."

She allows herself bitterness. "You mean you fucked it up."

"Portia, I know you're not vulgar. Why do you try to be?"

"Look, Saul, you came here to tell me I screwed up one of your peak religious highs by seducing you, a point which is debatable since you started the moves. Fuck off."

"Why do you think none of the rules apply to you? God's laws, man's laws. You can't just say the hell with them."

"Try me."

"Portia, that is what has always scared me about you. Why do you think I came back? I could have stayed away; just sent Mother checks. I couldn't shake you. I'd like us to try with each other. But there are things you have to accept."

"Like . . . ?"

"Would you like to marry me? Would you like to get married?"

A resounding thud jolts her stomach. The baby cannot be kicking yet. Her eyes fold in on themselves and she has a momentary out-of-body sensation, floating somewhere vaguely above, an observer.

"Are you serious?"

"We've already made a commitment. At least, I feel I did. There's the religion problem, but it can be dealt with. You're not a practicing Catholic anymore, but you are looking for something. You want something to believe in. I could show you the Way."

Portia disregards the arrogance of this statement as she considers both their natures, knowing them well. She will say and do whatever satisfies him and he will never understand the reason for it. But that's okay. She does not want a man who can follow her mind. She wants merely the sweetness of his body and the child's to turn to. It should be enough for her. It will have to be.

13 While no one expected the old man to kill himself, he had given his word. In the twelve-year wedge of time since she married Saul, little has happened and everything changed. Most particularly age has laid heavy claim to Tom, dragging him into his eighties. He had fought determinedly, drinking hard and generally raising hell, but time inexorably had its way. Always he promised: "None of this hooking me to machines." Tom had assured them, "I'll make my own way out. I'll know the time." But now he was doing it the hard way, digging in, oblivious to his own pain and everyone else's. The son of a bitch was enjoying himself.

Thoroughly pissed, Portia leans against the porch pilings, allowing Tom time to play out his routine with the current visitors. The old man has always been a show-off. She knows that. And he recognizes death as the final crowd pleaser. Many of the exploits of his eighty years have aggravated the family mightily, but none as much as this drawn-out dying. The ones who don't have to deal with him accept his cancer as an excuse for grandstanding. Sympathetic female visitors overlook his wandering hands. Husbands, if they notice his maneuvers at all, think the fondling harmless. Portia snorts, shaking her head.

The evening's lowering is heavy with late summer. Dusk rides night's cusp, drawing shadows into Appalachia's pockmarked hollows. Across the way, a game of sandlot ball scrapes along, the screams of fans and players weighting the already heavy air, oblivious to the rights of passage within the Crowe household.

The screen door behind her slams, belching against its wooden frame. Sissy Evans drapes her ever-tedious eighty-year-old body over the step and studies the sky.

"Think he's ever goin' to bring hisself to passin'?"

Portia shrugs, scattering loose paint with her shoulder blades.

"Not while he's having a good time at it."

"Oh, that's just Tom's way."

Picking up the scrapings, Portia crumbles them into a pale yellow pile. Porch hasn't been painted for years. Probably lead poisoning she's playing with. "Don't be so Christian, Sissy. He's enjoyin' himself."

"Don't preach religion to me, miss. You may be the preacher's wife, but you ain't no Christian. Tom's just actin' up 'cause he's scared. If a man knows he's got two hours to live, he can spend it thinking about death. Tom's got a little time to kill and he's playin' with it. When he gets serious about passin', he'll pick his moment."

"Some aren't so lucky. Some aren't even given two hours."

Sissy follows her thoughts. "Maybe your daddie was lucky in havin' so little time."

"My father would have used what he was given to ease his passing for the rest of us. That ol' son of a bitch in there has no consideration for anyone."

"Dyin's a lot more complicated than it used to be, before all these wonder drugs and such. Used to be when an old person got tired of livin', they could count on pneumonia. It'd give them a day or two to say good-byes before it snatched them up. Now things just drag on and on. And people thinks they know so much."

Portia's hand smacks the flakes off the porch. They lie uneasily on the clay-packed yard. "It's just he's done such a thorough job of livin'. I hate to see him have a sloppy finish."

"He's always stuck by you, even when you got knocked up by the preacher."

"I've had better moments."

"Well, you got a good man out of it, even if you did go about it the wrong way."

She ignores this. "You think Tom's done right by you?"

"To my way of thinkin', yeah."

"How about all them other women he was always sportin'? How about my grandmother?"

"Pansy had him for life and the others didn't mean nothin'. With your pappy, there was always easy women. Tom likes people. Women are people. But your grandma and I knew we was the only ones that counted. I always liked Pansy."

"That surprises me. You never seemed to have much use for her."

"I'll admit to that. She's not much for doin'. I always felt Tom coulda done better than your grandma."

"You bein' the better? Or maybe Maude?"

"I had more class. Maude . . . Tom just kinda used her for filler."

Portia shrugs, glancing at the hardened food droppings on Sissy's tight bosom. Maude's chest isn't much cleaner, but at least she is bountiful. The old man took his sex where he found it, philosophical about Pansy's coldness: "Your granny, she just don't like that man-thing. I always had to use the back door, sneak up on her. Guess that's why I only had the one boy, and your daddie, he wasn't much of a man, anyways. Too soft about people."

Daniel sure hadn't inherited old Tom's detachment where the pain of others was concerned Her father's sensitivity was as viable as his skin. You walked around him in circles, scared to touch lest he hurt; scared to get close, knowing if you hurt, he would take on your pain. Tom is a cat. Stroking is his due.

"Think those people will be leaving soon? I want to see him a minute and I'm gonna have to head home."

"You need to be givin' more thought to that man of yours. He is a fine thing to see and hear on Sunday. Even preachers can wander, you know."

Portia cringes. Over the past twelve years, Saul's moral fineness has deteriorated into spiritual Silly Putty. Belatedly she realizes she would have preferred a definable son of a bitch. But you can't argue that the man is still a thing of physical beauty.

"You people know him better than I do, Sissy."

"That's 'cause we listen to his sermons. You hardly bother to attend meeting."

"Maybe the preacher should try attending to his wife a little."

"I don't want personal details."

"Sissy, you and Cogan's Bluff want any damn details you can get. Let's just drop it. So, what do you think? How long for the old man?"

"When he starts talkin' about his mama, he's gettin' close."

She should've known that. She looks at Sissy with fresh resentment. "I'm gonna get those people out of here. Tom's had enough for this evening."

Portia moves into the downstairs room converted for sick use. The old man lies in a double bed spanning the hot-air grate, propped against numerous silk, fringed pillows printed with such phrases as MOTHER AND HOME or A SOLDIER'S GREETING FROM HAWAII, all souvenirs of Daniel's reluctant stint in the Air Force. She pulls an afghan over Tom's blanched body, more to relieve the tedium of white sheets than for warmth. His jovial court are some of Sissy's distant kin. He confers his favors gracefully, allowing them to touch the unknown medium of death. The old man is entitled, Portia tells herself, stifling anger. Behind him, goldfish stir the aquarium's algae scum, geraniums seek southern exposure from the windowsill, and a fan dilutes stale medication. He would have been better suited by a room with a street view, but Pansy will not have the house's dignity violated.

A bedside table bears prescription drugs in glaring new bottles and dust-covered containers of Aspergum and Preparation H. Nail clippers lie on a folded tissue beside parings. Yellow dentures are soothed in a cloudy jelly glass. Dingy Kleenex boxes flaunt their sale price: ten cents. Pansy cornered them at a Blue Diamond Department Store closing in the days before she became a recluse. A rolltop desk against the wall bleeds old lottery tickets, bills of questionable status, and Publishers Clearing House entry forms. Except for the pillows and throw, the room's colors are muddy.

Despite his banter, the sickbed literally has made Tom an old man. His foxlike features are blurred, the mane of hair thinned. Perversely, the wrinkles scoring his coal-pitted face have softened. But in his glittering eyes the canniness of some ancient Indian ancestor asserts itself.

Sissy's relatives Ed and May sit dutifully with required seriousness. They are well-intentioned individuals who seem to struggle against some vague opposing wind. May pats the old man's afghan-covered knee, eyes carefully averted. "Tom, you still look good to me. And you're eatin' well?" This is one of the few questions left about Tom's health.

Ed's booming voice gives testimony. "Too much Seagram's Seven out there just waitin' on you, old boy."

Tom matches them hollowly. "I'm doin' okay. Right, Mother?"

The rosary beads within Pansy's apron pocket begin to stutter. She nods resignedly.

Entering behind Portia, Sissy preempts the amenities. "Tom needs some rest. How about takin' us home, Ed. We got to be seein' about dinner."

Pansy recognizes her cue and tries to rise, knowing it won't be necessary. "I can get somethin' together. . . ."

"Not to bother." Ed is a man of occasion. "Aunt Sissy and May can get us a little something. We'll stop at the market on our way home. Now, is there anything you all be needin'?"

Tom thinks. "Maybe . . ."

"We're needin' nothin'," Pansy says.

"Check in with you again, ol' boy. Just you hang in there."

They exit. "Couple of drunks," Tom grunts at May's departing broad beam. "Too pickled to piss in a boot." The easing in the room is palpable, a mist coming in on the night.

"God, I feel old," he says. "So old it hurts."

He regards his wife. Pansy's mottled fingers have relaxed on her beads, her chins doubled on pillowed breast. Age has given her the fat puckered visage of a Navajo squaw under a recluse's putty complexion. Some lingering fragments of vanity prompt the woman to keep a little red print in her housedresses. Nah, Pansy won't die if something happens to Tom any more than Daniel's death altered her mode of living. She'd just shed her bit of red for a while and rock on.

"Yep. I figure this ol' fucker's been fucked. Anyways, you need to be gettin' home, sweetheart?"

"Not till dinnertime. Mays as well hang round a bit."

A soft breeze sifts in, lifting curtains, motivating the fan. The trio sit quietly. A drizzle gathers and Tom watches as Portia closes the window just enough to keep the moisture out.

"Smells good. Goin' to be a nice steady rain. We need it. Sweet God, I'm tired . . . tired of haulin' water to them tomatoes; tired of feedin' them damn goldfish out back. Contrary bastards. Go toss them some bread, would ya, Portia? And if something happens to me, just throw those squirts in that bowl in with them. Then eat the sons of bitches when they're big enough." Portia wonders if these are a man's concerns when he's dying.

A perfunctory rap on the door brings in the doctor, who takes a look at Tom and pulls open his bag. "Don't you go gettin' upset now, Pansy. I'll have him at ease in a minute."

Pansy nods absently and slips back into a snooze. Tom cackles. "Probably no need for that, Doc. Sissie came visitin' and I gave her a little feel-up. That always puts me to rights." The doctor laughs companionably in the way of men having a knowing, and Portia turns abruptly to feed the fish, damning her grandfather. How can he value people so lightly? What mourning, if any, did he do when Daniel died? The old should be exterminated before being allowed to outlive their young.

Remembering the goldfish, Portia grabs a handful of moldy bread from the tin in the kitchen. Passing into the minute backyard, she drops the crumbs into Tom's fish-pond, an earth-buried oil drum the mines have discarded. Immediately its slimy surface is broken by long golden slivers that rise to her silhouette.

Crumbs waltz downward, floating against the

rhythm of St. Bernadette's evening Angelus, and her stomach rumbles, thinking of the rectory and dinner hour. Then quietens, remembering Sarah's discount specials, which are standard fare. Portia sinks back into the rain-beaded grass. Drizzle wets her face. Grapevines stir, silver sheened against a filmed sky. The evening is cool. In the houses around her shadowbox figures move to the serious business of dinner.

Lulled by the day's mellowing, she allows her mind to free-float, willing it to sleep, to wander. From behind her eyelids, Daniel smiles knowingly.

14

I'm the original good ol' boy, was what Daniel Crowe had been thinking that night in 1963. Yes sir and right on. Good for what? Good for shit and that was about all. As he straightens up to adjust the miner cable, a roof bolt strikes his hard hat and he winces, shaking himself to straighten his brains. Straighten them. That's a laugh. He shoulda done that before he went into this hellhole of a coal mine to make a living.

Well, he hadn't had much choice in that, 'cept to stay in the service after the war. Re-enlistin' just meant losin' your life in a different hellhole, and Ida had been set on stayin' in Cogan's Bluff. Also that fightin' shit wasn't for him. God knows, mining meant warring all the time with the company, but at least those bastards have a face. And he had the union . . . and the mountains.

Someone had told him mountains were good for nothing except blocking the view, but Daniel knows few men who have the time for sightseeing. He himself likes the fact of them, the folds of Earth fondling a man, breaking the weather so's he isn't exposed. You have to be of the mountains to know; born and bred, a piece of them. Daniel always figured anyone who could leave never had the idea of them anyway. From his seat on the miner, Sootball maneuvers its metallic bulk into a new position. The machine's heavy cylindrical head is poised to bite into the coal seam, pronged bits flashing in the light from the operator's hard hat. Beside it, Daniel pauses, muddy cable in hand, thinking of the stark mounds of the Appalachians humping this burrow of Earth. Skeletal now with winter, their granite landscapes stretch starkly, perfect for tracking deer. And then spring coming, a bit of soft cotton taking a man from the cold, teasing him with possibilities of warmth and making him almost . . . just almost . . . lay back.

Yet to own this world a man had to literally work beneath it, making a living in a pit that all but rodents shun.

Angrily he tosses the cable aside and plunges a shovel into the offending rubble. Its blade glances off, jarring his whole body. This goddamn shit they call coal! Couldn't light it with a blowtorch. He looks upward, playing the beam of his cap light over the top. The debris he is clearing has come from the gaping hole overhead, which still sighs. The ugly wound of its leaving scatters his light beam over jutting rock, intense depths, protruding bolts holding nothing.

They . . . the company . . . had said they'd get a bolter in there to secure the top as soon as they dug a little deeper. And his crew got the job of clearing the heading. The foreman laughed when he protested. "Hell, that's supported top, Danny. Look at them roof bolts stickin' out." Small matter that most of the rock they had held was on the ground and the rest leaning to come down. A few support timbers would've made him feel better, but the company hasn't gotten around to purchasing posts twenty feet high, and that's where the top begins.

The crew ignores his complaints. Union or no, times are hard and the company finds ways to rid itself of men who bitch too much. An angry man quickly becomes a hungry one. He looks to Sootball, who steadily returns his gaze. "I don't like this, Danny. I don't like it one bit. It's not just the top. This place has a feel to it today."

Dan shrugs. He agrees but there isn't much he can say about it. Not that they'd send him down the road. The company knows the value of subtlety in getting across its message. They'd go for his daddie; send Tom to the coldest water hole in this pit. The old man is just puttin' his time in now, stretchin' himself to the retirement he's bought with thirty years of his life and both lungs. In a few years, after Tom retired, he'd show his son, show all of them what a union man was.

Digging the rubble, Dan concentrates on keeping the top put, knowing if he lets his mind slip, his concentration lag, somehow it will come down on him. Yet he can't help thinking . . .

Union! The union is beyond understanding, an entity existing outside of men and dues. The UMWA is not effective in peacetime. The coal companies know a dubious tranquility works to their advantage. Give a man a little here, a little there. Enough so's he won't notice they are taking it away with both hands. Subtle trespasses, a day-by-day erosion of a man's rights molds his hand to the shape of a number-ten shovel and his mind to the company's dictates. Dan knows his working under bad top will make it harder for the next man to say no. But what can he do, what with the old man to think of, a family to support. "Mechanized" mining, they call it. Hell yes, it's mechanized. Without the union, they'll drive a man like a machine.

He checks his watch. Four A.M. Almost time for a break, and he looks to the crew, seeing the same thought on their faces. Every time the section silences, he hears an underlying quiet. The mountain is tense. Life has evacuated. Well, he'll be out of it soon enough. He thinks of the look of the night mountains humping a dense sky, maybe himself humping Ida in the morning, their Friday special, the one he can count on. Tomorrow evening he'll drop in at Whetzel's with Robert and the old man and hoist a few. He likes watchin' the boy tryin' to score. Maybe the boy will get lucky, bag something. Nineteen. He's at that age.

He knows Ida is upset over the boy runnin' with that girl he met in a roadhouse, which is what she calls anyplace that serves liquor. Well, there is no tellin' her that the only place around here wheres you can meet anybody is a roadhouse. That's why most guys either marry their high-school steadies or leave the area. Maybe you can meet "a nice young thing" at church, but he married a churchin' woman, and God bless her, he isn't goin' to put that on his boy. Dan leans onto his shovel and the top speaks. Looking up quickly, he sees the furtherest back rock seems to have shifted some. He turns to Shinbone, who has left off running the miner to help him clear up, and nods toward the fresh fall. They both move away from the slip in the rock. Dan wipes his forehead, his tension more tiring than the work. Bone weary. Mind weary. He thinks of the forty-some years' difference between him and the old man. No wonder Tom sleeps most of the ride home.

Father and son became close after he started workin' the underground. Only then did Daniel come to understand the barrenness of his father's life. But at least the old man can still put it to Pansy when he gets the chance. At least, to hear him tell it . . . Last week was their fortieth wedding anniversary, and Tom picked up a pint on the way home "to grease the skids. Give her a little nip and she'll still kick a bit. Shoulda had a bottle last night for her to suck a little. I told your mama, 'Roll over here, Pansy. It's our anniversary.' She says, 'I just can't, Tom. I can't get my legs up no more.' And I told her, 'You don't have to get your legs up, woman. I just want to put my hand on it and wish it well.' "

With his easy ladies and feel for living, the old man has done pretty well with the hand he's been dealt, but by God, he himself is going to do better. Though he can't quite figure how, having started down his daddie's path. But one kid is gone already and Harriet not far behind. In a few years, he and Ida will have that little extra to play with. Maybe when he retires, he'll do somethin' he enjoys, invest in a sports shop. He'll think of something. Forty-eight and life still confuses him. He gets moved too easily; he knows that. Dust in sunlight, a woman's dark red warmth . . . even this hellhole under the mountains gets to him. Last year a torn ligament kept him out awhile, and when he came back to the mines, to the sulfur dust prickin' his nose, when he listened to a dripper's moan, felt the cool, soothing black dampness of the coal, he knew he'd come home.

Even as he holds this thought, the top cracks and Daniel starts, jumping back and looking to the rest of the crew, who have instinctively retreated. His cap light shows no obvious movement. Must have been the top relaxing. Darnell, section foreman, addresses the situation.

"I don't know, boys. We gotta get this sandstone outa here or it's our ass in a sling. But this don't look good. I figure we're due a cup of coffee about now. Little bit of work after that will get us to shift's end and then we'll get the hell out of here."

The crew moves from the rubble into the crosscut with their lunch pails. Daniel doesn't feel like socializing. He leans against the rib and pours a mug of hot liquid from his thermos. Steam laces the mine's damp. Sipping the brew, anticipating its bitter bite, he makes a face. Ida has slipped tea in on him again. Times must be hard. He listens to the men embroider old themes.

Nathan, the crew's self-designated philosopher, begins his harangue. "Well, boys, are you all enjoin' this New Frontier? Kennedy sure enough has us back eatin' hardtack just like granddaddie did. When old Joe Kennedy started buying up votes like graveyards was extinct, I thought maybe he'd pump a little of his own money in the state after we voted for his boy. Well, I did get me a couple of hotshot autographs, which maybe I can sell."

Joe shakes his head. "Autographs. Get real, Nathan. They probably had some flunky sign something, thinkin' you couldn't read. Democrats consider Mountaineers unpatriotic if they're literate. You got to be barefoot and retarded these days, boys. Keep up the image. Give the Party somethin' to cry about."

Sootball nods solemnly, encouraging Nathan to continue. "West Virginians have a duty to the Democrats. They depend on us bein' broke so's to get them sympathy votes when they pass these bills to help buy bathtubs. We got a responsibility to keep that assistance comin' in. I'm tellin' you, boys, the trick is to live in some beat-up house in a worked-out coal town. In Cogan's Bluff, we got that part licked. But you gotta keep it lookin' depressed. Neat, but depressed. If you've got plumbing, cover it up and build an outhouse. If you have to, put Christmas lights around it. That gets their attention and they think it's cute. If you're gonna go out to grab a bite to eat, be careful. . . . If they catch you, just say somethin' like, 'Well, thank you kindly, ma'am. Sorry you ain't got no slops for the hogs today. If there's a TV in the house, try to make it look like you bought it in a fire sale. Lay some lit cigarettes on it. Bring in the neighbor's young'uns. Kids impress politicians, 'specially when they's tryin' to get the Catholic vote."

"You got such a line of shit, Nathan. How come you never went into politickin'?"

"Takes more than what I got. Man needs a rich daddie like Kennedy or damn strong piss like Johnson. What if Jack did get us what he said he was goin' to. Hell, I'd have to leave all this." He throws his cold coffee against the rib.

The foreman rises, signaling time to get back to

work. Daniel contemplates the shovel and sledge leaning against the miner. His arms pull at his shoulders, their deadweight almost impossible to lift. The nagging tiredness that has been on him lately returns. One minute he's fine, then weariness fills his veins. Sometimes at night he wakens with a jerk as it passes over him.

Now his reluctance to go back to work is a thing beyond tiredness. Does he sense something? He'd think on this if he had time, but the sledge waits. God, he does not want to get back on it. But he must. Always a man must. Years of mining have conditioned him to that.

Everything is a matter of time. Time to be back at it. Time to pick up the sledge. Time to study the rock, to judge its jagged edges, finding the just-so-weak spot where it can be busted. Time for a quick glance at the top before lowering a blow primed with his diminishing manhood. He sees it come at him and makes a lunge.

"Sootball, get the hell out of here." The man jumps from the miner, perfect timing placing him under the tons of sandstone spewed by the top. Daniel feels a jagged pain in the midst of his back, and drops to the ground just as he reaches the supports, breathless but breathing.

He reaches out to the closest man. "Nathan, I think it got Sootball."

The big miner kneels beside him, gagging on the thick dust following the roof fall. "Shhhh, man. He's past bein' cared for. You okay?"

"I think. Just got me in the back."

"Don't move. I'll have them get the backboard."

"I'm okay. I don't need . . ."

"Just shut the hell up." His voice rises shrilly. "Joe. Get the damn backboard here."

They place the pallet beside Daniel, moving him with touching gentleness. "Now we're gonna get you outa here."

"But I can . . ." He silences himself. The tiredness of shoveling is back. They oughta be using this time to do something for Sootball, he thinks, not admitting it is futile. There is no time . . . God, he is sleepy. He is granted a flicker of recognition as the weariness claims him, a sense of clogged breathing, a moment to realize life is leaving him before being sucked into a long tunnel of lonely darkness. He travels beyond his tired body, beyond the reach of Ida, Portia, the old man. He is being cheated. "Those sons of bitchin' . . ." The core of himself melts into a pure energy that is not touched with life's distinctions but is yet a path of substance and peace. And there is no more.

The Federal Safety inspector kicks at the rubble covering Sootball. A rock dislodges itself and bounces against a steel thermos lying against the rib. Soot's hand protrudes from the pile of sandstone, luminescent despite its dust covering. Shrunken in death, it suddenly seems to twitch, grabbing. The inspector flinches. Just nerves, he thinks. The same nerves that prompt a snake to whip after death, a chicken to jump. "Never knew what hit him," he says.

15 Her reverie is broken by two hands leaning into her shoulder with precisely the right pressure, the correct touch trained for empathy. Her husband rouses her.

"What are you doing sitting out here in this wet? You okay?"

She turns to face Saul, and twelve years after the fact, is still stunned at the sight of him.

"Just getting some air. Death is starting to back up in that room."

"Portia, want me to talk to Tom? I could help."

"I don't think so."

"Counseling is part of my job."

"Not this time. Let him have his way about dying." Shaking off his hands, she looks at him, still duskily perfect, mentally keen, and all in God's own name. Some men make a pact with the devil for immortality; maybe her husband has made one with the Deity: He will be all things to all people if God keeps them at a proper distance.

She rarely admitted to herself that he offends her sensibilities; that she was embarrassed for him on the few occasions she has attended his services. This man, so sedate and passionless in her bed, indulges himself with sinners in an orgy of forgiveness. His parishioners respond with equal fervor. Life in Cogan's Bluff, as in all small towns, is desolate. Whetzel's popularity testifies to this. Religion takes the place of social and cultural advantages available in other areas. Consequently, the more colorful the religion, the greater its appeal. Despite their pomp and ceremony, Catholics are a bit too aesthetic for general tastes and the snake-handlers of the mountains a bit too exotic, giving the spirit-moved Pentecostals the edge. Saul's religion has displaced her.

Well, her life could be worse. He has always been considerate; thoughtful when he remembers to be. She is permitted to go her own way, filling life with teaching, books, whatever petty details must be dealt with each day for survival. The compromises she has made sometimes scare her. She has sold herself short. Sex has been unimaginative from the beginning, but the physical warmth of him in her bed and her life has been some comfort. Or at first, anyways. Sarah's inevitable residence in the parsonage has eroded any authority Portia had in the house. But she has tolerated this. At first. What she could never accept was her son's alienation. At twelve, Sam has long since discovered that his grandmother pandered more to his interests than his mother's and he is not averse to using this to his advantage. Portia would prefer a little active abuse from her family. At least she would feel connected.

"Well, let's head home. Mother's got dinner ready."

Mother. God! Even the way he enunciates that word puts her teeth to edge.

"C'mon. You need a break from this."

She shakes her head at his incomprehension. Does Saul realize the strain his presence imposes? Does he understand that this time away from him is a break? How can you tell a good man you are tired of waiting for demands that never come?

"Let me check on Tom. The doctor's in there with him."

"Yep. He's right on the job. I just can't understand why you people don't get someone with a little more expertise."

" 'Us people' like Wilson because he comes when he's called. And he's comfortable."

"Portia, the man still gives vitamin shots for cancer."

"Maybe he knows something. Lot of futuristic types are getting into that. Look, Saul, at Tom's age, it's not a question of treatment. He just needs to be eased out. The doc knows him well enough for that."

He shrugs and shakes his head, ever dubious at the Crowes' ineffectual approach to both this life and the next. "I still think I could help. I've done a lot of work with terminal patients."

"What would you say to him? He's seen everything but death, and even you can only theorize about that."

"Christians don't speculate. We know. We have the Bible's promise. We have Jesus."

"You have a book of fables written by four geniuses about a man who may have existed."

"Portia, I pray hard. We could probably eliminate some of this . . . strangeness between us if you'd see Jesus as your personal savior. I've spent so much time on my knees asking for this grace."

"You want to eliminate the strangeness between us? If we could eliminate your mother, we'd get rid of a lot of it."

"What's Mother got to do with this?"

"I don't want to get you more pissed off at me by talking about it now. Anyways," she says, shrugging, "it doesn't matter much anymore."

"It's this dying. Once we get past it, things will be better."

She rises, dusting off her jeans. The porch steps dance beneath their weight and an assortment of empty cans scatter as the back door opens to the clammy odor of death. Tom and the physician are intently discussing deer season, and over the old man's head, Wilson nods, indicating they should move on.

A pall of silence follows the couple as they walk to the rectory. Neighbors on porches quiet at their passing in deference to the death watch and the duo move at a self-conscious pace designed to satisfy. The rectory, leaning against the shingled church, is a worn clapboard of virginal staidness, its visage draped on two sides by a heavily screened porch. A drooping fern donated by some well-meaning parishioner pinpoints the door. Hedges and grasses are meticulously trimmed. No indignity, such as stray toys, bikes, or intruding flowers, clutter the lawn. Sarah O'Brian demands order in her life and on her turf, and so it is.

The front rooms of the rectory, those parishioners see, are modeled on the parlors of Catholic priests shown in the old movies Sarah has seen. Lace curtains and doilies give the fundamentalist sanctuary a Papist brogue, to Portia's malicious satisfaction. The scent of cleanser and sanctity is overridden by ground beef, the keystone of the O'Brian diet. Portia instantly recognizes today's variation: one box of macaroni, at forty-nine cents on sale, a can of kidney beans purchased at three for a dollar, half a bottle of generic ketchup (bought by the case), one pound of the cheapest hamburger, the grease skimmed off for future use, and salt and pepper. Such frugal maneuvering allows the pastor's family of four to subsist on the bounteous donations of Cogan's Bluff's parishioners. Portia's sparse frame is partially due to her aversion to this diet of meat loaf, meatball sandwiches, spaghetti and meatballs, hamburgers and hamburger gravy, occasionally relieved by a Sunday chicken or the yield of an arduous fisherman. Gifts of wild game, the backbone harvest of mountaineers, are not consumed, as Sarah deems them "unclean."

Entering the enameled kitchen, Portia finds her twelve-year-old son strategically slouched over his plate, shoulder-length hair drooping to frame Saul's black ghetto eyes. While his posture is not insolent, it is sufficiently reproachful to remind her that she's been keeping him waiting. Sarah also seeps indignation as she positions the casserole on a central hot pad. Seating herself to Saul's right, she indicates with a dry cough that the rites may proceed.

The minister's blessing is basic, barren of adjectives: "Bless this food, Lord, and those that eat it." The casserole starts its rounds, and Sarah begins.

"So, how is your grandfather?"

"Fading."

"Fading? You mean failing?"

"Fading."

"He should talk to Saul, you know."

Portia studies the slithering macaroni and says nothing.

"The most communication that man ever had with Jesus was taking his name in vain. He'll have to answer for that soon."

"How did you get to know my grandfather so well, Sarah?"

"Any fool's got ears."

Portia meets her husband's eyes across the congealing plates. Forks clink. She rearranges her pasta into a drab mosaic.

"I'm not very hungry. Tired, I guess."

"Living and dying's both tiresome but gotta be done. Just like eatin'."

The silence holds until Sam breaks it.

"Mother . . ."

And then, "Mum . . . we got basketball practice starting next week. I'm going to need shoes."

"You just got shoes, Sam."

"Loafers, Mum. I need tennis shoes for basketball."

"You got a pair at the beginning of the summer."

"Cheap suckers. The tread's already gone on them. I need traction."

She looks at Saul, silently chasing macaroni across his plate. "I don't think we can manage it."

Sam comes perilously close to slamming his glass. "I get so damn sick of being called the 'parson's pauper.' "

"I know not to believe that one. Your friends don't have *pauper* in their vocabulary. You only know the word because I forced Mark Twain on you."

Saul intervenes. "Your mum's right, Sam. No way we can afford new shoes. And you have to get over this idea that the more something costs, the more it's worth."

The boy swings his chair from the table. "Here we go again. Tithing!" He spits out the word.

Saul studies the macaroni in turn. "I don't tithe."

"Dad, you been preaching tithing for years."

"To my parishioners. But I don't tithe. I will not ration the Lord to ten percent of my bounty. He lets me know what He wants and I give it to Him." The other three look at one another, then at their plates, suddenly comprehending why they subsist primarily on hamburger.

Sarah assesses the situation. "Sam, you've got a birthday soon."

The boy preens.

"Mother . . ." Saul also sees it coming.

"This is between Sam and me, if you don't mind."

"You're thinking about your Social Security check."

"What if I am? If you're worried I can't keep up my end around here, don't be."

"Mother, your help is appreciated but not asked for. We can get by. You more than hold up your end with the housekeeping and all."

"Be that as it may, I pay my own way. I've enough

put back to cover next month, so that's no problem. Pick out the shoes you want and let me know how much, Sam."

"Good ones will run about thirty bucks."

Sarah's dignity almost flinches but she maintains. "Well, I'll clear the table and you take this stuff out to the compost, then we'll settle."

Catching Saul's eye, Portia shrugs and pushes herself from the table. He follows her into the yard.

"It is her money, hon."

"You know better. It's her keeping the upper hand. I never fight with her. I should."

"She treats you well."

"Sarah treats everyone well. Mostly because she doesn't bother to realize they exist."

"Portia, you know, even with your teaching, we're hard put. Mother's money has been a help."

"I know. And I hate it."

"You're out of sorts. Go lie down for a while. Take a walk. You've been in that sickroom too much."

"I'll take a walk."

"You're not going back to that house?"

"No. Not yet. I'll just walk a bit."

"You need to start thinking about the school year starting. New kids and all. Browning was telling me you'll have his daughter Debbie this year. She's rather precocious, he says."

"She's an airheaded little bitch."

"That's a bit strong. You don't know the kid."

"Saul, in a town this size, teachers know the kids

before they're potty-trained. Her and Sam hang to-gether."

"I haven't heard anything about it."

"Well, they are, and in this enlightened age, that probably means sex."

He turns from her, running his hands through heavy hair. "They're just kids. Have you seen them . . . touching or anything?"

"Watch them when they're together, the way they move toward each other even when they don't touch."

"That's poor reasoning."

"Maybe as a teacher I'm a little more in touch with reality on this than you are. Sometimes instead of the teachers' lounge, I use the kids' bathroom at school. I hear what those teens talk about when they don't know who's in the next cubicle."

"That's just talk. I remember jock bragging in the locker room."

"You wanta hear the latest story going the rounds at school? Sue Kelly's boyfriend supposedly pulled a muscle between his legs playing football, and he told her she had to massage it because he needed therapy to get it hard."

"Maybe the kid did pull a leg muscle. . . ."

"Oh, Saul. Grow up. We had two pregnant eighth-graders last year."

"Sam's been taught better."

"Most of them have. We need to think about getting him condoms before he screws up his life screwing some-thing else."

"Portia, that's encouraging promiscuity among children."

"Do you think these kids are going to go to their wedding night as virgins? Even you didn't make that milestone, and Sam sure doesn't have your conviction."

He kicks a clod of dirt spewed by the tiller. "So you've seen them fondle each other?"

"I told you. They just have that awareness."

Exasperated, he turns back to her, his anger palpable. "Take your walk. This is something we can't talk about."

"This has to be talked about."

But she has been dismissed. Dismissed, disregarded, and written off. She takes her walk as told.

Portia passes through the wet dusk, her adult appearance reflected in the thin silhouette on the pavement. Seeing the gangly shadow moving before her flare into a wild spray of hair, she falls into the old habit of tousling it to shield her face when threatened. The neighbors are still vigilantly keeping watch. Under the streetlight, her hair's redness is slightly subdued, flossing into wheat. She is too familiar with the face that is secluded in shadows and never appreciates how well it fits her, lean and gaunt, planes in balance, features not near pretty, closer to plain and easily beautiful. A few more kids, and toil and wear would have made it the sculpt of a woman of the Kansas dust bowl. Her choice of clothes is questionable. Since pants have become acceptable, "proper dress" can mean anything between polyester and jeans, but Portia dwells in an ambiguous area of cotton skirts and well-worn Levi's.

Necessity frequently forces her to shop at Goodwill, but no parishioner has been sufficiently embarrassed to increase his Sunday donation. Tonight her loose flowered smock billows in a late breeze.

The evening is liquid warm, rain's promise glazing the streetlights. Tom's need pulls on her but she delays, watching the kids cluster at the pizza shop that is their hangout. Most she knows; some few wave at her. Sam probably will not be there. She knows her son well. He will have called a friend with a car to head to the Crossville Mall for his sneakers and most probably has Debbie tucked in the backseat with them. She feels tenseness lock her jaws and angrily grinds her teeth to loosen them. How did she permit herself to become so ineffectual?

16

A woman swings into step beside her. P.J. Watkins flashes her shoulder-high, ever-present grin at Portia.

"God, girl. You look like your new puppy got run over. Want to go for a drink?"

P.J. masquerades as a lady of the night, a biker's bitch painted into black leather and spike-heeled boots. Overstated feather earrings frame her impish face, which gleams with the irrepressible light usually found only in very young children.

"Would, P.J., but ol' Tom seems to be on the brink. I'm just clearing my head before heading over his way."

"Heard he was pretty bad. A drink might help, ya know. I'm on second shift tonight, so I thought I'd get primed a bit before I go under." She laughs at Portia's blank expression. "You haven't heard?" P.J. licks each word: "The mines, sugar. I'm working in the mines. Thought everybody knew."

"I heard about the divorce. I didn't know anything about the other."

As they walk, Portia notices that the woman's eyes are red, coal-lined as Daniel's had been. New creases fold her face but most are laugh lines. Touching her own mouth, Portia feels the downward troughs forming there.

"Well, I've only been working two months. And Ben and I aren't really divorced, just separated. I ain't goin' back, though," she adds quickly. "It was an okay marriage. Ben was good enough and I got Clancy out of it. I just don't want to be married."

"So what made you leave?"

"I think it was that last can of baked beans I had to open that broke me."

She laughs at Portia's disbelieving face. "Ah, things just built up. All the cans and greasy skillets and scummy windows I spent sixteen years cleanin'. Clancy graduated in June and joined the army. So it was just me and Ben to do for in that big house."

"And you got lonely?"

"Hell, no. I started goin' out a bit. Joined a bowling league, got runnin' around with the girls in the evening, havin' a few drinks at the bar, maybe a little flirtin'. I liked it. 'Course Ben started ridin' my ass, said I was whorin' around."

"He's used to having you at home."

"Tough shit. It's fine for him to spend evenings with the boys at Whetzel's, drinkin' and checkin' out a little pussy. But he expected me to sit at home. No way in hell. What's good for the gander is good for the goose."

"If you can handle it."

"It's the other bit I couldn't handle. That last evening when I was fixin' dinner for Ben, I got to thinkin' about all the namby-pamby women's stuff I'd done: worked at the Bonbon Shoppe, joined the Soroptimist, the garden club, ran bake sales for the PTA. All because it was expected of me, but none of it felt right. I got disgusted with myself, upended the can of beans in the middle of the table, and got the hell out of there. Moved in with Daddie for a while and started lookin' for a job. But it was just the same old shit . . . waitressing or the sewing factory. I was killing time at Whetzel's when Alabama picked me up. That man, he was somethin'. Fuckin' him was fun, raunchy fun. And I hadn't had any of that for a long time. Dicks come in all sizes, you know: big, bigger, and oh-my-God. He surely was an oh-my-God, and what he could do with it . . ."

She laughs, animal pleasure rumbling through her. "Yep, screwed him first time in the cab of his truck and two days later we was in Florida. I left a note with Daddie sayin' I was on vacation. Alabama was the one told me to get off my ass. When we got back and he was gettin' ready to move on, he says, 'Where's the money at in these hills, hon? Mining. Then that's where to go.' Anyways, he dared me and some girlfriends to put an application in at Number Two. We drove over there and the rest of them chickened out, but I went in and applied. Got called a week later and thought, What the hell!" Her giggle is a frothy slide. "Best thing I ever did except for screwin' him, though I'll never regret havin' my boy. I was tired of livin' with Daddie anyways, so I got myself a room over at McDuff's, lived on nothing with only peanut butter to eat until I collected that first big paycheck. The money's damn good, Portia. Bought me a trailer and had a hell of a party."

"God, P.J., if I had your guts . . . Me going in the mines would rock the whole town."

"Just what it needs. And you could handle it. I

remember in high school how you always went your own way, never gave a damn." She shrugs. "It's something to think about. They have to hire women 'cause the government's on their ass. The company would really like a black chick, but your family's been working underground for years. They'd probably jump on you."

"I know I couldn't handle it," she says, but listening to herself, she hears a crazy woman talking, one who actually considers the underground as a possibility.

P.J. lights a cigarette. Its glow casts eerie shadows onto her creased face.

"It's no worse than the shit husbands give you. Any husband. And at least these boys don't backstab you like a bunch of women will. They tell you to go to hell straight to your face. Yeah, the work is hard, but it can't be any worse than dealing with those little assholes you teach. And the money's better. The funny thing is, you get to likin' the work in some strange way. 'Coal fever,' they call it."

Portia remembers the girl she was, listening to her father trying to explain the perverse lure of coal.

"Hate hearin' about your granddaddie. Guess it's been hard on you. You look kinda stretched out." She opens her purse. "Look, if you need somethin' to help you, I got some happy pills here."

"Nah, this was just a rough day. But look, you wouldn't have any rubbers on you?"

P.J. raises her eyebrows. "Good goin'. I always thought your hubby was a honey to look at, but a girl needs a little strange now and then."

"These are for someone else."

P.J. shrugs. "Whatever. This packet has twenty-four. Nah, let's make it twenty-three. Gotta keep one. Never know when you'll get lucky. If you want to keep it quiet, try gettin' them at the mall over in Crossville."

"I owe you."

"Forget it. Stay in touch. And don't be puttin' up with any shit. I know that mother-in-law of yours from way back."

The woman walks away, heels catching on crevices in the rough street, sturdy body swaying, hair spiking the night. Portia watches the red cinder of her cigarette disappear, then walks toward the stagnant Crowe home.

17 Letting herself in the open back door, she moves into the night-light's untimely dusk. Pansy slumbers in her rocker, rosary stilled, mouth open to small drool. Faded red flowers sprout on her purple housedress, its color deeper at the stretched seams and gaping neck, which is clasped by a safety pin. Opposite her, the old man lies quiet in the hooded white sleep of drugs, half watching as she sits at the bedside and picks up a hand to stroke his yellowed knuckle.

"How's the weather, girl?"

"Fair. Fall's coming in. Sam says there's lots of deer hanging at the waterholes."

"The boy likes his huntin', don't he? I won't be gettin' out this year."

"Then you're the only one who's sure of it."

"C'mon now, Miss Portia. We know how things are. But this hasn't been so bad. Gettin' old's made bein' queer-minded a natural thing to people. Lets me get away with a lot. And dyin' ain't as hard as I figured. I could enjoy it if I knew the endin'."

"How's the pain?"

"Not so bad. Doc says this is one of the 'easy' cancers. Anyways, every time I get to where I can feel somethin', he sticks a needle in me."

"He's just trying to help."

"Help! That's a crock. All of you are just tryin' to numb me so this dying won't be too hard on you. That old son of a bitch knows nobody can't do anything for me and it keeps him happy thinkin' I'm happy."

"You still have enough piss in you to give me a hard time."

"I take the trouble for you. And you'll miss it."

"Saul's pretty good at pissin' me off."

"Well, missy, you made a bad bargain there. I tried tellin' you. If God was so damn smart, he'd pick better men for preachers."

She shrugs. "Saul's like the doc. He means well."

"Yeah, and like Doc, leaves you feelin' nothin'. That mother of his wrung it out of him. Put him on the path to salvation."

"Hell, Tom, you know Sarah busts her ass."

"That woman thrives on being crucified. She sucks the pleasure out of life in God's name and has made the boy like her. Get yourself somethin' on the side."

It's too soon to hear this after listening to P.J. "We can't all get away with the shit you pull."

"You don't want to feel you missed anything when you come to this. Not that it's so bad. A dying man needs to die like a hungry man needs to eat. It'd be wrong to try and do anything about it even if I could. And I damn well can't."

She takes his hand, balancing it gently on her palm as he nods intermittently before drifting again.

"Before you drop out on me, let me see what Doc says here. Yep. Got a new one here, Tom."

"Man thinks I'm a horse."

"Horse's ass, maybe. Here. Just get it into you."

He pops it at one throw, ignoring her proffered glass of water, then resettles. A breeze from the hills brings in the sweetness of the rain, stench of the river, and ever-acrid sulfur of the coal. The old man is restless, eyes feverish, tea-rose complexion heightened.

" 'Morrow remind Pansy I want this bed turned round, facin' the window instead of these damn walls." New thunder plays against the mountains and the old man's voice comes fresh, tangled with the storm.

"Got Mama on my mind tonight. Been eatin' at me how she treated me. Water under the bridge, but some-times it gets to workin' on me. I guess she meant well. Lord, she liked to raise hell when I left home. But that was mostly 'cause she always favored Zachary. I never under-stood that. I was the baby, the youngest of five. Think she would have patted me a bit."

Portia rises and tucks a throw around the sleeping brown puck of a woman in the rocker, then settles to wait him out.

"I never took much notice of Daddie. He was just kinda there. Sometimes he'd give us a swat if we got in his way. But Mama ran things, said right from wrong. She always figured me in the wrong.

"I was fifteen when I went to Pittsburgh, but that was pretty much a man in those days. Had left school in the third grade after the teacher pissed me off and got a job as a cinder boy on the furnaces. Bought me this coat I'd had my eye on and then Zachary took it out for some sportin', and when I come home and raised hell about it, Ma beat me with a broom handle. Then Pap whammed me what-for and I decided the hell with it and took off for Salisbury. I'd heard talk of paper mills there.

"Had a few bucks on me, and when I got in town, caught a trolley to go lookin' for work. Didn't know you was supposed to get off the damn things, so I just kept ridin' it back and forth, back and forth. Finally the conductor, he says, 'Boy, you lookin' for something?' He lets me off at the paper mill where they was hirin' and I got on as a box handler. Spent twelve hours a day catchin' boxes some machine spit out. Them concrete floors was hell on my feet, but the evenings was real comfortable. Where I was boardin', the landlady's daughter took a shine to me. I did okay there.

"People was talkin' a lot about war, but it never meant nothin' to me till one day this cop comes around and says, 'Boy, your mum's huntin' you.' This old fart at the boardin' house had told them about me. The cop makes me call Mom, and what does she say but 'Zach's went and joined up. You gotta enlist so to take care of him.' What the hell could I do? Headed on home."

He breaks off, fighting the pills. She firms the blankets around him, noting his tiredness. "You want to try and sleep?" Portia asks.

"Feel like talkin'. Could use a shot of Seagram's, though." His eyes test her and she complies. Settling against the headboard, he downs the drink and studies the downpour.

"Always like a good rain. Makes you feel connected.

Was rainin' the day I signed up. H Company, where Zach was. Everybody knew I lied about my age, but they wasn't goin' to cross Mama. I didn't know what we was fightin' for, but I got to likin' it, the uniform and all. Got real cocky.

"Shipped us out in a convoy of battleships. We did a lot of gamblin' and fightin' to pass the time. I was a pretty good boxer and they had this stage, kind of a pit sunk in the middle of the ship. For this one fight, they put me, a blacksmith, and two niggers down that hole for what they called a 'battle royal.' Everyone kept throwin' money down on us and the last one standin' was to keep it. Well, me and the smithy knocked off them two niggers and then went for each other. Got so bad the chaplain had to stop it. God, I was hurtin'. Never did fight again after that. Not boxin', anyways. Just brawls here and there.

"We was in the big ones, H Company. St.-Mihiel, the Argonne. Belleau Wood. Brass wanted me to sign up for a sniper, but I had to keep an eye on Zach.

"I'll never forget one time. Me and Sergeant Peterson, my commandin' officer, was standin' in the trenches at the front. The Germans had flares bleeding all over the place and we got curious about what was happening at the front. So like damn fools we climbed over the sandbags and started walkin' across no-man's-land. Shell holes all over. It looked like them pictures of the moon except for the stinkin' bodies everywhere and the rats eatin' at them. Anyways, we duck into this trench and sees about thirty Germans lookin' at us. Thought we was goners, when all of a sudden they throw down their guns, up with the hands, and started walkin' out single file. We herded them back to camp and that was the last we heard of it. Somebody probably got a medal out of that one.

"Our battalion got picked to march in the Paris victory parade in front of ol' Black Jack Pershing. Paris was the dirtiest city I ever spent time in. Everyone pissed together in these long outhouses. Go in, pull it out, and might be some old woman or kid beside you. Girls, no more than ten, comin' up to you on the street and offerin' to sell their asses. We had a lot of fights with them nigger boys over the whores. French women hadn't ever seen anything like them, and when we'd hit the houses, all they wanted was a piece of nigger ass. I didn't fool with them much. Got me a steady girl. Nice and clean. We'd go on hayrides out in the country. The driver would blow a horn and everyone took off for the fields to play around a bit. Hour later, he'd blow again and we'd climb back on. Often wondered what became of that girl."

He frets at his chest, picking nervously, still uneasy.

"Still hurtin'?"

"Feel like I'm stuck on a barbed-wire fence with a fox eatin' at my gut."

"I'm givin' you another pill. Doc says 'as necessary,' and there isn't any sense you havin' pain like this."

He downs a fleshy capsule, hollowed eyes balanced against the darkened sky. "Think the Seagram's does more good." She ignores the hint.

"Now, what were you tellin' me?"

"What? About the war. Wasn't much more to it

'ceptin' I wanted to get out of Pittsburgh, get away from the heat of them furnaces. I came here with a buddy who said there was work in the mines. Married your grandma. She was a sweet little bit of a thing in them days. Later life got to her, losin' them two boys like we did, and she took comfort in what she could find, same as me. She took to food; I took to women. But I owe everything I got to her. Never could hold on to a penny myself. Woulda spent it in some saloon."

Portia studies his gaunt profile, lower on the pillow than yesterday. So many good yesterdays on that bed whatever comes at the end of it all. She has less sense of direction for herself than that old man lying there dying.

Tiredness settles her. She should call Saul. The hell with it. He'd know where she was. She lets herself drift on the sleep of the old ones. When St. Bernadette's sounds the midnight Angelus to the unhearing sleeping town, she dims the house lights and treks to her chaste home.

18 The next morning finds Pansy watching impassively as Sissy arrives at the Crowes' and begins cluttering around her kitchen to fix breakfast, before settling in front of the TV with her husband, clasping his limp hand. Disgustedly she hoists herself from the rocker and moves to the kitchen, clutching furniture and walls for support.

Before Tom's illness disrupted life, her days were centered around this room, away from the TV's murmur, where she dozed comfortably in the stove's warmth. The large room has windows on two sides softened by faded feed-bag curtains, their bleached-out pattern sodden with dust. Cupboards made by Tom a half-century before glow silkily from use. Within are the everyday dishes, a quilt of services used over the years. The oldest and smallest set is the plain-colored stoneware used by the kids when they were small. This was succeeded by increasingly elaborate patterns and gradually a scheme evolved as to who got which plate and cup. After Daniel's death, she put his set at the back of the cupboard. Ingrained thrift prevented her from discarding his dishes, yet touching them seared her fingers.

Pansy gets power from the room's accumulated clutter. Only she can pilot the maze of her kitchen. Debris tops the refrigerator, the floor, and all surfaces of the adjacent pantry: dingy boxes, plastics, pans, used tinfoil, and empty TV dinner plates, greasy and ungreasy. Home-canned goods routinely sprout colorful molds which are scraped off and the contents reboiled. The baking soda used to combat the resulting illnesses is bought in generic bulk. The Crowes are renowned as a family plagued by stomach disorders. The Deepfreeze is crammed with sale items, and only Pansy knows what lies beneath its immediate surface. She plans to excavate the turkey Tom received from the mines five years ago whenever the old fool finally passes.

The household eats its main meal at noon. Season and weather dictate the menu, and now facing the misty damp of the morning, the woman decides on soup. She plans: There is a bag of dog bones for stock and summer's leavings haunt the garden. Saliva fills her mouth; adrenaline thumps through sluggish arteries. Pansy relishes her eats.

Making the fire in the woodstove requires squatting, lifting, and rearranging her poundage, but she sure isn't going to ask Sissy for whatever. Grunting stressfully, she fits the dry wood into the stove and lights a perused sales circular, mopping her sweaty brow with the edge of her apron. The heavy iron pot is another struggle but she dislikes aluminum. Burns too easy. Four trips to the discolored sink bring the water in the pan to the required level, and in go the bones, heavily hung with shreds of beef and suet. The dog will cull the tasteless boiled remains. Tomatoes are carefully cut and cored, bad spots eliminated, soggy celery chopped and onions slivered. Garden herbs are added, then salt and pepper. Sinking in her rocker, Pansy takes a break before chopping other vegetables to be added for crisping at the finish. After consideration, she decides to use some of the frozen meat scraps she has hoarded. Though not a vegetarian by conviction, Pansy finds abstinence to be financially expedient, and rarely uses meat other than venison. She thinks pleasurably of the savings this practice has wrought, stashed in an empty Epsom salts box in her closet.

The bits of beef are embedded in the frost-crusted sides of the freezer and chopping is required to free them. Beneath lies one of her hidden prizes: frozen breaded shrimp. Just enough for one. Soon now, she thinks, patting them reassuringly before camouflaging the packet with a bag of okra. Slipping the meat fragments into the simmering pot, she settles back into the rocker with a groan.

Well, bad as times are with things so expensive and all, leastways she doesn't have to make do like when Tom was out on strike in the Thirties. That was when she learned to make do. Nothin' tasted better than barn oysters; just a matter of scraping a bowl of corn, adding a teaspoon of flour, a bit of butter, salt and pepper, and fryin' them up. For their bowels she gave the family "Democrat Sauce," cheese sautéed in prune juice. Make anyone loose as a goose. And as to Tom's drinking, she could fix him a brew cheaper and better than any shine. She'd take about eight gallons of water, add a pound of treacle, bit a ginger and a couple bay leaves, boil them about a quarter hour. After coolin', she added a little yeast, let it work, and watch out.

They never got down to chewin' coffee grounds to stave off hunger like some. The two of them held the family together, her and Tom. Now she wonders: Where did it go to, this time with him? Her mind slips further back, to gentler times before him.

She dozes into her girlhood in Harper's Ferry. Five of them there were. The four girls, Pansy, Rose, Violet, and Addia, and the boy, Daisy, who was ten years older than she. She didn't remember him well and he was only sixteen when he died. Run over on the railway trestle by a train. Some called it suicide.

Papa ran a tavern but Mama was really the proprietor, though no one would properly admit to it. Sherman held forth over a constant succession of beers while Mum was the one to keep glasses full, sweep up the sawdust, make change, and serve over-salty oysters to keep patrons dry. The tavern had been in her mama's family for three generations. Pansy's grandma was remembered for saving the last keg of beer in the county by hiding it under her hoop skirt during a Yankee raid. In her chest upstairs the old woman kept a fragile pair of wire-rim spectacles in a cracked leather case. John Brown had left them at the tavern a few days before his raid on the Federal arsenal.

They'd had such times in her girlhood: picnics on the river and beaus. Then came the tightening before the Great War, and her daddie moved to Cogan's Bluff. Coal miners had big thirsts, he'd been told. Her sisters and friends had married and Pansy was putting in time as a barmaid, so Tom Crowe looked pretty good when he started sparkin' her. Not that she wanted to get married.

Pansy liked her days to herself. But there wasn't much choice.

Tom was good to her but he always liked women. She ignored the humiliation and hid her relief. At least it spared her from havin' to put up with his nonsense. Things were all right until her baby, Mikie, died. She turned from the old man completely after that, left him to the others. And after Daniel's passing, she turned from life. Still, Tom was a habit of fifty years. She would miss him as one's tongue touches the gap left by a lost tooth. His passing would be an inconvenience but . . . she thought of the shrimp.

Rousing from her doze later, she rises to set the table, then settles back to wait out the ongoing television program. A jolt shatters her complacency. Daniel's plate setting is on the table square before Tom's chair. Surely her hand didn't put it there. What is happening? Something has changed, moved. She can feel it. A new sense of conclusion infiltrates the house. Pansy shuffles into the other room following some obscure scent. Sissy is determinedly watching TV, Tom studying the sky. He turns to the sense of her presence.

"Mother?"

"What's happening, Tom?"

"What do ya mean?"

"Things is different. Something's happening."

"The rain's a little harder, that's all. You ain't gonna get upset if I don't eat? I don't feel I could put anything down." He drawls out his sentences. "I am just . . . bone tired."

"You gotta eat, Tom. You've been doin' so good."

"I don't *have* to do nothin'."

As Pansy studies this, something unprecedented occurs. She loses her appetite.

"You go on in, Sissy. I'll sit here with him a bit. But don't go cleanin' up."

Sissy senses the tightened circle, feels her exclusion. "Well, Pansy, how's about I just put a cover on things so's Portia can heat them up later. Maude's gonna fix my hair about two. Think I'll be gettin' on." The woman pauses at the door to study their closed unit. Her time is past.

19 Night's blackness brings the soothing shadows of the mine, and on this familiar turf Tom quickens once more. A few old-timers stop by to shoot the shit, mostly bitching about the young strain of miners taking over.

Tough times and big money are attracting Vietnam veterans and college graduates. More sophisticated than their elders and with little reverence for the union, they have little to lose in challenging the companies. Tom revels in stories of how the boys are telling management to shove it.

"They never talk strike, these young ones. They just slow down, hardly seem to be movin'. Get what they want and never lose a day's work. Why didn't we think of that?"

"We weren't smart enough and too damn mean. Wanted the fast kick of seein' them suffer. We shoulda thought more of our own goin' hungry. Nah, couldn't reason with us. We hadda be hot shits."

Tom waves mutely as the pensioners shuffle out. Paddy Murphy takes Portia's hand. "That's a season passin' in there."

She sits with her grandfather into the night watching his body shut down, wondering on life's brevity. Sometimes it seems God went to a lot of trouble for nothing.

Tom slips back to the mines. "Tell Daniel to watch

that top in Number Two. Them assholes ain't usin' enough supports in there. That's sandstone over that coal. Damn it, Dan. . . ." He clutches Portia's hand, looks at her and shakes his head in disbelief. "Fuckers got him."

Tom's grasp tightens as death saturates the room. The old man has let them fool around with him long enough. It isn't fun anymore. His gaze suddenly focuses in on Portia and she kicks Pansy with her foot. "Nana, he's going now. Wake up."

The woman dozes on.

Tom passes at five that morning. It is done simply. He is there; then he is gone. The sound of his breathing quiets and stops. Whatever was, isn't.

Portia crosses the mangled hands, covering the gap where a bolter has torn off two fingers. Letting Pansy doze, she walks into the fresh dawn. It will be a stunner of a day, gold-coated and newly washed. Pete Turner's pigeons are circling, a graceful covey ringing toward the morning star. Momentarily she reaches out for the old man and instead touches the face of her father.

She returns to the house and forces Pansy back into life. "He's passed. I'll call the doc. He'll know what we're to do."

Pansy nods mutely, glad to be done with the whole thing. Now if the funeral and all that fuss were over, maybe she could get some peace.

The doc is brief; takes a pulse, ties a kerchief around the jaw, and arranges the body in a parody of relaxation.

"What time do you figure he died? I'll need it for the death certificate."

"About five o'clock. I thought maybe I should wait to call so's not to wake you, but I didn't know how they deal with these things."

"Standard procedure. I sign the certificate and you call the funeral home. Let the rest of them sleep through it. You told Pansy." He indicates the wizened woman in the stilled rocker.

"Yeah. She seems okay. Started on her beads and dozed back off."

"Pansy can sleep out her life now. And if Tom said anything to you about some offbeat funeral arrangements, like cremation or old Paddy Murphy playin' the trumpet, ignore it. You've got the living to think of and they like things done properly."

"He did want to be cremated."

"I know, but just forget it. It ain't gonna do him no good and will just upset everyone. I'll see you shortly."

Portia notices that her hands are shaking. She smoothes the sheets, thankful Tom's eyes are closed, and rearranges the get-well cards. They aren't many and they don't need rearranging. The faded snapdragons are pitched into the trash, then she has second thoughts and pulls them from the basket, pushing them into a tacky bouquet.

Saul is one who must be called. Portia rings Sarah, who says he is doing bedsides at the hospital but she will have him paged. He arrives with due solemnity, making noises about presiding, but Pansy shakes her beads at the proposed Pentecostal rites. "I don't know what my old man did believe, but he didn't hold with havin' fits and talkin' out of his head. He'll have a solid Christian burial."

Saul turns to his wife: "Portia, my being family, I could make it personal."

She sits down heavily on the now-empty bed. Tom's dentures still float in the cloudy glass. Almost everyone in the town had known the old man better than Saul. He will bestride the pulpit trying to find something good to say about a man who found enjoyment in about everything he, her husband, found sinful. But then, she has learned from Daniel's demise. All funerals are farces. Only the stage varies.

"It's Pansy's say. Frankly, I don't give a shit."

The look he gives her is a reprimand. "That's a sorry attitude."

"I suppose, but that's how I feel. Pansy needs someone here with her. I'll stay. Sarah will take care of you and Sam. Right now I am going to take a very hot bath and find a book that needs reading. If I am not around in the next few days, and I won't be when mourners start dropping around, I will be in the upstairs bedroom. At the moment I don't feel like dealing with anybody but my grandmother, and I would appreciate it if you would just keep the hell away from me."

A heavy dew on her face wakes Portia to the fading night and she twists in the sleeping bag to look at her watch as the six A.M. Angelus knells. She is on the side porch outside the upstairs bedroom with a clear study of the stars.

The hour is quiet and she drowses on, knowing downstairs the family is preparing Pansy for today's funeral. They have fumed with gratifying helplessness at her isolation, but she saw enough of the formal grieving process at Daniel's wake. Nonparticipation was so easy. She merely announced that she wasn't a participant in this rite of passage and the family declared a passing nervous breakdown.

Portia gives Pansy the rare comfort she requires, eats the food neighbors send in, and dozes through the three-day wake, sometimes reading, sometimes rearranging obliging water stains on the ceiling into a soothing pattern. Maybe this is a mental regression, but it certainly pays old Tom more respect than attending the archaic rituals he always despised.

Today is the finale. They will bury Tom this morning with popish rites and she has to resurrect herself. Moving inside to the bed, she pushes for a deeper sleep and is wakened later by fresh tolling of the bell. Her leg muscles are still cramped from her night on the porch, her mouth stale and stomach growling. The sun's angle on the trellised wallpaper indicates that it's about one o'clock. The knell was for Tom. Yep. She owes the old man; she owes herself. Now, what to do about it?

20 From her desk, Portia faces six indignant students who consider this Saturday morning's detention a violation of their rights. She stares back woodenly, knowing the practice of disciplining students by having them serve weekend time is a joke. Hell, we can take this, their faces say. We can take anything. And we will give you twice the shit in good time. Saturday school is always unpleasant, but this morning a winter storm has pushed the kids beyond edgy and irritable. They are plain mean.

The clock trudges through the last pregnant minutes of the session. Expectant looks hang on her as the hour hand hovers near one, and at five minutes till, Portia slightly inclines her head. The students erupt toward the door, frantically lighting cigarettes and, after a deep draught, dispersing like dim haunts into the heavy white flakes. Momentarily she sinks her head onto the desk, breathing air suddenly cool, then walks to the window, watching the curtain of snow obliterate existence. The outside world is an empty chalk box reflecting her own hollow interior. Ordinarily she loves a storm, its enclosing silence, the calm respite, but now Portia's thoughts are realistic: I'd better get the hell out of here before this gets any worse.

Changing Nikes for the rubber snow boots that embarrass Sam, she has a flash of parental concern. Please, whatever-deity-that-ruled, don't let Saul have given the kid the car to go to the mall in this shit. She opted to walk this morning, anticipating the predicted storm, but forgot her son's habit of Saturday cruising when a vehicle is available. Her head throbs. Surely Saul has enough sense to say no, but then Sam would have been smart enough to ask Sarah.

The school door bangs, echoing into the pooling snow. Little is moving on the streets of Cogan's Bluff. Telephone wires wear icy necklaces; trees grasp the flurried sky. Her lone footsteps stalk the nothingness of a white world. In the distance, four-wheelers scurry through muffled winter stretches.

She is supposed to . . . ? Yes. Regardless of weather, Saul wants her to pick up a solenoid for the Ford. She suspects his real reason is to assert some claim on her Saturday services, but being so conditioned, she crosses to the auto-parts store, an oasis of light on the deserted street. Ed Carter seems in fine humor as he thumbs his catalog. Instead of the usual coterie of wives acting on mumbled orders from husbands positioned under vehicles, there is one woman leaning on the counter.

"Oh my, such a day. Well, I guess this weather makes your life a little easier, Ed."

"Not really. People are always findin' something to get into."

An appreciative giggle is punctuated by a dramatic sigh as Emily Bircher tilts her body toward the parts section, flexing painted nails. Portia and Ed eye each other amusedly, knowing she is on automatic control. Emily's flirting is the reflex action of an aging Southern belle. "Well, I suppose. My Jim, he says he may as well get onto that clutch, snow or not, so he's on his back on that cold garage floor. Sometimes I just don't understand how men think. Do you, Portia?"

"People in general are beyond me, Em."

"Oh, c'mon now. You bein' a teacher, smart and all. And such a man as you have. A preacher and so good looking."

"So I'm told."

"Well, I'm sure after all those years of marriage, you've at least noticed. Now, are you givin' me the right part here, Ed?"

"From what you tell me."

"I certainly hope you didn't go by that or Jim might have to send me out again in this stuff. And he'd do it, too. Well, see you all later." The last of her to disappear is a fluttering scarlet nail. Portia and Ed exchange glances, acknowledging what will not be said, and move on to business.

"Now, how's about you, Portia?"

"Saul has Pete Evans workin' on the truck. Says it's the solenoid."

"For that old Ford?" He thumbs his book, skilled fingers agile, then moves to the shop's rear, searching shelves cluttered with the mysteries of the automobile.

"You lucked out on that one, Miss Portia." The gruff voice comes from behind her. Zanzucki stamps his feet, scattering excess snow.

She turns to grin at him, absurdly delighted. "You figure?"

"Yep." He removes the Russian hat posturing above snow-sprayed hair.

"Yeah, that year your husband's got is an easy piece. Few years earlier model and he'd have to tear out the starter. Have a real mess on his hands."

"Not his hands. He's got Evans doing the job."

"Somehow didn't sound seemly for the preacher to be dirtying hisself."

Her quick defense surprises her. "Saul doesn't mind the work. He just has too many other things going."

"I suppose. Guess savin' souls could be time-consuming. Sendin' them to hell is more my style."

"Well, everyone has their niche in life."

"Haven't seen you for a good while. How about a little drink? Brandy and coffee to warm you and we can catch up on the family."

The mental picture of her at Whetzel's with Zanzucki is a mind-bender. The town would suck on that one for weeks.

Ed is still in back of the cluttered shop rummaging for the solenoid. Zanzucki lowers his voice. "Tell you what. We'll just skip out to the Hole-in-the-Wall. Have a quiet drink where you won't be embarrassed."

"Oh, I'm not worried about that." She catches his skeptical eye. "Okay, maybe a little. Some blue-tinted parishioner will tell Sarah and my life will be hell. But a drink at the Hole would do." She modulates her voice to reach the approaching Ed. "Actually, Steve, a lift would be appreciated."

He plays. "Nothin's movin' out there. There's ice under that snow, but I think my ol' Jeep can get through."

Ed hands her the solenoid. "Anything else, Portia?"

"No, just take care of Steve. He's offered me a ride home, and from the looks of things we'd best get moving."

Ed shoots Zanzucki a glance. "That's so. What will it be, Steve?"

"I'm easy, Ed. Just some transmission fluid."

Ed snorts, bustles around, and rings up the purchase. "You take it easy drivin' now, Steve. Ain't no weather to be foolin' round in."

"That's why I want to get Miss Portia home. And it will give us a chance to talk. We're kinda related, you know. My boy married her sister."

Ed's face lightens, a burden lifting. "That's so, isn't it. Well, you get her back in one piece, then."

"Sure enough, Ed. It ain't far, you know."

Wind has added zest to the storm, flakes maddeningly alive as Steve helps her into the still-warm Jeep with the remembered touch to her elbow. The vehicle smells like him: oily rags, spilt beer, and sulfur. George Jones grates the radio. Spumes of snow encircle, isolating them from the frigid world outside the Jeep's confines. The five miles to the Hole is charged with tension that they try to bury under conversation.

"So, when is that sister of yours going to make me a granddaddie? She's had time enough for it."

"You probably hear more from them than I do. She'll get round to it when she gets the right help, I guess."

"Now, that just might be so. I never could teach Joey anything. His mama spoiled him. And how about you, missy? I thought your preacher man would keep you barefoot and pregnant." The heavy flower of sex suddenly spreads its musky scent within the vehicle.

"That's really none of your business, is it?"

"You two are high-profile church people, and that makes everything you do public business."

"Look, why don't we just turn around. This is becoming not a good idea."

He shrugs. "We're more than halfway there now. Mays as well go for it."

The vehicle continues to grunt forward, good-ol'-boy music covering the pitched awareness. The Jeep's headlights exaggerate falling snow. Life beyond the vehicle seems extinct. What's happening inside the vehicle will not be acknowledged.

Portia breaks the silence. "I hope we make it back."

"We will. Get something hot in you, you'll feel better. This is an adventure."

"This is craziness. What are they gonna think at home if I have to call?"

"Christ's sake, Portia. Grow up. They don't need to know where you're at. Those wires are covered with ice, anyways. Probably nothin' workin'. Just tell them I picked you up and dropped you off at your grandmother's. Then you found out you couldn't phone."

"I really should check on her."

"There. Just a quick drink and I'll take you to her place."

They pull into a parking area, plowing through the white crust to the cluttered building hunching itself into the ground. The Hole-in-the-Wall wears its name well, a bar/restaurant of the type that keeps cases of beer stashed in one of the booths and has two or three fistfights on a good night. Plastic Stroh's signs are mellowed by grease, and the cigarette odor has burrowed deep into the Naugahyde and will never be removed, even if somebody works at it and no one will. The owner doubles as waiter and cook. His sandwiches have an aftertaste of grease and red dye number two.

Steve sits beside her in the booth, ignoring the opposing seat. Her thigh touches his, stinging awareness arcing between them. As ordered, two coffees with accompanying slugs of brandy appear. Steve doctors the hot brew expertly. "Here's to adventure, Mrs. O'Brian." She takes a tentative sip and feels her peripheries reverberate.

"So . . ." Portia studies the bar and briefly ponders the possibility of buying it and moving in. "Damn, I'd like a cigarette."

"You smoke?"

"No. But situations like this seem to require it."

"Filthy habit." He speaks with the smugness of a quitter. "So how does teaching go?"

"I endure."

"Don't we all. And how does the marriage go?"

She shrugs, already brandy heavy, and fails to measure her words. "Again, I endure. Tell me something better about yours."

His eyebrows rise, making their sardonic statement. "She bitches. I run around."

"Well, he preaches and I don't listen."

"And you're not very happy?"

"So who's happy? You?"

He signals for a second brandy. "When you get near fifty, you don't have expectations. You're . . . what, getting into thirty? You should still be looking."

"Thirty isn't looking for answers. Thirty is wondering if they exist. People make my problems and being gutless doesn't help. What I want for myself is never what they want for me. So I change. It's easier than fighting."

"Don't go tellin' me they have you playin' the virgin. To me, you just look like a woman who's not gettin' any."

She reddens but grins. "Sure. And you're the man with the cure. That's an old one, Steve."

"Didn't think you'd let yourself get stuck like this."

"Who says I'm stuck?" Her belligerence is annoying but he always does this to her. "I just feel like I'm nothing. Technically I'm the Reverend Mrs. O'Brian, but Saul tells me I'm not making the grade because of lack of Christian sensibilities. I can't get a damn thing through to those thickheaded kids I supposedly teach. And I'm not even much of a mother. Ask my kid. He depends on his grandmother."

Zanzucki furrows his forehead, studying her, a bit unsure what he is dealing with. The expression of the waiter delivering the check leaves no doubt that he knows exactly who Zanzucki is dealing with and he should know better than to fool with the preacher's wife. As Steve stares through the grimy window at a snowplow flashing in the distance, Portia leans against him, adjusting her body weight into his. He shifts to accommodate her, putting an arm around her neck, where it rests heavily.

"I wish I knew what to tell you, sweetie. There's really nothin' I can say."

The owner is making none too subtle moves to close up, shutting off all the lights but the flickering Stroh's sign, and Steve pays. They cross the lot to the snow-encrusted Jeep. Steve opens the door, releasing a wet shower into its interior. He does not help her in this time. Driving home, he concentrates on the icy roads, but both are aware of their breath intermingling. Reaching the Crowe house, Steve lays a detaining hand on her arm.

"Listen to me a minute. You know there's always been something between us."

"Such as . . . ?"

"God, Portia. Sex. You can say it. It's three letters, not four."

"What's between us is a hell of a mess if we're not careful."

He stares at her, satisfyingly startled. Portia stomps into the house, pausing to reassure Pansy as to her presence. She manages a call home on Tom's decrepit CB. The O'Brians are worried but Sarah has things well in hand. Upstairs she sleeps fitfully, finding herself jolted awake by thoughts of another woman's husband.

21 A month later the alarm's four A.M. call wakens her in Pansy's upstairs bedroom. February's predawn cold hangs in the room and Portia wills herself quiet, allowing her metabolism to adjust to the hour, sensing the cloud masses plummeting through the mountains, their approach cold and blue. Today she reports to Cogan's Bluff Number Two mine as a trainee.

As P.J. had said, getting the job was easy. She submitted an application, went through a farce of an interview, and took a half-ass physical at the local hospital, where they called her back three times for X rays because of bad prints. She figures if she survives the mines, she carries enough radiation to finish her off.

Portia has acquired the singular identity she sought. She is an outcast. Community and family have ostracized her. Cogan's Bluff could have tolerated her becoming a miner had she been a back-hollow welfare mother, but the community has structured its life on predictable values and her defection is a judgment upon themselves. P.J. is seen as a good girl gone bad; Portia is making a statement they don't particularly like.

Saul's reaction is pitiful for an intelligent human being. He knows her soul is damned to hell, and without actually evicting her, strongly urges she move elsewhere. Now he broods in the parsonage, waiting for her to come to her senses and meantime figuring out a suitable punishment for her. Sarah's horror reflects the community's while Sam maintains an amused detachment, waiting to see where his interests lie. Pansy merely shrugs. "Use the upstairs bedroom. It's yours, anyways. Whole house is yours, comes to it. Tom fixed it up that ways. I'll do the cookin'. You buy the foodstuffs. And stay out of my kitchen." She slips back into a doze, wearied by this display of consciousness. Her seclusion is complete since Tom's death.

Robert is the one individual who can comprehend the alien territory she enters, and he is furious. She will be an embarrassment to him. How is he to react when the men he works with talk smut about his sister? "You don't understand, Portia. What do you think these guys do when they need to take a piss? They whip it out and let go. They won't care if you're standin' there or not. And the talk . . . It's 'fuck this' and 'screw that.' "

"Screw you, Robert. Always so supportive."

"You keep pullin' these half-ass stunts. Well, get it straight. I don't know you and I don't take up for you. You're on your own."

Portia's reverie is shaken by the room's cold. The fire has expired in the night. Wrapping herself in an old jacket, she pauses downstairs to tuck Pansy's blanket cocoon tighter before plodding to the basement to stir the banked coals. Her grandmother is the ideal roommate, leaving the rocker once a day to stew her concoctions in the kitchen, then returning to doze in front of the TV, days separated from nights only by the impertinence of test patterns. Stoking the furnace, she has a quick appreciation for the Crowe men's diligent shifts, which kept the home fires burning.

The heat pushes its way upstairs and Portia dresses over the hot-air vent: thermals, wool shirt, jeans, and hunting boots. Daniel's miner's belt has been scavenged to hold her battery and hard hat, the latter spray-painted red, marking her as a new miner. Sitting on the bed, she studies its surface and remembers Zanzucki's stickers, stashed in an old cigar box with other excess brought from the rectory, taken with no thought beyond a quick leaving. She carefully peels off their backing, placing the insignias on the unscarred hat. Their gaudy colors advertise machines that are extinct. Or should be. Companies are not prone to invest in new equipment.

Outside temperatures perversely drop with the rising dawn; the moon quivers in a halo of ice. Cold saturates the coal-camp house, little more than a plaster-lined shell, holding the heat momentarily before throwing it off with a shudder. Returning to the basement, Portia gives the furnace a final shake and puts an extra wrap over Pansy, wiping sleep's drool from her gaping mouth and placing the remote control within reach. She drinks two cups of coffee, pouring another for the road, wincing as she thinks of the inevitable scald between her legs. Lunch and a thermos were fixed the night before.

The porch light glistens on the ice-covered drive, where old snow founders beneath falling sleet. Portia tugs at the car door of Tom's warped Cutlass and it yields, ice falling in a glassy sheet. The vehicle reluctantly comes to life, steam rising against the cold. Tomorrow she will remember to warm it up. Tomorrow. The vinyl upholstery is hostile; the coffee cup takes its precarious position between her thighs.

Driving through the heavy quiet, she knows that across the mountains others are rising with the dawn, leaving sleeping spouses and children, passing into a different world. Insulated with starchy food and clothing, they leave the saltboxes and trailers bought with this labor, threading back roads and hollows before merging onto the main route to the mine. Turning onto the rutted company road to the site, she is trailed by impatient pickups and Blazers. Passing is impossible these last narrow miles. Cars file behind her, their frustration a tangible thing, until the Cutlass belches into the union parking lot. As she slows to park, frustrated vehicles screech around her taillights, lining up as close as possible to the shop building, which offers some protection from freeze-up. Engines are turned from the wind. One man gently tucks a blanket around his hood, weighing it with bricks. Bundled silhouettes clutch lunch pails and garbage bags of clean clothes. Some unseen signal moves clusters of miners to break simultaneously for the shop. She sprints behind them. A black hat obligingly holds open the doors for the oncomers but is startled to see her. A quick grin wraps his wind-pitted face.

"Little nippy, eh, puss?"

"A tad."

"First day?"

She nods.

"Heard we was gettin' ourselves a new puss. Old Man Crowe's daughter, ain't ya? Well, missy, he was a good man. You're probably a good woman, but this ain't your place."

She ignores the remark. "Where should I go?"

"You'll be wantin' the first-aid room. That's where they're havin' classes. Second door on your left. And if you want anything, just ask for Jason. I'll take care of you good."

Portia walks to the indicated door and pushes it open. A cluster of miners in various stages of undress gape at her. She has been directed to the men's bathhouse.

A few of the shyer, and there are very few, hold towels and coveralls in front of themselves. Gaping grins emit howls. One miner slowly pivots a plump ass, displaying his minute male organ. He keeps turning, alternating dimpled cheeks with gut and protuberance. Her feet can't find the ground. The howls crescendo and somehow she is out, running for the car, sweating despite the cold and giving herself hell. She should have known. The wind whips her back to reason, back across the parking lot to find the first-aid room, easily identifiable by its red cross. Faces confront her, laughing. They have already heard.

Seeking the most timid-appearing individual, Portia eases into a chair between him and the wall. Thirty pairs of eyes watch this maneuver, measuring hip girth, bust measurements, length of leg. Lowering herself to sit, she feels a sharp pinch on her posterior and flips her leg backward, collapsing the folding chair onto the lap of the offender. They watch in silence as she moves to another chair. A few giggle appreciatively. Then:

"Hey, Fred. Reach up there and get yourself a piece of that. See how far you can get your hand up that cunt."

The giggling escalates, misplaced and grating in this masculine preserve.

"Old Randy there is the ladies' man. He can poke it further than Fred can reach."

Fred finds his voice. "I ain't got much for sure. Ol' lady bitches about that all the time. But I could tickle her to death."

"Maybe she's got a cherry."

"You kiddin'? Ain't none of them things left."

"This ol' ding-dong here could handle it. So damn big I gotta put a sock on the end when I go swimmin'."

Life in a mining community and basic training at Whetzel's have prepped her to expect harassment, but there is more here: a deep resentment, almost hate. These are not the good ol' boys. This is killer turf. Portia turns to face them, recognizing a few who find other places to stare. They look at one another uncertainly, at the floor, and then carefully shift the talk to other things. Tension lessens as they expound on guns, hunting, stud tires, the ol' lady, the job.

"Fifty bucks a day sounds like a lot of money, but by the time you give Uncle Sam his dues, you'd do better jackin' off hoboes."

"Them guys in Detroit is makin' better than us, workin' nice clean assembly lines. None of this grubbin' underground. No worryin' about the top comin' in on them, fightin' the cold, the rats."

"The union's tryin'—"

"Union. Fat-ass pigs in D.C. livin' high on our money." The miner spits his wad into the corner. Momentarily the room is quiet.

"Manage, know what Jason told me? Said you raped a deaf mute, then broke her fingers so she couldn't tell."

They have heard it before but give the obligatory guffaw. Cigarettes and snuff are exchanged. The man next to Portia extends his tin of Skoal. "Try it, girly. Put hair on your chest."

"Not my brand."

"You'll learn, puss. Particularly if you're a smoker. Woman on third shift uses it. She can chaw and chew gum at the same time."

P.J.? Most probably. Portia grins. That is her style.

Someone is telling the inevitable hunting story. "So after ol' Kanute kills this bear, we goes to gut him. Just to see what was in his belly. Meat ain't no damn good. Kanute slits it open and the stink like to kill you, but he sticks his hand in there and starts pullin' out all this shit. Then he yanks out a tongue and a fistful of hair. He looks at us and everybody was thinkin' the same thing . . . 'bout that Jackson boy got lost up on the mountain beginning of deer season and they never did find him. Kanute starts screamin', 'God, it's him! That bear ate the boy!'

"My stomach just chucked up, I'll tell ya. I was pukin' to one side and ol' Barney to the other. When we straightened up, Kanute was there just laughin' his ass off. Wasn't nothin' but an ol' red fox the critter ate. Me, I didn't do much eatin' for the next couple days."

The class is laughing quietly as the instructor walks in, easily recognizable by his manner. He is a miner, but an educated miner. He has smarts, the kind Portia has seen over pool tables at Whetzel's. He can work this crowd.

"You boys doin' any good? Or just bullshittin'."

Portia smells their forbearance and has a quick sense of being one with the men. This boy is trying too hard. He's a college boy and he's had it easy. But for the next week, he holds the cards.

"Let's get to it. A lot of you men . . . and ladies. Excuse me, miss. I ain't got quite used to women around yet."

A voice from the back takes the opening. "Hell, she ain't no lady."

The instructor ignores this remark, sending a silent message. He is on their side about the woman.

"Well, I know you all think a week sittin' here, listenin' to me, is wasted time when you could just be goin' under and gettin' it."

Dutifully they nod.

"Just figure you're gettin' paid the same and givin' me a job. And what you learn here will make a difference. Sooner or later odds are—and I'm talkin' government figures—either you or your buddy is goin' to get hurt. What we're gonna teach you could save a life. At the end of this week we'll take you on a little tour underground so's you can get the feel of what you're gettin' into. How many of you been underground?" A few tentative hands come up. Portia does not raise hers. "Well, you might not take to it. Some don't. I had a boy last class . . . went underground for his first time. We got back up here and he takes his hard hat off, his belt, throws them in the corner and says, 'There they are, boys. Anyone wants them can have them. I ain't workin' in that hellhole.'

"Coal mining is damn unpleasant; hard work and dangerous. One miner a day loses his life. My job is to try and keep you from bein' one of them.

"You got a few things goin' for you. The government boys watch out for miners nowadays. Every once in a while they send a couple inspectors round to check things out." Snickers are heard. "Yep. That's right. You can bet every time one of them boys shows up, he's already had a good dinner and a few drinks, courtesy of the company. Those boys are in our back pocket.

"But then you got the union."

A shrug of the instructor's shoulders expresses his opinion of that institution, and the room is silent. "Some of their boys can tell you about their doings. So let's get to it. I'm like you all. I'd druther be down there gettin' it, but we're on company time."

They settle in their seats for four long days, learning the rudiments of first aid through tedious lectures and the more stimulating films of gouged eyeballs, crushed ribs, and amputated limbs. When the class loses interest, the instructor reclaims their attention by reminding them that when they are finished, they will practice intimate bandaging, and of course everyone knows who the lucky victim will be. At first this remark brings a chorus of good-ol'-boy chuckles, but by the last day of instruction the laugh has become obligatory and the men are restless. Aware of this, the instructor quickly moves to the promised entertainment.

"Okay. I've shown you all the procedures: bandaging, CPR, treatment for shock. Now we're gonna practice. Who'll volunteer as victim?"

Eyes glisten. This practice session has been the object of much bathhouse speculation.

"None. Well, I guess we'll use the lady."

"Yeah, puss."

"Get on in there, girly."

Knowing this is her baptism by fire and that she must comply, Portia shrugs her shoulders and walks to the front of the room. The instructor positions her on the backboard, hands lingering, another message to the trainees. She looks him in the eye. "You're bruising me." He backs off.

"Okay, Portia. Here's what's happened. Some fool has just run over you with the scoop. These boys are going to bandage you up and take you outside on the backboard. Fred. Come on up here. Start us off. What does she need?"

Fred leers, making it obvious what he thinks she needs. He is cheered roundly.

"C'mon, Donkey Dick."

"Don't rupture her with that thing."

The man studies the woman's rigid body, awkwardly sprawled on the backboard. "A crotch bandage, I'd say."

"Musta been a hell of a horny scoop."

Hubie comes forward to assist Fred. Tension mounts as men eye the strategic area. Rough hands catch at her skin. She realizes they are trembling.

Fred starts at her feet and slowly works his way up, sweat on his lip. Thirty eyes fasten on the delta between her legs. The attending duo is encouraged.

"Go for it, Hubie. You're an ol' muff diver."

"Look at the size of Fred's thumb. You can always tell how much a man's got by his thumb."

Smiling weakly, Fred ever so gently twines the gauze around her thighs. His face is pasty. No breath stirs the room. After a final square knot, he steps back with a sigh and it is done. The instructor has picked his man well. Unbinding Portia, he speaks low. "You did okay, girl."

The class grins at her with some obtuse pride, and one miner observes, "Ya musta got her rocks off somehow, Fred. Look at that grin on her."

Portia shakes her head, knowing there will be no end to it and knowing she is somehow part of it.

A union representative swears them in later that day as members of the United Mine Workers of America. He speaks briefly of their joining a privileged class. A month later he will go company.

She is assigned day shift, causing some red hats to murmur about the favoritism shown women.

Day-shift red-hat boss is Steve Zanzucki. Somehow she has known this.

22 Portia's second hands-on training is in bathhouse etiquette. Her instructor is P.J. and she learns that the criteria for women's cleanliness differs drastically from that for men.

Daniel had told her how the men's changing area was scrupulously washed down between shifts. An innovative system had been established for keeping clean and dirty clothes separate and coal soilage to a minimum. Each miner was assigned a wire basket attached to a chain that could be raised and lowered to the high ceiling of the shower room. At shift change, incoming miners lower these baskets, remove the dirty clothes placed there previously, and stash their clean clothing into garbage bags, which are then elevated to the ceiling. Men getting off work reverse this process. Every man has a security key to his rigging. Once a week, usually on Friday, work clothing is removed, taken home, hosed down and soaked before chancing it to washers. There are the occasional miners who ignore this ritual and continue to wear the same coal- and grease-encrusted clothing. They are invariably identified by such names as "Groundhog" or "Blackie."

Showers and floor are scrubbed down daily, the yellow plastic bottles of Joy used to remove body soot regularly replaced. Miners fought hard for the privilege of cleanliness and strike immediately if it is not honored.

The women's bathhouse is a fifteen-by-fifteen-foot

cubicle cluttered with greasy rags, tools, and the work gear of three female tokens hired for each of the three shifts. Hard hats and self-rescuers are piled in a corner and the floor is covered with the filth theoretically washed away in the sulfur-stained stalls. Although it kowtows to the men, the company feels that providing adequate bath-houses for the women is a major concession that will encourage hordes of females into their ranks. The women don't question the facility's cleanliness, not in the early 1980s. They just thank God for the privilege of work. The superintendent, in a rare moment of whimsy, has pro-vided a baroque mirror over the washbasin. Bright-red shower curtains frame the stalls and the general effect is of a whorehouse gone to hell. The mirror is a particularly cruel gibe. Though it may help the women to locate the coal dust that lingers around the eyes and under the chin, it blatantly reveals enlarged pores, bloodshot eyes, and what is left of the porcelain skin cultivated by their sisters in gentler professions. The underground is not kind to either sex. Men just wear it better.

After she steps into the bathhouse, Portia's street clothes are immediately scarred with dust. She is survey-ing the almost comic filth when a rush of cold air brings a new drift of snow through the door. P.J. Watkins, third shift's woman miner, enters, a coal-encrusted specter.

"So, you made it. Tried callin' when I heard you got took on, but that tight-assed female at the rectory wouldn't give me no answers as to where you were. Cold as hell out there. Underground too. Don't believe that shit they tell you about the temperature in the mines never changin'. Last night it was minus thirty at the pit mouth and icicles hangin' at the face. I sweet-talked old Forester and got him to let me go a bit early. He told the rest I was on the rag and had to go out. Doubt they believe him, but fuck 'em. They take any break they can get."

"This place always this dirty?"

"Hell, yeah. Shitty, ain't it. I wash the worst off here and then go home and soak out the dust. Bitchin' don't do no good. See that gap between the door and the floor." She points to the drift of smutty snow. "Some days we get ice in the toilet."

Portia catches her face, distorted by the cheap mirror and already scummed by the dirt she has picked up entering the bathhouse. P.J. hands her a garbage bag. "Put your clothes in there, hon. Only way to keep them from being destroyed. Seems like this place is gettin' worse, if possible. Cleanin' lady don't give a shit. She comes in, throws a newspaper over the dirt, moves things around a bit and says she's done her job. And you gotta watch out for holes. Those sons a bitches drill holes in the walls to watch us. Don't know what they expect to see that's new. I stuff 'em with toilet paper. Probably a few slip by, but it frustrates the bastards."

Trying to fasten her self-rescuer to her belt, Portia wonders if the few minutes of life its contents will supposedly provide are worth the ten-pound drag on her rear. P.J. moves to help and Portia feels the other woman's knowing concern. They are aliens in the world of the underground and freaks to those outside.

"Here, hon." A cigarette dangles precariously as P.J.

adjusts the straps holding the rescuer. "Once you get this thing fastened, leave it on the belt. Dunk it in water every once in a while to see if it leaks air. I'm gonna tell you, you're in for hell today, but you got one thing goin' for you. They won't forget your daddie died underground. That counts for something. Just do what you can without hurtin' yourself and stay away from the fuckin' bosses."

After blowing her nose, Portia sees that the mucus staining the tissue is streaked with black. "These guys are so damn hostile," she observes.

"They'll ream you out good today. You're a threat to them. A miner needs guts. You think they want to admit a woman has them? Other thing is, they get bored. You add a little interest to their work. Zanzucki's the drone boss. He'll be headin' your crew. He ain't too bad, but he'll try and get in your pants. They all do, but bosses are the worst."

Trying to relieve the drag of steel-toed boots on her legs, Portia sits on the toilet, the only available seat.

"Zanzucki's boy is married to my sister."

"Ooohh." Enlightenment flashes across P.J.'s face. She lights a cigarette and puffs on it with the deep satisfaction of one just having undergone eight hours' forced withdrawal. "Well. That always helps. Guess it's better than fuckin' your way in, which is what most of them have done. They don't stay, though. Put in a little time, then quit. The woman you were brought on to replace stuck around just long enough to get herself a new car."

"And how'd you get hired?"

P.J. laughs. "I asked for that one. I'm not above

doin' anybody if I want a little from 'em, but I won't fuck for my dinner. I let the boss man think he was goin' to get some and then threatened a lawsuit after I'd suckered him enough. Your best bet is to keep your mouth shut and steer clear of the bosses. There's some nice honeys you can play with in there without messin' with them." Cigarette finished, she motions Portia to one side of the toilet and discards the hissing buttsie, then turns on the shower and strips down. Her rotund buttocks protrude from the stall as she waits for the water to get hot. Portia shifts back onto the toilet, her self-rescuer dangling ominously into the bowl. P.J. sputters further instruction from the shower.

"Even if a boss gets down on you for not playin' house, it ain't nothin' to what the men will do if they know you're screwin' him. Gertie Johnson was foolin' round with boss-man Matheson. The guys shit in her lunch bucket, messed up her car, and spray-painted pictures of the two of them fuckin' on the ribs. She quit. Couldn't handle it.

"That son of a bitch Leo makes my life hell. He stuck me on the two-left belthead to clear up the shuttle car spillage. For some reason, the boys driving the buggies on that section can't hit the belt when they dump, and I did a hell of a lot of shoveling for six months. Leo figured if the boss man wasn't goin' to get any of my goodies, neither was anyone else. The rest of them at least get a shot at runnin' machinery, and all I can do is shovel. I won't be able to do shit when I do get a chance to bid. There's two jobs they don't post around here: shovel jobs and blow jobs. They just figure women can handle them both."

"Can't you raise hell about it?"

"Tried. Sometimes a boss will say, 'One of you red hats get on that scoop and move it.' If you jump on it to learn something, you catch hell for doin' some good man out of a job. If you don't move, you're just another lazy woman. Damned if you do, damned if you don't."

Showered and dressed, P.J. applies a carmine slash of lipstick across her still-grimed face. She points again to the shredded tissues in the wall. "Think they're real cute, drillin' them holes. They shouldn't have wasted their time. See that gap in the stairwell above you? That's what the bosses use. They can see everything. Watch us showering, scratchin' our asses, pickin' our noses, puttin' in Tampax. Goddamn sideshow. Bunch of perverts." She swings her bag onto her shoulder and totters toward the door in her trademark spike-heeled boots.

Portia has a quick sense of abandonment. "Well, see ya later."

"Yeah. I'll give you a call. See how things is goin'. Hang tight."

As Portia enters the shop where the men sip coffee while waiting for the shift change, she senses the crew's immediate awareness of her presence. Although indistinguishable from them in coveralls and hard hat, carrying bucket and thermos, she is covertly eyed.

"Here comes the puss."

"Ain't too bad."

"Look better when she gets a little dirt on her."

"You can bet goddamn well that's what it will be: a little."

She in turn studies them. Their bodies are belligerently draped over machinery, eyes lowered. Clothing varies from man to man, depending on where he works, his personality, and what he finds comfortable. Motormen favor heavy thermals with hoods because of their outside trips, passing through the pit mouth, where the windchill may fall to seventy degrees below. The long-wall boss depends on fat for insulation. His T-shirt, which brags on Maryland crabs, is separated from his pants by a protruding beer gut in the front. In the rear, twin moons gleam through the gap. Others wear hunting jackets, yellow wet suits, and coveralls, the latter indicating a female at home concerned with keeping laundry to a minimum.

Sipping her coffee with studied casualness, Portia watches a hefty male shuffle toward her, hands buried in bibs.

"Good to see a new cunt. Need a few women around to liven things up. They ain't good for much else."

Encouraged by background laughter, he continues. " 'Course I ain't ever had many complaints about my work. Especially when I use the main tool." He fondles the protrusion straining at the crotch of his bibs. Portia studies him momentarily before tossing her steaming coffee at the bulge. He howls, cupping the offended member as she calmly twists the lid back onto her thermos and walks away, muttering sotto voce, "Asshole hasn't got much above the neck or below it."

The crew huddles. Time to check this out. They send a wind-whipped man to approach her. "You local?"

"Yeah. My dad was Daniel Crowe. Robert's my brother."

"Bobby's a good union man. Your daddie passed, didn't he?"

"Yeah."

"And your granddaddie, he's the man I remember. Always liked him. I remember you now. You're that red-haired nub that used to hang around Whetzel's. My name's Pat. You'll do all right. Just don't get too down on the boys. And stick close to me. Zanzucki will be your boss. He ain't half bad. He'll cut you a break if he can, but he's got a loose zipper. Watch him."

The jitney carrying midnight's crew clatters out of the pit mouth and into the shop, releasing its cargo of third-shift miners, who immediately begin taunting their oncoming daylight relief. Crews squint at the seven A.M. winter morning, blackened and tired, yet boisterous at the thought of sixteen hours' respite.

"Damn this weather. Freeze a man's balls."

"Bein' you, I wouldn't worry too much."

"Dago! You gettin' any lately? Look at this here puss. Zanzucki's gonna have his own supply from now on."

"She's too scrawny. I like 'em with boobies."

"Ol' once-in-a-while made it today. His ol' lady must be on the rag."

The men rush toward the showers, eyes bright in coal masks, minds on home, beer, and ease. Zanzucki comes from the foreman's office and surveys his crew, removing the white hard hat in the familiar gesture of smoothing his hair. He dispenses tools, many of which will be "lost" before the shift's end. Miners always have exceptionally well-supplied toolboxes at home. Portia accepts the hammer he extends and stands silent as he confronts her, hands on hips, grinning and seeming to expect something. She waits, passive, and he turns abruptly to the crew.

"Okay. Let's go to work."

The miners pile into the vacated jitney, defaced with dents, grime, and the inevitable spray-painted FUCK YOU. Rolling out of the shop, the car collides with the day's bitterness, an intense cold increasing as they pass through the pit mouth, where the air intake aggravates the wind's chill. Portia closes her eyes against the searing cold, settling lower in her seat. Most of the men pull the parkas they wear over their hard hats. All are silent.

The cutting bitterness eases as they pass the portal, and the crew tangibly loosens. Portia opens her eyes. Again, as in childhood, she is Alice down the rabbit hole, the jitney's front headlights giving the only illumination. A long tunnel unfolds, black and mottled, wet drippings solidified into ice stalactites. The man beside her huddles down, his face barely visible. She can feel the hulking body heat of the miners gather around her.

The crew remain sexless clusters of warmth until well beyond the intake's bite when they relax into men who act and react differently from their outside personas, mutants influenced by this alien world. Voices are low, almost reverential, as they adjust to the underground. Speech is hesitant at first, then returns to normal cadence. Portia will learn that the mine affects men differently. To some, as to her, it seems strangely soothing, belying its reported vindictiveness. Others find it threatening and become bitter at being forced to work in a hellhole to maintain a life that doesn't seem worth it.

Each day of mining prods the cavern into a denser labyrinth, extending into new crosscuts and headings. Technically the expansion is planned, the result of the precise input of engineers and miners, but the underground workings evolve into an entity beyond its creators, much as a child becomes independent of his parents.

The jitney stops at the track's end. Portia grabs her lunch bucket and follows the crew into the dinner hole, an abandoned crosscut reeking of the garbage that overflows a corner barrel where luncheon remains are haphazardly tossed. Mice scurry at their approach and the miners relax for the traditional short break they take after going underground. The transformer, the large gray box that relays power, hums in their midst, giving some semblance of warmth. The men quickly down a sandwich and clamber onto its surface, an illegal but accepted practice. Zanzucki runs the faces, checking for gas, and Portia squats against a rib next to Pat, a black hat who has been around and knows his territory. Her fingers have rimmed her vanilla cupcake with coal smudges.

"So, Zanzucki isn't too bad? He was head man when my daddie worked here." She dislikes her curiosity, but a visceral need to know pushes her.

"Steve, he's okay. Just a little beaten around by mine politics." Pat belches comfortably, inserts a wad of snuff between lip and teeth, and relaxes.

"But he's a boss."

"Red-hat boss and that's about the bottom of the heap. The guys who count are those in there gettin' it, not towing around wet-ass repair crews. A lot of tools disappeared when he was heading things. And he'd get bossy, piss the men off, then they'd break up the equipment. And he's got a temper. Things like that add up."

She tries to equate this image with the amusingly tolerant man who wandered the mine that long-ago Christmas with her and Daniel. "He seems pretty laid-back."

Pat snorts. "Never forget one time I was ridin' with his old lady and him to some shindig Charleston throws for its company people. She was puttin' it to him, really bitchin'. He didn't say much, but steam was rising from that ol' head. He takes the cutoff road through the cemetery, stops, reaches over and opens the door on her side, and boots her out. Just puts his foot to that broad old ass and pushes. Shuts the door and keeps on goin'. Never did find out how she got home. I know he never went back for her 'cause both of us got drunk as hell that night. May as well drink up the company's money when you can get it."

He chuckles, spits, and opens his bucket to contemplate a moon pie. He appears to have second thoughts about eating it, and settles back against the rib.

"No, workin' for Steve ain't half bad. If he sees an easy way, he'll take it. He don't push his men too hard, and he sure as hell don't push himself. Right now he don't give a damn about this job, but give him a chance to get back on top and he'll turn mean on you. Long as they keep him down, he's no trouble."

The heavy dank air of the crosscut is stale, sleep-clogged. The men continue to snore on the transformer, cap lights off as mice scurry through the renewed darkness, nosing out crumbs scattered around the garbage barrels. Portia is strangely peaceful, childishly contented. Zanzucki's lone beam comes down the tracks and turns into the cut.

"Okay. Let's hit it."

"What are we doin' today, boss man?"

"Shootin' off a rib. The inspectors jumped the company's ass about that overhang up near the one left-track cutoff. Guess one of them had indigestion from that rich dinner they gave 'em. There's an auger down by the face. Couple you boys go get it."

A collective groan arises and Pat explains to Portia. "Auger is a ten-foot hand drill and a real bitch. You lean a couple men into it and screw it into the coal. Breast auger, they call it. Don't let them put you up front. God didn't design women for that. You can't take the pressure against you. Steve will most likely put Dutch and a couple big boys up there, get the job done fast. He'll be wantin' his nap time, bein' Monday. Man usually has a rough weekend."

"Well," says the hefty black hat called Dutch, "nobody can say we're not progressive. Nineteen hundred and eighties and they pile us behind an auger to drill holes so red hats the first day out can learn dynamiting. Some smarts."

Two miners return lugging the auger and the crew trudges back to the track. Drill and bodies pile back into the jitney. As they roll, Steve quizzes one of the black hats.

"Missed a little time there last week, Mike?"

"Had a couple days' sick time."

"Bring in a doctor's slip. You know that bastard Snyder will insist on one."

"Ol' Doc Walters covered my ass."

"The old man's still good for a freebie, but they're gonna catch up with him."

"Where'd you hear that?"

"Foreman's shower. Talk gets around."

"Ed here missed a little time, too. Wanta tell them about that, Ed?"

"Hell, you know I was sick. Couldn't sit down for a week."

"Somebody poke the wrong hole?"

"That'd been easier. No, I got a hide full of BBs."

The crew draws in tighter, smelling a good one. "Old lady catch you with that little piece from Whitter?"

"I'd be dead if that ever happened. No, me and Ross went fishin' with that damn fool Foster boy from Clarksville. We was drinkin' a bit and Foster starts in on how he's gonna knock off fish with this BB gun he brought. He begins to get on our nerves, so Ross and I row him over to the beaver dam and let him off. Told him to do his thing. He sits there for a while, starts soberin' up and gettin' madder and madder, screaming for me to come pick him up. But we was gettin' a few bites and told him to fuck off. That gets him to hollerin', 'I'll shoot the both of you. I swear I will.'

"About which time I hook a big one and make the mistake of standin' to reel it in. He peppered me in the ass real good. I'll tell you, before he could get off a second round, I had that boat right there. Got the gun, got the man to shore and beat the hell out of him. I kinda had to laugh about it. 'Fuck you,' I says, and *bam!*"

Steve laughs a bit too hard, and raising her head, Portia sees him studying her. He quickly becomes absorbed in the toe of his boot, scraping blackened mud from it with great thoroughness. He is angry. The emotion is not directed at her yet somehow she is involved.

They stop to load rock dust, and as Portia gets back into the mantrip, Zanzucki motions for her to sit next to him, a move not lost on the crew. He positions a strip of cardboard between the cold seat and her rear.

"Ain't no sense freezin' your ass any more than need be."

The men's silence is heavy until the jitney starts, its clatter masking the couple's conversation.

"Well, this is one half-assed stunt you've pulled."

She shrugs.

"Leavin' the preacher was smart. Now you need to

find yourself a real man and get out of here."

"I'm not lookin' for a man."

"Shit! Anything would be better than this hellhole."

"Maybe. P.J. seems to handle it pretty well. The money's good and I think I can handle their shit."

He removes his hard hat and traces his mane. "Hell! You haven't even begun to see their shit yet. And P.J.'s always been a little nuts, runnin' off with anything that comes rollin' down I-79."

"Well, it's a done thing."

He grunts. "Bet your old man didn't take it so well. Heard he ran you off to your grandma's."

Unsure what to say, she says nothing. Quiet settles as they go deeper into the Earth. "Next crosscut!" Steve yells at the driver. "Should be spad sixty-eight." They slow and stop where a prominent rib extends into the track.

"Well, that baby's got to go. Pat, you run down to the face area and tell Harmon we'll be shootin' up here in about three hours, so he better get his men out. Rest of you guys, let's gets her drilled and wired for shot. Quicker we're done, quicker we'll pull some downtime." He turns suddenly. "Portia, go on with Pat. You ain't ever seen a working section yet." He is postponing the indignity of the breast auger.

Ed gives her the obligatory leer in front of the crew, but when they are alone, becomes sudden consideration. "Slow up there, woman. You're walkin' into a sump hole. If you get lost, and that's easy to happen, just follow the power cables. They always lead to the face." They progress amidst rising noise and thickening dust. Through a coal fog she sees the blinding light of the miner as it mutilates the face. The minute figures hovering around the equipment are tensely concentrated as they move cables and adjust supports, all the while eyeing the top. Ed motions Portia forward and yells to the foreman over the machine's din. "Old man sent me to tell you! We're shooting up on one left in about two hours, so get your boys cleared out."

The white hat checks his watch and waves a hand in acknowledgment. "Happy as hell," Ed tells her. "Means a break for them."

At the outcrop three miners are sandwiched against the auger, attempting to puncture the coal. Steve motions her toward them. "Portia, take your turn on the outside. You don't have enough weight for the front."

She leans into the last man on the auger, who rolls his eyes in delight at her body pressure. Her work on the drill is a token gesture; they all know it. But she is expected to take a turn and calmly accepts the few derogatory remarks about her boobs. "Never get mother's milk out of them things." Drilling finished, the crew shows her how to tap the holes with powder and rock dust before stuffing them with dynamite. Steve checks his watch. "Ten o'clock. Harmon won't have his men out till about eleven, so we mays as well grab a bite."

They return to the dinner hole, where the men eat quietly, thoughts elsewhere. Relieved at their preoccupation and in spite of herself, Portia drifts off into a stale half-sleep to be wakened by Steve's voice and a flurry of activity. "Let's get movin'. We'll catch some more time later."

He wires the protruding rib to the detonator. "Okay. String her out." Trailed by the umbilical wire, they move the box up the tracks, where Zanzucki motions them back into a crosscut. Three times he sounds the cry: "Fire in the hole." The detonator handle is plunged and the rib spreads itself across the track. Zanzucki goes down to survey the damage. "Looks good," he says, kicking a hunk of coal. "Second can clean up this junk. We've done enough."

The miners immediately disassemble to the transformer. Some drink coffee; most sleep. Portia shivers and crawls up on the forbidden box. Its gentle whine combines with the warmth to soothe her into a sodden sleep. Part of her listens to Dutch's account of a phone number he will share guaranteed to get a man off in less than five minutes. Zanzucki rouses them near quitting time to check on a faulty pump, and the crew then crawls into the jitney for the mantrip out. Portia stumbles into her bathhouse in a half-daze, the bone-weary tiredness of a survivor.

23 Portia can never quite figure how she endured those early days. Physically she is racked. Her bones and muscles scream. The outer skin peels back from her bleeding fingernails. Her body can never adjust to the mine's fluctuating demands: fatigue beyond sleep, hunger satiated by quick fixes of junk food, skin scrubbed raw and bloodshot eyes. Underground, sleep hunkers like a weighted specter. The few moments' rest she catches at break time are never a gentle easing but rather a knockout punch that leaves her head reeling, saliva acrid in the corners of her mouth. Yet she is constantly wired, her body tense and swollen with carbohydrates even as her skull sheds flesh until red eyes hang in black pouches. The physical deterioration embarrasses her. Meeting Sam on the street, she cringes from his gaze as he tries to be cool, ignoring her death's-head appearance. When she calls the rectory, he is rarely there and he never calls back. She knows she is in trouble.

The harassment, as promised, is hell. Long afterward, when faces and names have merged into one unidentifiable black-faced entity, she will remember the abuse: a miner's self-conscious gentleness exploding into crucifying profanity; the physical assaults in dark crosscuts; the stalking when she attempts to relieve herself, the excrement in her lunch box, the grabs for her ass, and the constant drilling of new peepholes in the bathhouse.

The verbal assault is unrelenting. "How's your puss, babe? Gettin' any?" Heard once, it can be dealt with. Heard twenty times, it can be endured. But heard endlessly and continuously throughout an eight-hour shift from the throats of three hundred men, this primitive brainwashing scrapes her mind raw.

The shit over taking a good man's pay continues, the general consensus being that women are an unpleasant fact of life pushed on the innocent male by the government. "You wanta make some money. Just put up a cot in the pit mouth. You can make more on your back in a day than in a week down here." Hatred is viscious. The men bond against the hostile underground, leaving her to survive if she can.

Outside life offers no easing of the pressure. The community continues to shun her while the miners' wives openly refer to her as "the whore." Portia becomes a recluse, sharing Pansy's solitude and venturing out only when necessary.

Years afterward an enlightened generation of women will ask her, "Why did you take it?" By the time of such questioning, women have memorized Friedan and canonized Anita Hill. They are saturated with righteousness. She attempts to defend her peers as having been programmed since birth to remain barefoot and pregnant by well-meaning parents, spouses, and communities. Steps to independence took incredible guts. But the exploited female of Portia's generation is considered a primitive and vaguely stupid being.

Her sense of humor is her salvation. While the guys are crude and offensive, they are also funny, often unintentionally. Each of them feels an obligation to hussle her as a passage of manhood, and most would be stunned if she agreed. They do so jocularly, with increasing acceptance, much as they joke with a brother about his private endowments. And then there is the occasional dense individual who hasn't realized his mates have ceased believing she is going to bed them. John Stephens is one miner who is very serious in his wooing.

"I tell ya, girl, that thing will get sloppy if you don't use it. Remember, you can't wear it out." Stephens stalks her from bathhouse to shop to dim crosscut. The mine foreman knowingly sends them on joint work assignments, to the crew's great glee.

"C'mon, honey, just a little kiss. I ain't ever been kissed underground."

She ducks behind some tattered brattice to elude two hundred pounds of frantic fumbling. "John, c'mon. How's about your wife."

"Hell, she'll never know. Wouldn't care anyways, long as she gets that paycheck."

Echoes of John's pleas follow her as she rejoins the men. "Think of the fun we could have makin' babies. I'd even leave my old lady for you. And with the big money we'd be earnin' together, we'd clean up, girl."

The crew takes it up:

"Ol' John proposin' again." Blackie manages the words by shifting the wad of tobacco swelling his cheek.

"What's he after? A piece of ass or a piece of that paycheck?"

Zanzucki finally does the wrong thing. He blows. "Look, assholes, quit riding her. I got no complaint about her work, and I'm not goin' to have any discrimination case on my back. So shut the hell up, do your job, and we'll get along. Push her and it's all our butts."

The men exchange significant looks. Zanzucki sounds concerned. They know where that leads.

"Ah, Steve, we was just kiddin' her. Keeps her on her toes."

"And off her back." A miner giggles.

"That's enough. There's a shuttle car broke down in Number Two with a full load. Blackie, you and Ed grab a shovel and start unloadin' it. I figure there's about seven tons there. You shouldn't have time to run your fuckin' mouths."

Word travels fast. Zanzucki is taking up for the woman. The next day the foreman reassigns her. She is to go with Gorilla Watson to unload cinder blocks. Gorilla has the sexual finesse of a wandering wallaby. In the shop, men snicker with anticipation. Steve kicks an oil can in frustration. Watson strolls up and pats him on the back. "Don't worry, Zanzucki. I'll take care of the woman tonight. Don't want you to wear your dong out."

They ride underground with Steve's crew and he is obviously in a pout. Catcalls follow Portia and Gorilla as they jump off at the designated crosscut and watch the mantrip disappear into the dark funnel of coal. Watson grins at her. "Wanna have a little fun before we get to haulin'?"

She turns her back and begins moving blocks. By pacing herself, she finds she can make her trips in opposition to him. They unload the flatcar too quickly, both sweating, aware of the undercurrent of tension. Gorilla sits down and motions for her to follow.

"Take a break, woman. You work too hard. This job is supposed to take all night. We're almost done."

Exhausted, she sits against the rib opposite him, tired beyond argument. The miner studies her with new respect.

"You move this fast on your back? Never thought a woman would tire me. I'm a pretty good worker. In fact, I'm a pretty good man. You should give me a chance, girl. The ol' lady, she was never one for cuddlin' or such. I had a hard time gettin' them girls I do have. Had to use the back door. I'd like a woman I could hold to once in a while. I don't mean just sex, ya know. Just havin' someone around."

She nods and, embarrassed, he regroups. "But I think we oughta fuck first."

"Can't, Watson."

"Shit! I thought you were one of them wild college girls. Marriage to that preacher stiffened you up. But we can fix that easy."

"Well, there's more to it than that."

"You ain't a cold one, are you? I've heard them religious are dead fish."

Portia rests her head on her knees. The miners know

she has left her husband but are unsure what that means. She herself is unaware of the status of her marriage, having been too busy surviving. There has been little time to think of the family she has left beyond sloppy calls to Sam.

"Smart man, Watson. You guessed it. I'm shipping to Africa to join Holden as soon as I make the bucks."

"Who in the hell's Holden?"

"My fiancé. Another man of God. A missionary."

"You're hell for them preachers, ain't you? You ain't gonna be a nun or nothin'?"

"No. But he is a minister in Africa. Wants me to marry him."

"So?" He is treading on unfamiliar territory. "Thought you wasn't gettin' any. Heard you had a thing for old Zanzucki. Anyways, what this Holden don't know won't hurt him. I'll break you in a bit, slip you a little now and then."

"Nah. I wouldn't feel right. God would know."

"Yeah, but ol' Holden wouldn't. God ain't no problem. Besides, I thought some of them preachers couldn't marry or screw."

"Priests can't. Holden's Pentecostal."

"God, that's worse. Bunch of Bible-beatin' hypocrites got their hands in every man's pocket and up every woman's skirt."

"Thing is, Watson, I can't lie to him. If I cheated, I'd have to tell him. He'd go crazy. How could he continue savin' little black babies knowin' that?"

Watson does not have religion, but he is superstitious and is not going to chance hellfire for a quick fuck. Quieting for a few minutes, he draws on a cup of coffee, then rises and stretches. "Well, let's finish movin' them blocks. Sooner you get that paycheck, sooner you'll be out of here. Mines ain't no place for any woman, 'specially one with religion."

Thereafter Portia has her champion. When she is taunted about how many little half-black babies she can expect her missionary to bring home, Watson casually drapes an arm around her shoulder and straightens his bulk. "You men leave my woman alone. Bother Mama here and you'll deal with me." Portia is never sure if his tactics are because he believes the story or is impressed with her imagination. But she learns the wilder the tale, the more it is appreciated, and her mouth becomes a bathhouse fable. "You should hear the story that woman came up with last night. You can't believe her shit, but you gotta hear this one."

P.J. and she frequently compare their situations. Both find the older miners treat them with cautious courtliness, frequently offering to help, assistance that must be denied because of the resentment it causes among the younger men. These boys are vulgar and abusive in a group, but as individuals they converse respectfully, deferring to Portia's reputation as educated and P.J.'s as nuts. P.J. mothers the guys, bringing in cookies and lasagna, while Portia finds her best defense is a wisecrack that reduces the harassing individual to a fool. She becomes very good at being the smart-ass.

Coming into the shop for her shift change, Portia is

routinely greeted by the men with, "Hey, puss! You get any good cock last night?"

One weary morning she decides to shut the boys down.

"Yeah. I took home a beer delivery boy, tied him to a chair, and played with his bottleneck. You guys do any better?"

Looking to her union for support, Portia finds the United Mineworkers hierarchy as confused as its members in dealing with the ladies the government has forced onto their rolls. Officials at union headquarters are prone to treat the phenomenon as a freak occurrence of the times. At the local level the men either support the women as members of the exploited rank-and-file or harass them, depending on their mood, management's stance, and the situation. P.J. and she agree. Abuses dealt out by foremen are protested, while the same treatment coming from the men is accepted.

A scant five percent of the work force attend local meetings, most showing the effects of the previous Saturday night and some coming to avoid the obligatory Sunday visits to the wife's relatives. P.J. is always a no-show. After fifteen years of enforced abstinence, Saturday is "skin night." She is all for union, but a girl has her priorities.

At Portia's first local meeting, thirteen members out of three hundred loll around. The president is reviewing some minute change in the grievance procedure while

Robert, the recording secretary, scribbles. Bored, the brothers decide to liven things up.

"Hey! Let me interrupt you a moment here, Elwood. Are there any boys from Crutchard here?"

The boys from Crutchard slouch lower in their seats while other members straighten up at the prospect of some diversion.

"Okay, chicken asses. I know some of you are here and I just want to tell you. I heard what you boys were sayin' about my ol' lady over the CB the other night. I didn't appreciate it one bit. Ain't one of you sons of bitches got the balls to say it to my face, have you? Gutless pussies."

"Shut up, Brad. We got a woman here. Elwood, keep him quiet."

The president shrugs. "Hell, he's takin' up for one of her kind, ain't he?"

"I'm takin' up for my ol' lady. I got the right to say anything I want about her, but the rest of you assholes keep quiet."

The president shifts his tobacco wad to the other cheek and nods. "Sounds about right to me. Got that down, Robert? Good. I'd say that concludes business. And remember it's Ace's turn for the first round at Whetzel's."

The union's backbone is the men who do not participate in meetings or hold office, but carry the spirit of the UMW. These are the boys who work the picket lines, the men trusted to carry it on. These men are not elected but by consensus speak for the brothers on arbitration and contracts. The miners listen to these voices with a respect they do not give to their elected officials. On Portia's crew, reports come from Clyde, who attends whatever company sessions his clout as a committeeman will get him into, then passes the word along to the men in the dinner hole.

"Them dumb sons of bitches of ours," he says, shaking his head over the three-tiered sandwich necessary to sustain his energy until lunch. "Company's got them so outwitted, it's pathetic. You know what we had representing us at the last arbitration hearing? One loudmouthed president and this dizzy little fart sitting up front who didn't know a damn thing. I sit through a full hour of shit before I got around to asking who the little redheaded fink was. Hell! He was our district rep.

"And there's our honored local officials sittin' around with the district reps, collectin' our good money for attending that meeting, watching out for our interests. And they didn't say nothin'. Just picked up a little extra jack while they sat there dozing. No wonder the local's going broke."

He chomps down on his sandwich, then disdainfully throws it into a corner. "Goddamn Spam. Got enough of it in the army. Well, I did get them to push one thing through for our little lady here." He smiles benignly at Portia. "Told 'em we wanted a flowered Porta Potti with a pretty red curtain round it put up in the returns. I told 'em, 'How would you like it . . . seven guys puttin' their light on you every time you squatted down?' Hell! Even I wouldn't like it.

"And, Miss Portia, I told 'em we wanted an electric outlet run over to the returns from the power cable so's you could fix your hair, pretty up a bit. Gotta keep the main lady happy, I says."

The Porta Potti joke is an old one. Law requires underground johns, but the maxim is "Use 'em, clean 'em." Consequently the miners find a vacant crosscut where they can relieve themselves, covering their leavings with a rag as a courtesy to others passing that way. Stepping in unmarked crap has the same result as being shut in a closet with a litter box.

Clyde has moved to solve this problem by building a privy with old timbers, complete with a pile of rags, a stack of *Playboy*s, and a plastic cup, where he insists the men leave a dime for usage. The last shipment of rags to the mine has came from a ladies' underwear company. The men tend to hoard them, pulling them out to sniff the crotches.

The second-shift woman has quit, and Portia and P.J. are the only women at the mine. The woman said heart trouble made her leave. "Heart trouble, my ass," comments the Dutchman. "What she's got is dropsy. Every time she sees a man, she drops her drawers." As the survivors, the women are subject to increased attention. Men watch to see who they'd pair off with. Females always did. Portia closes even more into herself, saying only what is necessary, particularly to Zanzucki. Sometimes she'd watch him, studying her feelings, trying to learn his mind through the transparency of his face. And sometimes he returns her study. The crew instinctively sees what is developing.

"If you want somebody to play with, hon, you could do better than that old fart."

"How's it feel to run your fingers through the wired-up mop? Bet it's like fuckin' a hippie."

"Missionary, my ass."

Robert has avoided Portia since his angry words at her hire, but he now attempts a counseling session, visiting her at the Crowe homeplace.

"There's plenty of talk around, girl. I know there ain't nothin' to it, but for God's sake, watch yourself. They'll crucify both of us if you take up with a company man. And Zanzucki! He's pretty much family."

"Oh shit, Robert. Nothing's happened."

"Well, you're just makin' a hell out of your life for nothing. And mine."

"I know."

"If that's regret talkin', you'd better do something about it fast. Saul's hired Wayne as an attorney and he's movin' to get a divorce. And you got Sam to think about."

"Kid won't talk to me."

"Can you blame him? Everyone callin' you a whore, includin' his father."

"That's Saul's revenge. He doesn't believe in turning the other cheek despite what he preaches." She lays her head down on the kitchen table, suddenly tired, even beyond the physical hell of the past months. "I'll try callin' Saul tomorrow. If I can get past Sarah."

"Portia, I do hear he's keepin' company."

"With who? Well, never mind. Didn't waste any time, did he."

"What did you expect? Man needs some now and then."

What about a woman? she screams to ask. Why are his needs excused? Where were they before?

Saul does not accept her calls, nor does Sam.

The laborious drudgery never lets up despite physical conditioning. Her nails are black-caked, fingers turgid, skin curling in wood-shaved bits leaving tracks of spottled blood. Work gloves don't help. Maybe endurance is a sexist thing; maybe she can't take it.

Trudging through coal-sodden sump holes, each foot up an accomplishment, a forty-pound belt structure eating into her shoulder, she hears an old song, seemingly filtered through her teeth. Is she hearing this? Maybe she is going crazy. Somewhere she has read that dental fillings and air conditioners pick up radio waves. Whatever. The song rotates, saturating the few brain cells receptive enough for life.

> *Walk like a man.*
> *Talk like a man.*
> *Walk like a man, my son.*

She looks to the male on either side, sweat beading strained faces. Nobody, neither man nor beast, should have to work against nature to make a livelihood. Animals adapt physiologically to unnatural conditions. Of course, it takes thousands of years: supplementing gills, figuring out the appendix, developing appendages they do need. All a man can do in a short lifetime is pack himself down with cumbersome mechanical devices that mar his efficiency while attempting to up his chances of survival. The self-rescuer bangs against her ass with every step. Steel-toed boots suck up black mud. The hard hat has left a stigmata on her brow. Clothes layered for warmth entrap wetness. Life doesn't have genders. Life is a bitch. Portia catches herself. Another contradiction in terms.

Yesterday her class of miners took their black-hat quizzes, state-administered tests given each man at the end of ninety days to determine if he is qualified to shed his trainee status and become a licensed, card-holding craft worker. Portia's stomach still churns remembering her tension. These men have grown up speaking the language of spads, brattice, and ten-inch cuts. Some of this she has heard from Daniel, but the sons of miners carry their knowledge of the underground as an extension of their persona much as she has been versed by Ida in the lore of separating whites from darks or using milk versus water in making gravy. But she passed. She is a miner and today is the day of reckoning. Today the new miners will be greased, a rite of passage initiating them into the brotherhood. Squirming men will have their pants forced down and dicks heavily coated with lubricating grease. P.J. has warned her of this: "Them sons of bitches came at me. Was gonna finger it into me. I had ol' Pete's buck knife and told them, 'C'mon. Just one of you bastards try it.' They backed off but you can count on it. They'll go for you."

Dutch's moon face swells heavy-jowled with anticipation as they ride in on the jitney. He says nothing, just placidly regards Portia. The rest of the crew lean forward tensely, salivating.

When they arrive at the dinner hole, Dutch companionably drapes an arm over her shoulder. "Guess you're legally one of the boys now," he notes, shifting his wad of tobacco. "Treat you just like a brother."

Blackie is working on his pant legs, wrapping the electrical tape tighter around their rims to keep water out of his boots. "What you always wanted, isn't it, Miss Portia. You passed the test. Guess that shows you can do the work. Least as well as ol' Tip-Tap here." He points to the diminutive seventeen-year-old, glasses dripping over a would-be mustache. The kid made a name for himself his first day under when he commented on the decaying feces littering the rib, blossoming into powdery white fungus. Douchebag, a jaded veteran of twenty years, is quick to grab any chance at relieving the job's tedium. He makes his move at break time.

"Hell, boy, ain't you ever seen them flowers before? No. Guess not. Them's moonflowers. Sunlight kills them. That's why you never see them outside."

"My mum . . . she freaks out on flowers. Man, I'd like her to see these. Bet she's never grew nothin' like them."

"Probably not, kid." The other men study their

sandwiches intently, an errant smirk stifled with bologna. "Tell you what. Wanta try gettin' some home without them dyin'? Put a couple in your lunch bucket. Just keep the lid closed so they stay in the dark. That usually keeps 'em fresh."

Dutch expells a mouth of Spam and white bread that disintegrates under the glare of the other men, whose sandwiches move faster, hand to mouth. The boy is contemplative. "Yep. Guess that would do it."

Dutch rises. "Piss time." His back shakes as he retreats to the returns. Tip-Tap is using a shaft of cardboard to scrape feces from the rib, dropping them into his bucket. Determined to keep the silence, the men eye Portia. Their looks have an edge of fellowship and she slowly peels a banana, commiserating with the boy but knowing she will not break the pact. The sweet pulp slides easily down her throat. Snickers rise and they are not directed at Tip-Tap. "Lordy Lord. I do love to see a woman eat a banana."

Dutch stretches and walks to the jitney, returning with a grease gun in hand. The crew's glee straddles the moment of reckoning. Standard procedure. No exceptions. And how in the hell will she handle this.

"Well, Portia, guess it's time you became a professional." He pumps the handle suggestively. "We don't want her squirming too much. Any of you boys want to help?"

With a whoop, Douche dives for her legs and she sidesteps, allowing him to skid on his gut. But her arms are pinned. From behind Blackie has her trussed and off her feet. The rest of the crew laugh, in no hurry to get past the moment, as Dutch advances, leering, eyeing her flailing legs, bobbing and weaving as if approaching a boxer. "Hold on there, missy. Ain't no one ever died of this. Least as I knows. Makes a boy's pole glide a little smoother. Once we get a bit up yours, it'll be grease on grease. Smooth as silk. Zanzucki won't have no problem with friction when we get done with you."

She wishes Steve were away, wouldn't hear of this. She wishes he were here. Maybe he could stop them, but it would only mean more hell at some whenever. And Harvey, the foreman, is conveniently absent, running the faces. He won't stop their fun, but he doesn't want to see it. He is covered.

Blackie yodels. "Mama is hot. Get some grease up her. We'll all take a turn."

Not giving it conscious thought, she back-ends her leg, up and into his crotch. Blackie releases her in a rush of pain, a blast of air. "Goddamn bitch . . ." He sputters further epithets, rolling on the ground, dangerously near to a cluster of moonflowers. "Get her, Dutch. Put it to her." She hears his teeth grind.

Dutch looks at her with pained fury, with shadows of respect. "Fuckin' woman. Best not try that with me."

She remembers how P.J. bought salvation with a buck knife and dives for her lunch bucket. Only the fork for her cottage cheese is there, but she grabs it. "Okay, bastards. Try it. C'mon. Just try it."

She and Dutch glare at each other, the incongruity of the dripping grease gun matched to the fork. He shakes his head, laughing. The tense wire slackens. Somewhere the gods are smiling. Blackie still writhes on the ground, cradling his crotch, but the tears come from disbelief. The big miner throws the gun into the corner. "Silly bitch. Can't do it to you after that fight you put up. Tell you what. Just let me smear a little . . ." His hand slips down her coveralls, passing through the neutral territory between her breasts. "And we'll call it done."

She recognizes the indignity and knows she is compromising, hating herself for it. Portia gives the smirking crew a halfhearted smile and picks up the fork, tossing it back into her lunch bucket. Its rattle echoes her anger. She is getting damn sick of playing their little games in order to survive.

The men's hazing intensifies. Someone nails spikes into her hard hat. Foremen assign her the heaviest jobs. The Cutlass begins to have frequent flat tires and she puts a lock on the gas tank. Her lunch box is filled with grease and she sniffs the contents of her thermos before drinking. Aggravated men have been known to piss in one another's coffee.

The men's harassment pushes her to Steve. Why the hell not? It can't get any worse. Tension grows; between her and the crew, between her and him. One night while she is rock-dusting alone, a light comes up behind her. She knows it is Zanzucki.

"Brought you another bag of dust." He throws it down, busting the thin sack, then sits upon it. "How's it goin'?"

"You know damn well how it's goin'."

"Puttin' it to you pretty good, ain't they. Well, I told you how it'd be." He is self-satisfied.

"But it's gettin' worse and you know the reason for that, too." She sits across from him.

"I've made a point of not doin' anything."

"Yep. That you have."

"You know what would happen if I put it to you? You really want to see some real hell around here?"

"Can't be no worse than what it is." She hears her backhanded assent.

"Portia, you know how this goes. Company hires women to cover their ass, give the guys something to fool with. If these boys think you found a company playpen, we'll both have hell to pay."

"Are you worried about me or yourself? I know I can take it. Either we do or we don't. It's something that's always been there."

Zanzucki preens, pleased with himself, with his role as the chosen. He knows he is one son of a bitch, but she still wants the son of a bitch. "We'd better be headin' back. They'll be wonderin."

"Let 'em wonder. They're gonna think the worst, anyways."

"Portia, look, I'm a no-good bastard. But I like it that way. Maybe if the ol' lady had been different, maybe I wouldn't have gotten into always bein' into heat, runnin' around, the drinkin'. I might have been different, but I'm not likely to change now. I don't know if I could treat any woman decent."

Suddenly she is just tired of it. "Wanta come by later?"

"Sure. As long as you understand."

"I understand." They both know exactly what is being said.

"Okay. Four-thirty, then?" She assents with silence.

"Well, c'mon." His slap on her thigh is companionable. "Let's be gettin' back. Don't want to give them too much to mouth about."

Conspicuously trailing her rock-dust bag, she follows him back to the crosscut. The crew, sprawled in the darkness, rouse themselves sufficiently to stare and grunt. Avoiding their accusing looks, Portia throws herself against a rib and turns off her cap light.

24 She drives absently, thinking about what is to happen. The April day still holds the light and in other circumstances she would have enjoyed the release of the ride. Cats moping around the short driveway scatter at her arrival. Inside Portia pitches her grimy jacket and lunch pail into the corner, and moves to check on Pansy.

"Nana . . ." She hears the name, one she uses only when upset.

"That you, hon?"

"Yeah. You had anything to eat?"

"That boy of yours, he brought me some kinda hash. It weren't bad. But tonight you get that ham outa the freezer. Time we ate it."

"You feelin' okay?"

"Fine, hon. Just turn on my shows."

"We might be gettin' a little company later. Remember Steve Zanzucki?"

"Sure. Joey's daddy. You watch that old fart."

The woman's instinct always amazes Portia. "He's just stopping to talk a little family."

"Humph . . ." Pansy passes into the world of the tube.

Sitting in the bedroom, head in hands, Portia studies the situation. It is all wrong. Despite the cold, she pulls on a pair of cutoffs that display her bruised and unshaven legs, a T-shirt that emphasizes her nonexistent bosom, and frizzes up the carroty mass of hair. The mirror's image discourages seduction.

Zanzucki's big green Pontiac self-consciously creeps up the drive, and she watches him walk toward the door, head tilted, studying the surroundings. He looks old, tired. The rakish appeal of work clothes has been replaced by double knits, white belt, and nylon socks. He knocks, cautiously extending the bag he carries to her. "Wasn't sure what you drank, so I got Stroh's and Bud." His discomfort relaxes her. Maybe this is nothing.

"Never could taste much difference in beers."

He shrugs. "Mind if I have one of those Stroh's?"

"Go in and say something to Pansy first. I told her you were coming."

Steve obliges and for fifteen minutes a one-sided hum harmonizes with the TV. He returns and opens the beer. "She fell asleep on me. Or pretended she was. Think she just wanted me out of there."

He sits in the kitchen's warmth with some approval. "Plants. My mom was always crazy about plants. Had the damn things everywhere. We kids got stuck watering 'em. The ol' lady, she can't keep nothin' alive. Kills snake plants. Never knew nobody could do that."

Portia sprawls on the rag rug in front of the fire, sipping a beer, allowing its malty graininess to fizz up her nose. She doesn't feel at all sexy, but she does feel curiously comfortable, shut off from the lowering night. The house has been lonely with just the old woman. Maybe companionship is all this will come to.

"Your grandma been much trouble? She tie you down?"

"Give Pansy some food and keep her warm and she's fine. She just doesn't want to bother."

Steve moves up behind Portia as she throws a piece of kindling into the woodstove, his arms encircling her body. If the thought of Pansy blundering into the kitchen has hindered him, it does no more. The old ache rumbles within the woman. A storm begins to clutch at the mountains. Shredded clouds coagulate, drifting past the window. Tension gathers as he roughly fingers her breasts through the T-shirt. He will not be a considerate lover.

"Steve." Her squirms are childish. "I don't know. About this, I mean."

"C'mon, Portia. Don't be a cocktease."

"Pansy . . . ?"

He rises and looks into the other room. "She's out of it. We'll go to your room upstairs, keep it quiet. I know she can't take those steps. Look. You tellin' me this doesn't feel good?"

His callused hands graze her nipples. Portia has been thirsty since Saul; even with Saul. Yet she still looks around in her mind for a reason to say no. He is married, but that doesn't really concern her. She is married, but that's a technicality. She doesn't think of herself as Saul's wife anymore. There will be hell at work, even if he doesn't brag. Which he will. But she can't catch any more shit than she is already getting. And his roughness is exciting, a far move from the tepid coupling of the past years.

"Well, what the hell," and they walk up the steps.

He laughs, feeling her quicken now under his hands, moving with them, into them. The musky odor of sex rises. His shirt opens to surprisingly thick body hair and hard arms, visibly muscular but not offensively so. These things excite Portia, which bothers her in turn: that she is the fool to be aroused by such macho traits. She traces the coal dust lingering around his eyes. Miner's mascara.

"You didn't wash very well."

"You know that stuff never comes off. Besides, I was in a hurry for something."

Portia's laugh signals that the preliminaries are over. He makes a quick motion and her T-shirt is off. His hands drop to her cutoffs and he fumbles at the catch. "Rabbit's ass. You get 'em undone. And get under the covers while I strip. This place is colder than a witch's tit."

From under the blankets she watches him undress, thinking that grand passion would have been preferable to this systematic disrobing, the careful folding of clothes. His feet are yellowed, callused. The gut is that of a drinker. Shivering, he moves under the sheets with her.

"God, it's cold! How can you stand it?" He pulls her to him. "Let's get warm."

Momentarily she lies against him, feeling his hardness. Then they move into each other. His sexuality carries them, a domineering maleness that grasps for what he wants, making her move beneath his hands and rise up to him. His power excites Portia, but he is not really concerned with her pleasure. As selfish in his sex as in all things, he is unintentionally good.

She gives, and then gives, the both of them taking from her rather than merging. She rides him hard, lowering and raising herself, the waves wrenching her body, then passing on to him. She pleasures in the look on his face, the sensual dominance.

"Goddamn, you are fine." His hands roam her body as he pumps, calluses catching her skin. Seeing him beneath her, she has a sense of displacement. Always before it has been younger men, smooth bodies. What is she doing? What has she done? Satiated, she rolls next to him under the now-warm covers.

"Goddamn. . . ." He gives her the ultimate compliment. "Goddamn. . . ." The covers are kicked to the floor and a sheet swathes them lightly. She watches the disappearing day leave the wall as he sleeps, lips reverberating with semi-snores. The light dissolves and the furnace slips into life, gathering itself against the dark. Reaching down for the blankets, she falls back into his unconscious arms, and when he wakens later, it is to night's black. Mumbling, Steve stirs, then sensing his displacement, jolts upward, staring at Portia and shaking his head.

"Christ! What time is it?" He squints at his watch in the bedroom's darkness. "Ten o'clock. The old lady will have my ass. Or maybe she'll be too drunk to notice."

Portia is not prepared for her sudden hurt. She has asked for this. She knows his domestic scene, the easy ladies on the side. She is just more of the same. He reads her face.

"Portia . . . c'mon now, babes. You know I gotta live with that woman, and that ain't easy in the best of times.

We'll manage. I'll work somethin' out. I ain't walkin' away from you. But you'll probably be gettin' a lot of company out here when them union boys get to sniffin' around. You ain't gonna want no old man then. One of them will just sweep you off your feet."

She turns into the pillow.

"Rabbit's ass, woman. I'm just talkin' common sense. You think you're tough. Big-time coal miner. But you need a man."

"Thought I just had one."

"Look, all I'm sayin' is, let's take it one day at a time. See what comes of things."

She rises on her elbow, purposefully letting the blankets fall to expose her breasts, but he tucks her in absently, his mind already elsewhere as he dresses, moving to home, excuses, dinner, work.

"Might have to move that transformer in southeast mains tomorrow. That'll be a bitch. I'll have to pass on a nightcap, puss. Tell you what, next time I come I'll bring us some kielbassy. We'll roast it on your woodstove. Now, that's eatin'. Okay, babes, now settle down and get some sleep. You'll need it for that move tomorrow." He kisses her forehead absently. And he is gone.

Portia is sure of nothing except that she has been screwed more ways than one. And that some jesting God is laughing his ass off.

25 For a while, a short while, things are as she supposes they should be. Steve comes when he can and she is always there for him, whenever and for whatever. She doesn't realize what she is missing and he appreciates what he is getting. They eat at dingy diners, screw at sawmills, and explore old hunting camps. The sneaking around necessitates comic couplings within the limitations of his Jeep. They do it front seat, backseat, under the steering column; in the parking lot and behind the railroad depot; under blankets and in sleeping bags on the grass. They have it all: passion, panting, splinters, mosquitoes, and startling horn blasts. They laugh easily and laughter covers their sins. As the fun grows, so does the illusion of permanency.

Portia has studied Freud 101, basic psych, and knows she is acting out a father hang-up, probably even a grandfather hang-up. The relationship is bizarre. She and Steve have no common ground beyond his lust for youth and hers for reassurance.

Compatibility is frequently a function of silence. When they talk, it is mostly of work, and then there is little that can be said that is not already known. Still, he is a touchstone for her and she gives him another chance at youth, therefore they pact with the devil. Steve grows careless, flaunting her at bars, prideful of his new acquisition and perversely giving her a twisted pride in herself.

He doesn't want marriage. "I'm not ever for marryin' again, even if I get out of this mess." She agrees, which confuses him. He does not believe her. Her ease with the situation makes him wary. He would feel a lot easier if she would just talk about getting married once in a while. While Steve scoffs at kids who live together openly, he cannot comprehend a woman who is not frothing for matrimony.

The taunts increase.

"Hey, Zanzucki. Day shift doin' anything but fuckin' these days?"

Steve preens. He gets uptight. He worries about losing his job. "They're gonna fire me sure as hell over this. Just been lookin' for a reason, anyways." He combs his hair with his fingers, taking a drink from the brandy bottle he now keeps at the Crowes'. "The old lady's been up at the mine raisin' hell. They know she's nuts, but they're listening."

The grapevine extends to Charleston. Harriet storms into the homeplace, seething and posturing, her staged voice a shrill reflection of herself.

"My God, Portia, Robert called to ask me to try and do something with you. Steve's my father-in-law. Your boss. Everyone's talking about it. He's at least as old as Dad was."

"He's seven years younger."

"Don't get cute with me. He might be related to me by marriage, but he's no good. You know that. He's been screwin' around for years."

"She drinks."

"He drove her to it, always runnin' around, beatin' on her."

"So she says."

"Well, you ask around about Meg Riley's kid, see who he looks like if you don't believe me. And as for the beatings, I've seen Peg with bruises and black eyes. Not that you'd know about that. You've never seen him at home, but I have. I don't blame you. I know how smooth he can be, but he'll get tired of that. Steve ain't one for makin' an effort. No woman could stand him long. Now Peg's sayin' she'll kill herself because of you."

"If he's such a shit, why does she care?"

"She's had twenty years of him and now he's all she's got. He's messed her up so bad she might just be crazy enough to do it. Get away from him, Portia. Before something really bad happens."

"I can't."

"You can't! Look, come to Charleston with us. There's nothing for you here. You can stay with Joey and me till you get a job, get a life."

"I can't."

"You can. That's what I'm tellin' you."

"Harriet, I'm pregnant."

When did she first become aware of the baby, of this unique physical churning within herself? There was no one moment, rather she saw textures and colors had developed new undertones. The lines on her palms rearranged themselves into different extensions. Her emotions were erratic, and some untried instinct told her it was a baby.

Portia began to wear a bra to contain her swollen nipples, and her breasts hurt pleasantly as she drove the rutted mine roads. Two missed periods and a doctor's appointment only confirmed what she knew by instinct. Within her is a quarter-inch of new life.

"Abortion," Harriet dictates.

"No way."

"Stop it. This is craziness, crazier than going in the mines. Or getting involved with Steve. He won't marry you, you know. When he finds out about this, that'll be the end of you seein' him. A baby means money and Steve ain't gonna have any part of that. Maybe you could force him into something, but he'd hate you. A baby! You don't even understand what a baby is for a single mother. You had Saul's support when you had Sam. Friends and family backing you. You'll be on your own this time."

"That is exactly why I want this child. I'm thirty-five and I don't have a family. Not really. I see Sam once in a while, and if he wants something, he's decent to me. You have Joey, and Mom now that she lives in Charleston, though I don't envy you that. You don't know how it is with just Pansy. This baby is mine. Not Sarah's, Saul's, or even Steve's. Mine."

"God in heaven! And you were always 'the smart one.' Well, if you think Joey and I can help you, you're dead wrong. And Robert's too busy with his union, not to mention how this will embarrass him."

"I'll manage. I'll work as long as the doctor lets me.

I've saved, and when I can't work any longer, I'll get a medical slip until I can go back to the mines to support him."

"Portia, they'll tear you to pieces. The miners and the town. You're not even divorced."

"They can't do much, and as for what they think, I don't give a shit."

Harriet's heels click smartly in leaving. Portia hopes that one of the cats has relieved itself near her car. But her sister is right about one thing. The prospect of a baby sets Steve off.

"Didn't they teach you anything at that college, woman? What the hell are you going to do?"

"Nothing."

She watches his coy flirtation designed not to provoke her as he eases out of the situation. He requests, and is granted, a shift change. Visits to the Crowe house cease. There is no confrontation.

She didn't expect it to be easy. It isn't.

Mornings, the odyssey to the mines is thick with fatigue. Every muscle protests. Her mind aches to shut down. She wants sleep, a deep fall into softness. For the first few hours underground, she is nauseous, clutching her stomach in crosscuts, dry heaves shaking her and the fetus. Eating is misery. But not eating can hurt the baby. She operates solely by rote, moving one foot in front of the other. The evening drive home, formerly a release, becomes a dreary fight to stay conscious. She cares for Pansy, does a little washing, then collapses, waking in the middle of the night, tired beyond sleep, counting and timing each penny while studying the rose-trellised wall-paper she will always remember.

Rumors begin. The woman was seen at the obstetrician's office. She has upchucked all over the dinner hole. Her boobies are fillin' out "like little ol' goose eggs." The company, seeing a potential embarrassment, wishes to avoid it and subtly conveys this attitude to the men, who begin harassing both parties, pushing them to quit.

"You shoulda just sucked that thing, puss. Saved yourself a lot of grief."

"Hey, Zanzucki, don't go pushin' that woman of yours too hard. She just might drop little Stevie there."

"Guess you didn't wear that thing out after all. Just filled it up."

There is one taunt Steve cannot take. "Child support is gonna be one bitch, old man. And you're gonna get hit for alimony on top of that. But when our sister here decides to put the screws to you, us boys are all gonna testify. You better hope this kid doesn't have your ugly mug."

Now that Portia has passed her miner's exam, she is permitted to work on her own. Management consistently gives her the hardest, wettest, and most solitary jobs. When Robinson, the shift foreman, approaches her in the shop with a gleeful look, she knows she is in trouble.

"Portia, my girl, this is your lucky day. Now that you're a black hat, we're gonna give you a shot at being pumper, see if you got natural talent. Go sign out some tools."

Portia flinches. She knows little about pumps and is

still unfamiliar with many of the dark passageways the pumper must travel.

"Who's to be my helper?" Two men are always put on this job because of the extensive distances that must be walked and the weight of the pumps.

Robinson shrugs. "Ain't gonna be none. Ain't nothin' in the contract says we gotta give you a helper."

"Pumper always gets a helper. No one can move two hundred pounds of machinery around in that muck by themselves."

"You're gonna have to try. Them's orders. Use a comealong if you have to. Big girl like you shouldn't have no trouble."

She attempts nonchalance as Robinson slaps her on the back. Never let the bastards see they've got to you.

The crew has the grace to be embarrassed, averting their eyes as they watch Steve cross the shop to where Portia stands hanging tools on her belt. "That son of a bitch! He asked me for somebody to do the job, and I said none of my crew knew their way around well enough. So he picks you. That asshole son of a bitch." Just as she begins to be pleased at his concern, he walks away. "Well, you dumb cunt, I tried tellin' you what you were gettin' into."

Robinson rallies the miners. "Okay, everybody. Let's go to work." And the shop disintegrates into a frenzy. Picking up her bucket, Portia strolls through the pit mouth as the jeering jitneys pass her. Once inside, she crosses to the beltline, leans against a rib, and turns off her cap light till the sound of the mantrips fades. Smitty, the shift fire boss, walks the entire mine checking for gas and must pass here. She waits.

He appears, a stocky older man, identifiable at a distance by the reflector on his walking stick. She lunges from the crosscut. "Smitty! Hey, Smitty. Wait for me."

"What are you doin', hangin' back there by yourself, girl? Can't be waitin' round for an old man like me."

"They put me on as pumper, Smitty. And I don't have a helper. They know I can't find my way around these sections. Let me follow you. Just for tonight. I'll learn my way quick."

"And what are you goin' to do if you have to move one of those big blue boys?"

"I'll wiggle it or maybe use a comealong. Contract says I don't have to move more than I can lift, so if I can't, the section will have to flood out and that's their problem."

"Ballard will have my ass if he finds out about this. You know he wants things as hard as possible for you. Duck out of the way if you see another light comin'. And I wouldn't even attempt those heavy ones if what I hear is true."

"About a baby? Yeah, Smitty, it is."

"Goddamn. You do like to keep things stirred up, don't you? The hell this is gonna make."

"Well, I'm passing the word. If those bastards cause me to lose this baby, I'll sue their asses to hell and back."

He grunts and hits his stick against the rib, dislodging loose coal. "That's your business. I don't hold with women in the mines. It ain't the place for them. But since you're here, they oughta treat you decent."

Smitty keeps up the talk as they move deeper into the underground. "Cut through the bleeders here and it'll take you to second left. That saves a mile of walking. Southeast mains is the trick section to find, but if you get that down, you'll have no trouble." He shakes his head. "Been in this man's mine thirty years and never thought I'd see a woman workin' here. I'd shoot my wife before I'd let her go underground. Even these young boys who'd do about anything for a buck, they wouldn't let their wives work here.

" 'Course things now ain't as bad as they was when I started. Those days we loaded by hand. A man got paid by the ton, and only ten cents a ton at that. You took chances to get that coal and get it fast. Many's the time the chances got the man. Now we get better wages for sure, but conditions still ain't what they should be. Hell enough for a man. Ain't no place for a woman."

They cross to southeast mains, avoiding the crew working there. Smitty helps her maneuver the pump into the face area, black mud oozing around their legs and sucking at their boots. He has no rain gear and his coveralls are sodden.

"I surely do appreciate this, Smitty. Usually I don't take help from nobody, but things bein' what they are, I kinda have to."

He waves her thanks away. "Wife is goin' to bitch about these coveralls. I shoulda wore a wet suit. Remember to wind electrical tape around the bottom of your trousers. That'll keep the worst of it out. Meantime, let's hit the transformer and dry a bit."

They sprawl on the humming gray box, cap lights out, absorbing its warmth. From someplace within this surrealistic world, she hears rocks fall into water. The creases and groans of a working Earth sing around them. Finally Smitty sighs, his raspy breath breaking the druglike trance induced by the transformer. "Well, girl, I hate to say it, but we better get movin'."

At the day's end, he leaves her with a promise. "I'll watch for you. Ask the belt men for help if you get lost. They're pretty much a good bunch."

The next day, Portia rambles a bit, but by the end of the week the job has become merely a cold, wet hike She moves the pumps when she is able. If not, they sit. Management gets the message.

Portia's personal demons on the job are the unblinking eyes that watch her from the crosscuts. Rats, she tells herself. But these eyes aren't paired off. They crouch on the facets of coal and watch her in clusters or in a single cold glint. She doesn't know what they want and doesn't try to find out. Her only escape is to turn off her cap light, taking her breaks in the safe blackness. The dark void holds no threats. She is alone then. Almost.

It is these times that make the baby a reality to her. Gently she rubs the bauble of life under her miner's belt. The swelling cups to her hand as she trudges toward the next section and begins to position her body in ways that protect him. The child is no longer shapeless protoplasm.

Portia develops a sense of "us." She and her boy converse. She has no doubt as to her child's sex.

At the end of the month she bids for pumper on a permanent basis. The company turns her down, citing inexperience. Without union support, management quickly takes advantage of her ambiguous status to assign her to a faceman's position.

The faceman's job is a vague job, as easy or difficult as the foreman and crew want to make it. They make it a bitch. Portia is then in her third month.

"Hey, woman, bring a few roof jacks over here. And some bolts and resin."

"Puss, that buggy needs about fifty gallons of oil, and you'd better check the other one."

"Gotta get that brattice hung in Number Three."

"There's about ten bags or so of rock dust up by the track. Get 'em."

"Hey, woman! Clean up the dinner hole."

The crew lays on the transformer and watches as Portia sifts through the garbage littering the crosscut, picking up chicken bones and rotten sandwiches with a churning stomach. Occasionally she has to sidestep a "fuzzy flower," the decaying fecal matter left by another shift as a calling card.

Time is passing fast, too fast. Her savings are adequate but not to the point where she feels secure. She will push herself to work as long as it is possible without damaging the baby. After studying the embryo's picture in a physiology book, she knows at four months he is a tiny gilled entity resembling a tadpole. She consciously tries to will her womb deeper into herself, centering the baby and praying he will stay intact. Each shift becomes a gamble for that day's pay. But as the child grows, he no longer fits securely under the wide band of the miner's belt.

"That ain't beer showin' down there, puss," observes John. "Looks more like a watermelon patch, and I don't think no missionary planted it."

The end comes on a crisp September morning.

Section is down that day and the crew lounges around while the mechanics work on the broken buggies. An occasional snicker rises as the woman passes by the lazing men, lugging the heavy belt structure through the muddy section, its rollers digging into her shoulders. Studying the situation, the foreman chaws down on his sandwich. "Portia, we're gonna need those jacks in five moved to Number Three."

She grunts and moves to fetch them while the Dutchman leans against the buggy, regarding her. "Ah, the wages of sin. You know, hon, if I had to take all the shit you do, I'd just grab my bucket and head down the road. You oughta think about it."

Shrugging, she trudges to get a jack as the men watch. Bending to pick up the third support, a cramp grabs at her stomach.

"Sweet Jesus." Sweat beads Portia's forehead as another pain pierces her womb. She drops the jack and walks over to the foreman. "Goosie, I'm hurtin'. I'm outa here."

"Little Stevie actin' up? You know the rules. You go outside, you gotta have a doctor's slip to get back in."

"I'll have it."

Clutching her stomach, willing the boy to settle, she goes to the dinner hole for her bucket. The men watch, confused. They never really thought it would come to this. Goose follows her, flustered. "You want one of the boys to walk you out, Portia? You been workin' pretty hard. Go and have a laydown on the transformer for a while before you try goin' out. Now, you're sure you're okay?"

The other bastards avoid her eyes, grabbing jacks, suddenly working at nothing. Turning to face them, she raises her middle finger, salutes them, and departs.

26 The doctor is visibly relieved as he gives her the sick slip. "We just don't know anything about pregnancy in women miners. I'll feel a lot better with you out of there. I've worded this to say you can't work until 'further notice,' which in your case means after the baby. Six weeks is the standard time off, but considering the circumstances, we'll see how things go."

She pictures him and his wife discussing the matter over dinner with much shaking of heads and murmurs of "Poor woman. Well, you know whose it is, don't you?" She photocopies the slip, sending the original to the mines registered mail. Best to cover one's ass in these matters. As Portia watches the letter slip into the postbox, the physical and mental tensions of the past months suddenly loosen. She knows she will have to fight again. But not now. Later. When she is up to it.

Pansy asks no questions, merely regards her expanding stomach. "Figured that was what was goin' on. Ain't the preacher's, is it? Thought not. Well, it'll be kind of nice having a young'un around again. Just don't go bringin' in no man."

Autumn has a good taste that year. Portia blessedly settles into her "confinement," a term still used in Cogan's Bluff. Her heightened senses find everything surer, clearer. The day's clarity rises into nights capped with stars. She has not traced the constellations in years, not been aware of missing them. Many warm evenings, the embryo and Portia wrap into a blanket, sleeping on the porch. It is there, as frenzied insects cry against the coming winter, she feels the child's first teasing flutter, a tiny fishlike movement that grows daily, strengthening as the fetus impatiently gropes for life.

Time, as measured by how far up she can zip her jeans, passes quickly. Portia stays to herself, making only a few necessary trips to grocery stores and the library. Edith has passed and the new librarian seems professionally remote. What reading she does do is mostly "how-to" books, enumerating the endless paraphernalia a baby now requires. She is amazed how much more materialistic newborns have become since Sam.

The developing child is dominant. She becomes a spectator at her own pregnancy, a host organism for this parasite who eats at her essence, gives her heartburn, punches her insides during the nights, and slumbers through the days. While she begrudges him nothing, the kid is beginning to push his luck. Why doesn't he get on with it? The baby cooperates. He arrives early.

She has paced the house in exasperation all day, unsettled, impatient, although the child himself is strangely quiet. Grabbing a coat and giving the door a healthy slam, Portia begins to walk with no sense of destination, merely following the silent weight of her body. March's barren promise chars the woods. Her movements stir lifeless undergrowth. She returns, unusually threatened at the prospect of another solitary evening with Pansy, and is suddenly angry at the child for his stubbornness about being born. Her steps into the house ring firm, a silent complaint to her unborn companion.

But he hears and answers. Moisture saturates her jeans. Has she wet herself? Water puddles on the linoleum, gathering in its cracks. Nine months climax quickly in a gentle flow of water. After reading about one's water breaking, Portia has expected an explosion, not this gentle tide.

"Pansy."

The woman is unusually alert, her face instinctively lighting.

"I'll be goin' to the hospital now. It's time."

"Honey, you take anything they give you for pain. Scream. Don't try to be strong about it. And you have one of them nurses call me when the boy gets here." She rubs her hands. "Ah, this is a good day. A new young'un. I've been sewin' a few things for you. Tucked them in top of your bag."

"And you've been strainin' your eyes doin' that?"

"I may be an old woman, but I still see. I just don't see no more than I want to. No use gettin' uncomfortable."

The prepacked suitcase mandated by textbooks is under the bed (that seems to be the custom). Outside of the discomfort of the wet car seat, saturated with her fluids, the trip to the hospital is painless. She is studied suspiciously at the admissions desk. Pregnant women are invariably accompanied.

"Are you sure this is it, Mrs. O'Brian? Have you had any pains?"

"No, but . . ." Portia lifts the legs of her jeans. Her shoes squish. Water flows onto the glassy floor.

"Yes, I'd say this is it. Orderly, get a wheelchair."

"I can walk."

"Hospital policy, Mrs. O'Brian. We'll need your insurance card and the keys to your car. It has to be moved to a permanent place. Also the hospital requires a name to contact if problems develop." Obviously she sees Portia as the problem.

Portia gives them Sam O'Brian's name. There is no one else and she hopes he will realize it. The birthing room is white, sterile, and seems an unlikely place to encourage new life. A nurse extends a hospital gown, the open back an indecent proposal. "Best be getting into this. We need to get you prepped."

"What's 'prepped'?" There was none of this business before. Nothing in the books.

"We need to prepare you for the doctor with a pubic shave and enema."

"C'mon. Is this really necessary?"

"Well, honey, the shave's for you so's you don't go gettin' your hair pulled, and the enema is for the doctor's benefit. You'll be doin' a lot of bearin' down and we don't want any accidents."

"Okay. I understand what you're saying."

"So, let's get things moving. Any pain yet? No. It may take a while. You just relax."

Portia is shaved down to bristles, purged and tucked into the antiseptic bed. She pulls out a book, eyeing the nurse in an adjoining room who is reading a magazine while picking at Fritos. Another joins her and they briefly discuss ordering a pizza. Mercifully they decide to pass. Medical apparatus gleams. A clock bestrides the room. It will dominate her life in the following hours. Portia studies her silent stomach. Is this all there is to it the second time around?

The nurse enters, pulling on a plastic glove. "How are you feeling?"

"I'm not feeling anything."

She wets her lips with satisfaction. "That'll change soon enough." Spreading Portia's legs, she studies the vagina, probing a bit, extending the slit, and then sits on the edge of the bed. Within minutes she gets what she is waiting for. Portia's face registers more remembrance than pain as the first twisting contraction hits her, leaving a sensation like that of a bowel movement. Yeah, this is how it starts. Soon there is another, stronger, grabbing. The nurse feels her taut stomach and nods. Inserting her gloved hand into the womb again, she probes the dilation.

"Something wrong?"

"We may be at this awhile, honey. You have an inverted womb and it'll take some time to come around."

"They didn't say so last time. Will it hurt the kid?"

"The babe will be fine. It's just the way nature arranged you." She pats Portia's knee. "If the pain gets too bad, I'll get you a little something, though we don't want you too doped up. I'll be in the next room if you need me."

"How long do you figure?"

"Pardon?"

"How long do you think this will last?"

"Hard to say. May be over by midnight. May take until tomorrow morning."

Tomorrow morning. Sweet Jesus! A spasm grips and holds, and the nurse visibly mellows before her pain. She thinks longingly of the saddle block she had with Sam. Damn progressive thinking!

"Felt that one, didn' you? Well, let's try and keep your mind off things. Here's your book. Or do you want a nice magazine? Let me wipe your face. Wanna talk? I'll be off at eleven, but Alice will be comin' in and she's real nice. Had twins herself last year. She thinks she's got trouble now, but she doesn't know what she's in for. Like those boys of mine. Friday night and they'll be out at all hours. I have to lie there, one eye on the clock, thinkin' the worst. My husband, George, ain't no help. He says I go on too much. Every time the phone rings tonight I'll figure it's somebody sayin' that those kids got drunked up and killed themselves or somebody else. You'll be learnin' about it soon enough, girl or boy. Sometimes I think girls might be worse."

A pain sears her insides and the nurse ceases prattling. She pushes the hair from Portia's forehead where it is wet and matted. Portia's body extends as she strains.

"Would you rather me just shut up, hon? Some likes talk, some doesn't."

"Yeah. I do better alone." She doesn't want to alienate this woman who controls her world.

"Well, I'll be right next door if you need me. Just

give a yell, but I think you'll have to put up with this for a while."

The nurse departs, slightly affronted but consoled by Portia's pain. She settles herself on a sofa in the adjoining room, picks up her magazine, and dips back into the Fritos, occasionally wiping her fingers on the glossy pages or her uniform.

As much as Portia wants to realize the child's coming without the smallness of everyday talk, her aloneness is stark. Birthing is too intense an experience to be borne by an individual alone. She thinks of Steve. He has been transferred to night shift, another step down, and most probably because of his hassles with her. He will fault her further for that. But he remains a reality while the child is still a straining bulge, and Portia times his night shift by the stalking wall clock that marks her pain.

Ten o'clock. He would be making a stop at the Hole, ordering coffee or a glass of Dago Red, depending on the weather and his mood.

Eleven-fifteen. The pains are two minutes apart now and Alice, the relief nurse, must still probe for the opening. She touches Portia with a new gentleness. "The cervix is dilated, but it just doesn't seem to want to come around. We can give you something, but it'll be better if you try and go with it, better for the babe. Breathe deep now. Pant."

The nurse demonstrates and Portia imitates her sweaty gasps. She hears herself, an animal struggling for air, but some relief comes.

"Good. Another pain building? Let's try again."

Eleven-thirty. Steve would be dressing now, trading vulgarities with the other foreman. "Poked a little bit too deep that time, heh, Zanzucki? You gotta know how to use that thing."

Twelve o'clock. They would be loading into the mantrip.

"You're dilating well now. Just hold on."

As the next pain begins, Portia begins to breathe fast, trying to beat the hurt back. She wonders, rather abstractly, if she should call the whole thing off.

"You're doin' fine. Just be a little longer." Portia nods. She really has no other choice at this point. The clock continues to push pain upon her.

Two o'clock. Steve is trudging the slimy mud. She hears his hacking cough and remembers how wracked her father's lungs were those last years of his life.

Three o'clock. Lunchtime. Beantime, Steve calls it. He does love to eat. Basically, he is a good ol' boy, loving all the elementary pleasures. Does he feel pain as intensely as the good times? She is locked into her own.

Four o'clock. The nurse probes and nods her head approvingly. "You've come around, honey. Time for the finish. I'll have them call the doctor." Portia is wheeled through a corridor of white and green into the delivery room. The gurney pauses and a shaggy head bends over her. It takes her a moment to realize it is not Steve.

"Mom. You okay? The hospital called the house. They were worried when you came in by yourself. I got here as soon as I could."

She looks at Sam's acne-ridden face, rimless glasses riding his nose. May this one coming be as beautiful as her boy-man. . . .

"Sam, you need to wash better. Have you been using your Clearasil?" A pain grabs her. "Christ! That was a rough one. Hold my hand a minute."

"You hurtin', Mum?"

"I've had better times." She touches his face. "Hey, it's not so bad. Look what I got last time."

"I wish I could do something."

"You came. That's the big thing."

"And I'm stayin' right here."

"You don't have to."

"I have to. I'll be down the hall. Yell a little so's I know how things are comin'."

"Believe me, I'll be yelling a lot." He clutches her hand, trotting alongside the gurney. "Sam . . . how's your dad?"

"He's okay, I guess. He never says much. It's like you never existed. Once in a while he'll say, 'your mother,' but he won't use your name. Do you want me to try and get hold of him?"

"No. We two can manage."

"You shoulda held on to those rubbers you gave me." He grins.

The delivery room is an engulfing white cavern, stark lights accentuating pain, chrome stirrups an awkward indignity. Sheets drape her legs. The nurse leans over the gurney with concerned eyes as she inserts a breathing apparatus over Portia's nose. "Okay. Now a deep breath."

A sweet, giggly gas saturates her brain, and the pain relaxes.

"Okay, hon, now bear down. Push." White-coated figures coax her, exhort her as the doctor moves to a crouch position beneath the dust covers draping her legs. "Gonna be a blond," he announces.

How can he tell that? She looks to her belly, where the bulge is still intact, though slightly lower. Tensing, Portia pushes, arching, trying to expel this intruder. Soaking with sweat, she hurls herself into a red-black bordello of pain and emerges at an extremity beyond endurance. Strangely, she likes this being on the edge, but she is not crazy about having so many individuals clustered beneath the sheet. She wants them to leave and bears down, locked in a vise of agony. The white-masked galley cheers her on. "C'mon. Push. Push and breathe."

In a gush of water, blood, and flesh, Portia expels her insides and there is a new voice in the room.

"A boy. Looks fine."

The doctor says this easily. He must know these few words have redefined her life.

"Yep, this one's going to be a real chow hound. Hear him smacking his lips." Portia raises herself but is blinded by the glare and restricted by the stirrups, sees only the nurse carrying a raw morsel of flesh to a heat lamp, where she wipes it off.

"He's okay?"

"We'll check him out in a minute, but to all appearances, he's a perfect little fellow." He kneads her stomach for the afterbirth, which emerges in another red gush. She leans back. The clock reads 5:07 A.M.

"Doctor. Thanks."

"You didn't do too badly yourself." He puts his hand on her shoulder and withdraws it gingerly. "Now take a look at what you've got."

They lay him in her arms.

This child, this tart and wrinkled persimmon, has come so far to get here and already he is groping, reaching for the breast. She wonders at him; wonders at herself. How was she so audacious as to will him into being? She must be relevant, to have such power, and she must not make any mistakes with this one. She must make him understand his own relevancy. She must not hand him over as she did Sam.

The nurse takes him. "Time for you to get a bit of rest. We'll clean him up and you can nurse him later."

"No. I want him now."

"You'll have to wait, honey."

His going creates a void, but the line of tension holds, a cord of awareness connecting the two of them. She dozes easily in her room of sea-green drabness, waking in the early light as they bring the child to her. The nurse coaxes the nipple to his mouth and his instinctive sucking becomes greed. Raising her eyes, she sees Sam watching the two of them curiously.

"You're not supposed to be in here while I'm nursing. One of their weird rules."

"It's nice. I've never seen it before. Did you nurse me?"

"Nah. You were born with teeth."

Awkwardly he plops down a candy box, fumbles with the wrapper, and extends a piece. "Nursing is supposed to make you hungry."

"How'd you get to know so much? Debbie hasn't been misbehavin', has she?"

Sam grins and makes no comment. He eats the proffered candy himself.

"Someone needs to call Pansy."

"I did. She's pleased as if she did it herself. I told Dad. He's trying to be Christian and all, but I don't guess he'll ever understand. What are you going to call the kid?"

"Jesse."

"Biblical. Pretty far from Sam." She knows he is testing his position.

"I don't think so. Samuel is biblical."

"Yeah, it is. Hey, Mum, I'm sorry for being such an asshole. Staying away and all. It was just the kids at school were gettin' on me pretty bad. You know how that is."

She looks at his gauche freshness, thinking what beautiful children she makes. "Forget it. The three of us will be okay now. Maybe you can help me out with the baby-sittin' once in a while."

"That might work. The kid looks neat."

"Well, don't get any ideas about one of your own yet."

"Nah. You know Debbie and I fool around, but I'm careful."

This talk has been vital, but she is bone tired. Seeing this, Sam strokes her hand momentarily before moving to leave. He turns at the door. "You ain't figurin' on goin' back to the mines?"

"The kid's gotta eat."

He shakes his head and returns suddenly to rub a timid finger across Jesse's cheek. "I'll be here to drive you home Sunday. See you then."

She touches his hand as gently as he has touched the baby.

"Okay, Sam. Oh, and tell your dad—"

"I'll tell him everything's fine."

27 In the six weeks' interim granted her, Portia finds she has lost her independence to a world of opportunities. Pansy enjoys the child, but Portia can count on her for nothing but that pleasure. She dotes on the boy as the mood takes her and then signs out to wherever her mind dwells these days. As there is no Sarah to coach her, Portia is mother as she never was with Sam.

She becomes familiar with Jesse's moves, moods, and demands, and as her respect for him as an individual grows, she finds new confidence in herself. Which in turn moves her to write.

It is hard. Probably the hardest thing she has ever done. But now her love for the boy pushes her to it. As Edith has promised, the words come. Wide awake after the four A.M. feeding, she sits at the noisily intrusive typewriter, aware of the coming dawn, of the men rising to forfeit their day to the underground. Sentences crackle, sometimes in a haze and at times clearly dictated. She reads them later with the same creative pride and wonder with which she regards the child.

Portia knows she must return to work as soon as possible. Time moves smoothly to the day she packs Jesse off to a sitter while she again tracks the rutted mine road. The spring solstice has just passed. Clouds move to shred the sky, loosing unserious rain onto the mine buildings that squat gray and quiet between shifts. Cap lights flicker around the pit mouth. Men crossing the parking lot to report for work seem weary already. They regard her curiously, particularly the new hires as the veterans point her out and tell her story. The foremen's office is to the side of the shop. It quiets as Portia enters, their curiosity a tangible thing. She approaches Blanchard, who sits behind a steel desk, dust-covered and belligerent. Other foremen are scattered around the room drinking coffee and smoking. She ignores Zanzucki in the far corner.

"Well, Robinson, I'm not sure what the protocol is on this, but here's the doctor's slip. When do I start back?" Her hand trembles as she extends the paper. He regards her incredulously.

"Well, puss, I'll tell you. Bets was we'd seen the last of you." The foreman fingers the note, squinting and muttering, then shakes his head. "It looks in order, but I don't know if I'm the one to be handling this." He calls the super, then turns to her after a huddled conversation over the phone. "He's phoning Charleston."

She prods him a bit. "I thought this was standard procedure."

"Honey, not a damn thing you've done's been standard."

She bluffs again. "Do you want to give Charleston my attorney's number?"

"No. No, why don't you just wait outside till they figure this thing out."

Leaving, she hears, "Fuckin' broad. Thought we were rid of her. Damn you, Zanzucki. Next time you go screwin' around, pick a dumb one."

Portia leans against the battery rack, watching Blanchard's movements through the glass partition. He gestures over the phone, hangs up, is silent, shuffles papers to avoid looking at her, answers the phone, rereads the doctor's slip, confers with the contract book, and slams down the receiver. She can lip-read the expletives. Forcing a smile, he beckons her into the office. "Charleston says to start you back Monday. The new pay period starts then."

"Shit! Great!"

"Well, there'll probably be plenty of shit, anyways. See you on Monday."

"P.J. tells me you've changed locks on the women's washroom. I'll need a key."

"Oh, yeah." He fumbles beneath the pile of Twinkie wrappers in his desk drawer. "Have to hide the damn things. Somebody got ahold of the old key and distributed copies. You know how boys are."

"Yeah. I know how boys are."

Outside the foremen's office, night shift is coming out placing batteries into their racks, and she is confronted by a cluster of mine-blackened faces. She holds up her key, not sure what to expect. "Well, looks like I'm back."

The men surge around her. "Good to see you, Portia. Things were gettin' boring around here."

"Hey, woman, you gonna bring that kid to work with ya?"

"Sure, she is. She can nurse him on section."

"Yeah, if the roof falls in, we can live off mother's milk."

"Look how those boobies have filled out."

The Dutchman grabs her and swings her newly lightened body in an arc. "Girly, next time you want a kid, come to me. I'll show you how a union man does it."

The hazing of the early days continues, but with a gentle hand. Either motherhood has touched some inbred reverence or the miners are impressed with her staying power. They become even more adamant that she should get herself a man and stay home with the babe, where a woman should be. Men who think nothing of gutting a deer are very impressed with the mundane demands of motherhood. They laugh at their own limitations with kids, most of which seem conveniently self-imposed.

"Change diapers? Maybe if it's just wet and the old lady's not there. But with shit in them? God, I'd puke."

They speak with awe of how their wives feed babies at night, clean up vomit, and rise to a sick child's cries. Their masculine egos will not recognize the fact that on top of attending to these distasteful tasks, she works the underground, doing what they pride themselves on as being a hard job.

Occasionally Portia's seniority qualifies her to be

straw boss, the black-hat supervisor of some inex-perienced new hire who, after loudly advertising his dis-dain at working for a woman, invariably proves to be good company underground. Soon after Portia's return, they send her to boss a job with Jeff Ashton. They are to haul cribbing from the long wall. Ashton is a freaky six-teen-year-old dropout who reeks of pot, which the older men write off as aftershave.

Long-wall mining features a new technique devel-oped in Europe, and the men distrust it on principle. A one-hundred-foot or more stretch of supports called chocks extends across a face stretched between two en-tries. The chocks are fronted by a belt. This moving belt receives the coal cut by a huge cylindrical wheel that guts the face. As the mined coal is removed on the belt, each chock moves forward to support the newly mined area, frequently releasing a shower of sandstone. The injury rate on the long wall is high.

Chrome supports gleam eerily as Portia and the kid stand at the long wall's head, allowing their cap beams to play down its length. Jeff has all of youth's bravado, but she can smell his fear. Sitting in the dinner hole for a sandwich before starting the job, they hear rocks escaping the supports, clattering onto the panline. Ashton talks to ease himself.

"You know I'm only sixteen? Youngest damn kid in the mines. Had to lie to get on. 'Course Blanchard knows, but he's friends with my mum. We don't have much comin' in since the old man took off. Blanchard's been pretty good to us, but I think she slips him a little somethin' on the side, ya know? Can't blame her. Person gets horny. Guess it's my age that makes me that way. Always horny. Can't get enough ballin'." He eyes her curiously. "Are you like that?"

"I take it when it comes. I don't go looking for it."

"Well, you're gettin' up there. Thirty-somethin', ain't ya? I started messin' around pretty young, so I may burn out early. When I started I wasn't tall enough to reach a rubber machine, even if I coulda came up with a quarter. Then I quit high school last year. They wasn't teachin' me a damn thing, anyways. Bummed around, got smoked up. Blanchard got me on here after Mom went cryin' to him. Guess he figured he was doin' me a favor. Shieeett."

He shifts the wad of tobacco in his mouth, releasing fresh spittle. "Anyways, I got it made now. Big coal miner's paycheck. Slip Mum a bit and I'm sittin' pretty. The chick I live with, she's a bit of a dog, but she does keep the place clean. Kinda clean. Packs my bucket, washes my gear. Picks up the cat shit. Stuff like that. And it's nice to have a piece hangin' around. 'Cept she won't swallow the stuff. Says it's ucky. There's others out there that ain't so particular. But they all bore the shit out of me once they get talkin'. Never did find any of them interesting enough to marry."

She looks at him. Sixteen. Sam is already fourteen, soon to be his age, and another man-child with a limitless sense of possibilities.

They leave the dinner hole. The blackness seems to have coagulated. Illuminated by their cap lights, the chocks stand like columns of some ancient temple deifying a subterranean god. The boy shakes his head in awe.

"Goddamn! This is one mother machine. Can you imagine figurin' out something like this? That must have been one mother-fuckin' smart man. Hope he was smart enough to keep us from gettin' killed."

Rocks fall at unexpected intervals, rattling on the panline, and they seem to Portia like meteor showers of shale and limestone. The kid has no such romantic images. He freezes at each random sound, squats, looking up to the chunks of rock resting on the support tops, tensed for a plunge to a safety that doesn't exist.

"This place is spooky."

"They call it progressive mining."

"Progressive, hell! Spooky."

"That might be about right. Meares told me the second-shift pumper quit because he saw ghosts in the returns. They found him running down the beltline in the dark, screaming. Said he turned his cap light off so the 'things' couldn't get him."

"This place would do it to you." They study the rock dust curling in wraithlike specters. "Fuckin' shit. They ain't puttin' me down here again. I'll quit first."

They shovel. The kid paces himself to Portia, who knows the ploy: "I'll work with that woman, but I ain't gonna shovel my ass into the ground while she sits on hers." He keeps up a more or less steady monologue though his voice quickly dwindles to a whine. "Hey, slow down a bit. There ain't no boss standin' over us. You don't have to work our butts off. I'd like a smoke."

"Just don't do it in front of me. I don't want to bitch about it, and I don't want to know about it."

"You'd say somethin'?"

"Fuckin' A."

"Hey, can you imagine gettin' stoned down here? That would be a freak-out. Or gettin' laid?" His mind backs up. "Does it bother you swallowin' it?"

"Supposed to be pure protein."

"Like vitamins, huh? I'll tell the ol' lady that. She might listen, you bein' a college girl and all. Ever try speed? Man! I get some of that shit, I could shovel a whole cut by myself. Oughta put it in those little jugs of water they give us. That'd get 'em some coal. Coke's what I'd like to get into. Supposed to really move ya. 'Cept I don't like needles, and sniffin' tears up your nose."

"Wouldn't it make you paranoid? Scared, I mean. Usin' that stuff down here?"

"Hell, no. The only time I get scared is in the bathhouse."

She looks to see if he is kidding. He isn't.

"There's some bad-ass dudes workin' in this mine. That son of a bitch Anton. That Dago wants to rape me. No, woman, I ain't kiddin'. That ol' fucker wants my ass bad. 'Course I brought it on myself. He called me 'honey' one day. I hate that shit. They all call me 'honey,' or 'sweetie' or stuff. And I says, 'Anton, only two people calls me "honey." One's my mother and the other's fags.' I was too damn stupid to realize he really is queer. Now he chases me around the bathhouse, screamin', 'Get me that boy. I want that little ass.' The other day he ran me down and kissed me. That bastard is even hornier than I am. I've seen him hump knotholes. I've been gettin' dressed in the car, but God help me if that bastard ever catches up with me. There goes my cherry. I wouldn't be able to walk for a week."

Portia knows Anton is just trying to get to the boy and doing a hell of a good job at it. A week later she is riding out with the crew on the mantrip when a yellow slash of color sears up the track, arms and legs moving like propellers. The mirage fades just as she has time to realize it is the boy, streaking by in his wet suit. Anton plunges behind him, two hundred pounds of shaking laughter growling, "Get me that kid. Pull down his pants. I want a piece of that little ass." Jeff never comes back to the mines and his mother claims his uncollected check.

28 Life settles into a strangely satisfying monotony. Work even becomes boring at times. She has heard all the bullshit before, and the job is often repetitious. But Jesse is ever changing. Following the habit of kids, he grows, becomes more demanding. Portia sometimes resents defining herself in terms of the child.

The weariness of motherhood shows in the new planes of her face, the tenseness in her body relaxed only by sleep. She studies herself in the mirror, sometimes glancing quickly to catch her reflection unawares. Often she appears effervescent, a flash across silver. Occasionally she has a coarse ugliness. Mostly she isn't too bad, though she is still not overly fond of her body. Its frame has a tendency to flesh out if not kept lean with work and living, but the overall structure is good, a throwback to Tom's fabled Indian ancestor. Femininity lurks in the highness of her cheekbones, the hollow of her back, and the curve of her hip, which gives the illusion of a Rubens.

The blue in the eyes that study her reflection is not the incredible azure of Daniel's or Jesse's, but rather a blue that has found character and deepened. Her skull's structure has improved. The bones are starker, closer to the surface. Her mouth and chin are Ida's legacy, a combination of firmness tempered by womanhood. Still her hair remains a corona of orange fuzz that will not be controlled. All in all, a rather unremarkable appearance, but her features wear well.

Much of this she sees in Jesse, the strength and length of herself muted by Steve's fairness and vitality. Watching the boy develop, she sees what her mating with a man of much style and little substance has produced and is satisfied that it has strengthened the Crowe line, weeding out some of the introspection that haunts her breed. She is pleased by the boy, his becoming.

At night, going to the crib to check his existence, she asserts her own. Mothers never tire of spying on their children at sleep and trying to read their secrets. Often he thwarts her by being awake, quietly studying the plants with Chinese eyes, grinning fuzzily as she invades his world. "Shhh," she whispers to him, acting out their mundane private joke. "You must be quiet. The baby's asleep." He soon drifts off and she stands there, watching the small creases on his soul fade.

Yet this tranquillity is continually jarred by the restlessness that prevails at work. The weather has been good, prime fishing weather. They have run into bad top on the long wall. Real bad top. Manage, who has worked the mines for years, shakes his head. "I've seen it bad, and I've seen it real bad. But I ain't never seen nothin' like this." The men's tension tastes alkaline as they move softly beneath the dangling sandstone, eyes up and watching. The crew is identifiable on the outside by their sandstone-pelted hard hats.

Portia is faceman, and on the long wall that means endless shoveling of the chocks, allowing them to move forward without obstruction. It is heavy going. Most of the work falls to her, as the other faceman, Avery, has an agreement with the crew. He takes the chances; they do the work. Avery moves the chocks under bad top with the understanding that nothing else is required of him. He laconically sprawls in a safe area and watches Portia shovel, emerging when a chock is ready to be moved. One lazy flick of his wrist sends it forward while he stands under a sandstone shower, then he returns to the sidelines and his semi-slumber. Avery justifies himself. "Hell! If the company was smart, they'd just hire a couple of chimps to move these things, and pay them a few bananas. Or maybe they oughta recruit some midgets. 'Course the chimps might be too smart to work down here, and they'd have to pay the midgets the rate."

Contract time is coming round and the men are anticipating a strike. Bets are they will be out for a while. "You bet your ass," says the Dutchman, "if we're out two weeks, you can figure on four months. Better be savin' your dollars, boys, and get your old lady's ass to working the streets. It's all that son-of-a-bitchin' governor's fault. Gonna use the state boys to break us, he says. Well, I ain't worried. Heard they're gonna put in a factory for designer jeans over to Grafton. Figure I can get hired on there. Hear they use the governor's name on them and they're sure winners. They have a zipper up the ass."

Avery could give a damn. Stretched over the transformer, he combs his locks with a coal-grimed hand. "Strike suits me fine. I need a little vacation. Pick off a few deer. Maybe sell some of that copper I've been savin' for a rainy day and use that for beer money. I had a pretty good crop of wacky weed this summer, so I won't be hurtin' for smokes."

"Might suit you, boy. You ain't got no payments to be worryin' about. Mummie and Daddie will take care of you."

"Ain't my fault you assholes got married. Anyone can get a free piece."

Kotex shakes his head. His name has evolved from his constant complaints that his wife is ragging and won't give him any. "Sorry sort of woman who'd have you. Couldn't tell what she was gettin' with all that hair hangin' in your face."

"Women likes that hair. Tickles them. Besides"—he gropes his crotch suggestively—"I got what it takes."

Manage glances at Portia and swings the talk from Avery's privates. "You was with us last contract, Dutch. Remember how we went down to Whitefield and talked Dickens out of haulin'?"

The crew relishes the big man's memories. "Yeah. Really got the ol' boy's dander up. We told him we didn't want any more coal goin' out of there till we had us a contract. 'It won't, boys,' he says. 'I'm done haulin'.' And two hours after that a convoy of his trucks come up Main Street, all full loaded." He laughs with relish. "Joe Elliott was with us. We waited till they got dead under the stoplight in the middle of town and told 'em to dump her.

"The man drivin', he says, 'I can't do that.' 'The hell you can't,' we says. 'But the cops will kill me,' he whines. 'So, you're a dead man either way.' We stuck that ol' shotgun of Elliott's under his nose and he dumped her quick enough. Shoulda seen that pile of coal sittin' square in the middle of town and them pensioners haulin' it off as fast as they could. Dickens didn't take to it kindly. Said he was gonna put the cops on us. Shit! We had rags over the license plates. I had my hair all greased up under a cap, and we was wearin' ski masks. Town cops don't give a damn, anyways. It's them state boys that get nasty. We just eased ourselves on outa there, and he didn't do too much haulin' after that."

They laugh fondly and Kotex keeps it going. "Briggs and his bunch didn't take too kindly to gettin' shut down either. We'd send out pickets. He'd close down for a day and then start haulin' when we sent them somewheres else. But he had this big ol' yellow end loader sittin' out in the shop yard. All pretty and bright. Brand new. So one night we make us a couple of cocktails and . . . *ooomph!* Up she goes." He pitches a rock against a rib for emphasis, releasing a shower of cinders onto Portia's hard hat. She shudders. "Yep. Ol' Man Briggs shut down the next day. He was pretty much shut down when we blowed his 'dozer to hell."

"What time is it?" The question is asked by Earl, the ever-practical foreman.

"Two-fifteen."

He grunts. "My watch says two-twenty, and we don't want to get out there too early. Robinson will get scared we're shortin' him. I'll run the faces and then we'll pull." He walks into the darkness, the glow of his bug light banging on his hip. The men watch him approvingly.

"Good man, that one," notes Manage. "Nothin' like the rest of the lot."

"Didn't let it go to his head. Earl will put in a hand to help a man."

The crew relaxes now that the day's end is in sight. Some sip a bit of lukewarm coffee left in their thermoses. A few still have cakes. Avery prowls hungrily. "Anyone got any extra feed?"

"Portia still has her lunch box," one says, leering, eyeing her crotch.

They quiet, fatigued with the day and, despite the talk, apprehensive about the strike. Or something. The Dutchman voices an instinct not yet spoken. "Somethin's out there waitin' to happen. I can feel it."

Later Portia only remembers that she herself had no such foreboding.

29 The mutilation and death of its men is a way of life in a mining community. For coal miners, accidents are more than a possibility. They are a probability. As the strike approaches and tension grows, injuries become more frequent. Some are staged to get workman's comp during the downtime. Most result from stress. Some just happen.

Miners generally don't talk about the accident itself but rather what might have happened. Say, an inch to the right, maybe to the left. Up. Down. What if. If only. Thank God and amen.

Portia wonders what passes through a man's mind as he is ground senseless by some cannibalistic machine. She blesses God for Daniel's quick demise and tries to put her mind elsewhere. But she cannot release the thought. Her father is a haunt she walks with.

The day goes as usual. She maneuvers the shuttle car to the face, concentrating on the machine's movement, making a smooth turn, sighting for a man or obstacle that may block her. The car whines its way to the feeder. She is contented. *Happy* is too extreme a word, but things aren't bad: with the baby, the job, the life. Portia drives the car into a break, sighting the turn with her cap light from beneath the overhanging canopy, which protects her from roof falls.

Suddenly there is agony on the periphery. Something is drastically wrong. Turning her head, she sees the flesh of her right arm ripping, bones snapping. The posts supporting the canopy are crushing her arm, moving toward her head. She is going to die.

Death fills Portia's mouth, a stale bitter taste. Her system is beyond registering pain, crazy with the shock of torn nerves, crushed bones. A nightmare of black and red moves to her head.

Sounds tear at her throat. She listens with the curious detachment of a spectator. Suddenly there is silence. It is not happening anymore. The car has stopped. She is not going to die. But the remainder of her life has been dissected in those few moments.

"Oh my God! Manage. Joe. Somebody help me. Aieeeee . . ."

Her keening cuts across an abrupt quiet, all machinery inexplicably stopped. At the opposite end of the buggy's canopy, her arm protrudes at an angle designed by neither God nor man. Detachedly she notes that her elbow, which hangs loosely from shattered skin, resembles the knob end of a chicken bone.

"Help me. Somebody." Voices echo her own disbelieving horror. "The woman's cut all to hell. Earl! My God, Earl! We gotta do something."

The crew assembles and disassembles. Earl turns his back and gags, heaving his lunch. Voices and people are thick, but nothing is happening. The men cannot move the machinery, as her buggy has sliced the main power cable. This has saved her life, but now the crew has no way of lifting the machine off her mangled body.

Portia knows the arm is somewhere on the other side of the canopy. Torn flesh and bone fragments pollute what was the sleeve of her hunting jacket, but she is confused about the limb's exact location. Her senses position it high, shoulder high, yet the cap lights of the frantic men show it hanging. She knows it is a phantom limb. Gone. Its ghost will ache in the damp. The specter will try to reach, experience. That's what they say, the amputees.

"Did you check the transformer to see if it's kicked power?" She can't tell who is speaking.

"It's not that."

"How about the tricycle?"

"Ed was down there. He says no."

"Christ, you assholes! Don't you got eyes? She's run over her power cable. That'll take hours to repair."

Remembering his first-aid training, Joe bends to press a finger against her collarbone where the artery pulsates. "We're gonna get you out of here, baby. You'll be okay. Just don't panic."

Portia stirs. "I'm not pinned, Joe. It's gone. Just take me from this side."

His eyes flatten. "Jesus. Shhh, now. We'll get you out." Turning, he screams in a voice belonging to another man. "You sons of bitches get a jack. Get something, for God's sake."

She thinks it curious how often God's name has been invoked during the last few minutes. Just make it for Jesse's sake, she thinks, and sinks back into Joe's arms. His cap light is the only illumination. They remain quiet in a dark void of panic.

"There ain't no jack on the jitney." Manage speaks in the midst of a sprint across the section looking for something . . . anything. Everyone is moving swiftly. Nobody is actually doing anything, but continuous movement gives the illusion of constructive effort.

Manage sputters. "We've bitched and bitched at them about bringing in a mantrip without a jack. There'll be hell to pay for it this time. At least we've got transportation on the section if we can get her to it. Much bleeding?"

Joe shakes his head, unconsciously grinding his teeth. The rest of the crew keep their eyes averted from her body, warped between the coal and the machine.

"Even if we get the power back on, we don't know what's gonna happen. The buggy could move forward and take off her head."

Earl is there, two bars in hand.

"You gotta be kidding." Joe shakes his head. "This thing weighs thirteen tons. Ain't no way."

Earl hands the other bar to Manage, and the two men insert it between canopy and rib. They pry, bending into the buggy with their body weight. Tears and sweat mingle on Manage's face, following lines gouged by labor.

The machine quivers, sliding some little way from the rib. Hardly believing, Portia looks at Joe, but he is watching the two straining men, willing the buggy to move. Manage strains as he dissolves the laws of gravity. Eyes bulge with effort; prayers are spit between clinched teeth. "Now, in the hour of our need. His will be done . . . the shorn lamb . . ." Shorn, Portia thinks. That's me.

The opening around her arm widens and she takes the bloody remnant in her other hand, moving it upward, seeking an out. The buggy moves some little space more. The limb slips into the space. Free! She falls back into Joe's arms, and amazingly she is shattered but whole, and sinking. Unconscious? No. It's just the sense of relief spreading tangibly through the crew that reaches her. "The stretcher," Earl says. "Let's get her out of here."

Strapped on the backboard, Portia sees only dimly. Someone has removed her cap light and hard hat, eliminating another whole sense. Voices come to her darkly, through the passing light thrown by others. Shadows accentuate the unreality of a scene that can only be happening in her head, anyways. Portia knows she is indestructible. She has spent the better part of thirty years proving that. The shadow sitting on her shoulder is not real.

But the pain is. Her nerve endings scream. Torn flesh protests: too much, too much. Pain builds on pain as shock recedes. Reality and illusion take their corners. She lifts something from her chest, a fragment of bloody bone, and closes her eyes again. This time around she will have to get used to being the victim.

"Easy now. Easy." She is lowered into the jitney. Joe's hand follows the artery, compressing, dipping and swaying like a dancer as they edge the stretcher into the mantrip. Wood clambors against metal and she is in. Earl climbs on one side of her, eyes brilliant in coal-grimed face. Joe is on the other side, his ever-present hand on the artery.

Manage calls back from the driver's compartment, "You ready?"

"Let's get it movin'."

"We're on it. Tracks have been cleared the whole way out."

The jitney clatters out into life, moving fast, cross-cuts whizzing past in the darkness. Portia loosely figures they will be outside in ten minutes at this pace. The men's silence confirms the reality of the moment. Nothing less than a crisis would still the horseplay that marks each mantrip outside, each release from the blackness that is a third of their lives.

Earl shifts restlessly, eyeing the bloody attachment that was the woman's arm, then quickly looking away again. Joe is quiet but Portia can feel his heart in his touch. It is firm, penetrating the pain, and this caring starts her first tears as she remembers the real victim of this accident.

"Jesse! Oh, Jesus, I want my baby. What's going to happen to my baby? I want Jesse."

Joe pushes the hair back from her face. "Quiet, now. Go thrashin' around and you'll hurt that arm. You don't need to be worryin' about your baby. He'll get taken care of."

"But he's only got me. And I need him."

"Christ!" Earl mutters. "I need a drink."

Shock, the crew is thinking. They have been trained to expect this. A person may talk quite lucidly and still be in shock. A woman who has just had her arm torn off and is calling for her baby. Gotta be shock.

"Something on the tracks up there. Thought you called for clearance." Joe's hand tenses on her collarbone. Screams pour from the jitney. "Injured man! Clear the tracks, you dumb son of a bitch."

The impeding vehicle moves. Earl mutters, "Zanzucki. That bastard stopped to listen to the phones. Wants to know what's going on so he can cover his ass. Probably left his red hats on their own. Wait till I get him outside, foreman or no."

Both men are silent for the remainder of the ride. The pit mouth comes closer and a faint light creases Portia's eyes. She pushes against the pain. Black becomes gray. The glare of daylight erases cap lights. They are outside.

The sudden brightness seals her eyes. Brakes squeal. People gather. Faces peer into the jitney. Familiar voices merge with new ones in the same refrain: "accident . . . woman . . . arm . . . don't know."

"Where's the damn ambulance?"

"Give 'em time, Earl. We only called about twenty minutes ago."

"Look at this fog. Ain't nothin' gonna be movin' fast in this shit."

Portia opens her eyes, avoiding the faces and looking into the sky. Sure enough, it is raining. The brightness that seemed like sunlight when leaving the pit mouth is really a thick weeping mist. That seems appropriate. Rain has always eased her.

A new voice cuts into her reverie. Lester, the company safety man, moves to assert management's interests.

"What happened?"

No one answers. The son of a bitch hasn't even asked how she is.

Portia studies the flaking yellow paint on the side of the jitney. Someone has spray-painted the standard FUCK YOU there. Fuck Lester, she thinks.

Murmurs start. "Found her wedged between the rib and the buggy."

Voices rise. "Cut off. Damn straight. She'll lose it, sure as hell. Seems steady, though. 'Cept she keeps callin' for her kid."

Who else is there, she thinks, and remembering Sam, feels strengthened. The rain is cool on her face as they lift her from the jitney. She would have liked to linger there under its ease.

But she is moved inside. The crew is still with her, jamming the small first-aid room, hovering protectively. Lester attempts to take charge. "Put the stretcher on the table. Ray, get me some scissors and sterile wraps. I got to take a look at this."

"Where's your ambulance at, Lester?" Joe's grip tightens on the artery. Dutch has appeared from somewhere, and he takes her good hand to emphasize his presence. He is union committeeman and he is there to witness. Brothers all, thinks Portia.

"Should be here by now. Guess this fog slowed them up. Ray, call the rescue squad again. Find out when they left. The rest of you, get out of here. Give her some air."

The men filter out, leaving Dutch to keep watch. Before going, Joe directs Lester's attention to the need to compress the artery. Portia's gaze follows the man as he leaves, trying to say . . . maybe thanks. Maybe that she loves him for his caring. He trails the crew out the door.

Lester hacks away at the jacket while Ray calls the rescue squad. "Yeah, ambulance. Girl has her arm cut off."

Lester turns to him. "Shut up."

Portia grins, if faintly. "C'mon, Lester. I know."

He treads these verbal waters gingerly, strain showing on his face. "We don't know nothin'. Ray is lettin' his mouth get carried away. It might not be gone, and you're tough. You can beat this. We don't even know what happened yet. What did happen?"

Dutch squeezes her hand warningly. She meets Lester's look and holds it. He glances back to the arm in confusion. The jacket is almost off. He tries again. "Did it throw you?"

"I don't know. I don't know what the hell happened. That buggy's a piece of shit and my arm is gone." Tears start as Portia remembers. "I want my baby. Get ahold of P.J. for me. She'll take care of him."

"Ray, get the woman on the phone. Her number's in the directory there. Now, where's he at, Portia?"

"Mrs. Johnson. P.J. will know what to do. Have her call Sam, my other boy."

The calls are made. Lester nods. "P.J.'s on top of it. Now hold on. I almost got this jacket off." His fumblings are increasingly nervous as he folds back the shattered cloth. She sees the arm.

Red flesh. Prime sirloin. Unmarbled but charred

crisp and packed with coal dust. No filet cut here, what with bone fragments splintering the meat.

The door flips open and Portia turns her head to see Steve Zanzucki approach the table where she lies. His walk indicates a wary man nearing a wounded animal who may attack. Their eyes meet and his fall to the mangled flesh. He looks up again in calculated horror. Does this man ever react spontaneously, without watching his tracks? She knows him so well. He is worried. Is he covered? Can this come back on him in some way? He turns suddenly and bolts out the door. She hears him:

"Get those men back underground. We got thirty minutes till shift change, and they ain't gettin' paid to sit around on their asses." She sees the fury on Dutch's face. Although Zanzucki is technically correct, the men aren't in any shape to go back underground. Pain disappears in anger. She screams at his disappearing back, "You fucker! The only thing you ever did give a damn about was your fuckin' coal."

Lester and Ray freeze, then quickly resume working on her arm. Suddenly Lester's monotone accelerates. Excitement alters the pace of hopelessness.

"The artery's still there! God knows how. Another quarter of an inch and it would be gone. See it, Ray? Beatin' right behind that mess there. They oughta be able to do something if they still have the artery."

A red flashing light bounces off Ray's face. "The ambulance," Lester says, tearing at a blue paper package that ejects a sterile towel. As he places it over Portia's arm, red splotches dot the surface.

"It's here!" someone yells. Renewed confusion agitates the pain. As the nerve ends regain their consciousness, she feels herself sinking. It is good, the blackness inviting. Temper the wind to the shorn lamb.

Portia wanders along the back roads of her mind. Dying, when it comes, will be a secondary shadow to the present. It will not be now. She knows this. Maybe not for a long time. But on its day, death will recognize its spores as ashes on her forehead, coal in the pores, flecks in the lungs.

She is being moved through the weather into a glittering vehicle. White-coated attendants flash across her sight. Her brother's face comes into view. Robert's hands leave grimed imprints on the attendants as he climbs into the ambulance beside her.

"I'm goin'," he says gruffly.

She manages a feeble grin. He is her brother. His ways differ from hers, but his presence buttresses her strength. And she needs him. Someone will have to make the decision about amputation.

Portia concentrates on fighting the pain yet keeping it in her sights. If she quits looking, it will take over. If her attention swerves, the unbearable will worsen.

The forty miles to the nearest hospital stretch over potholes and broken roads. Thick fog nudges the windows, trying to infiltrate the vehicle and obliterating the world outside.

"I ain't seen it this bad in years," the driver complains, inching the vehicle along. "Not since that ride to the Ridge in 'seventy-three. Remember that one? Picked up that kid who got eat up by the feeder. Didn't have to worry about speed that time. He didn't have a chance."

Arrival at the hospital brings more trundling and bundling. Eyes strain to see Portia, and in them she can read curiosity and scorn. A woman working in the mines eventually gets what she deserves. Probably brought it on herself. Some eyes mirror her shock, and they have pity. As always, their compassion is the most difficult emotion to endure. You can turn away from scorn but not compassion. It hurts both receiver and giver.

Emergency-room nurses avert their heads as the arm is unwrapped, then look back again. They stare at the limb, make a face, then find themselves drawn to look again, deliciously horrified, fascinated. The doctor is blessedly brief.

"We can't handle this. Make arrangements for transport.

"Morgantown?"

"No. Try Union Pacific in Baltimore. They specialize in orthopedics. If the arm can be saved, they'll do it. Tell them we have a patient with a partially severed right arm and a high chance of infection. We need the medevac." A nurse cuts off the remainder of Portia's filthy clothing, touching it gingerly. Another tugs at her boots, the expensive miner's boots she has just bought. Each jerk is agony. "Cut the damn things!" Portia screams. A doctor sinks the first of many needles into her good arm. She raises her eyebrows in question. "Morphine," he says. "Should cut the pain." It cuts nothing.

A nurse swabs at the wound to clean it. "Don't."

The doctor's voice is sharp. "Don't touch that arm. Pack it in ice, start an IV, and we wait."

Wait? She must see to Jesse. "Where's my brother? I gotta get a few things straight with him." The doctor nods his assent and Robert is ushered into the emergency room. He shakes visibly.

"We gotta get somebody to care for Jesse. He's at Bess Peterson's now."

"Would she . . ."

"No. Bess is good, but she has her own to tend to when they get off school. I want P.J. to have him."

"That trash."

"Shut up, Robert. That woman's got more heart than the lot of you. Make sure she gets him. She understands."

"Okay. Are you sure that's best?"

"I'm sure. And promise me it's done."

"Okay. But I don't like it."

"You never showed any concern for my kid before. Give him to her."

Word comes on the medevac. "Fog's too thick. You'll have to go by ambulance. It'll be a hell of a trip, I kid you not. We'll send along a nurse to give you another shot. You'll need it."

She is back in the ambulance. Morphine has blunted the pain somewhat, clouding her awareness, but still the agony is there, gnawing, without site. Hurt envelops her body, centering in no particular area. She wants unconsciousness, but it doesn't happen. Her mind is too disciplined, gripping reality despite herself.

After five hours on the road, which Portia believes to be fifteen, Baltimore's lights tint the sky pink. Despite drugs, the pain has escalated, taking on a razorlike quality. The other passengers in the ambulance are silent, and the forehead of the nurse gripping her hand is beaded with sweat.

"Supposed to be a police escort," she mutters.

Finally spotlights gleam down from the tall brick walls of Union Pacific Hospital, and the nurse speaks for all of them: "Thank God!" She detaches the IVs. Doors are thrown open and Portia is lifted out, but her senses register a difference. Hands here are smoother. Floors have a high polish. Lights are brighter, voices lower. White coats unwrap, X-ray, evaluate, page. A doctor removes some of her pain and most of her mind. "Move your fingers," they say. "Strange break. You shoulda lost that artery by all rights." God and she acknowledge each other.

An Oriental gnome introduces himself. "I'm Doctor Kim. I'm going to put you to sleep."

His moon face beams against fluorescent orbs. She likes this man and smiles through the gathering dimness. He pats her cheek. "You don't look like a coal miner. Too pretty."

"You don't look much like a doctor."

He laughs merrily, a yellow Santa Claus in blue scrub suit. "Little stick," he warns. A needle is inserted in her arm. She is slipping. Despite herself, she is pulled in. The blackness of the mines returns.

Later they will ask Portia, "Do you remember?"

She says yes, but it is a qualified affirmation. A series of surgeries are punctuated by segments of dimness in which things are viewed obliquely. Portia has never realized such pain existed. Nights span trips to the operating room and days are broken when the last shot wears off, leaving her to lie there, waiting for the next fix and oblivion. The people in her world exist only from the waist up.

Before each surgery, sweet-smelling gas lulls her to sleep and she wakes in hell. They call it the postop room, but it is Satan's antechamber, populated by monitoring equipment that follows her fight back to life with beeps and lights. Nurses hover, monitoring the monitors.

The sterile environment is frigid, designed to discourage microbes. It discourages Portia. This cold existence does not seem worth returning to. She wakes frozen, teeth chattering. Each tremor pushes pain through her body. Her mouth is dry and she looks up into the bright lights knowing she is back for another go at it and wondering if it's worth the effort. But the boys wait. Licking her lips, she finds even her spit has evaporated and manages a dry call. "Water."

The nurse confers with another nurse, who pages the doctor. An eternity later she rubs ice over Portia's parched mouth, then allows her to suck a few chips. The woman's system goes crazy. Cells stampede toward the moisture.

Little by little each teasing drop is absorbed. Finally she is allowed a sip. Then a swallow. The dryness relaxes some.

Her teeth chatter against the glass and she asks for

blankets. Nurses pack her in warmth. Her senses cease complaining about drought and chill, and she relaxes . . . enough for the pain to reassert itself.

"Can you give me something?"

"Not yet. We have to wait till they get you upstairs and check the doctor's orders."

"How long will that be?

After what Portia judges to be four hours, she timidly dares to catch the nurse's eye. The woman glances at her watch. "Oh yeah, sweetie. I'll call for transport."

A half hour passes. Chances are the floor nurses are catering to the needs of others and are hard put to find the time to release her from hell. Finally Mary, God bless her, appears and moves Portia, tucking her in and giving her medication and soothing words. The worst is over, at least until the morrow.

IVs empty into her system, one clear bag following another. Glucose. Blood. Antibodies. Her system disgorges fluids through a catheter into a bag where the yellow contents are embarrassingly visible, the stuff Ida told her was nasty.

On the third night—at least Portia thinks it is the third night—they set the bones. The doctor tells her they will use a Hoffmann apparatus.

She nods, comprehending nothing. And wakes to find a madman's Erector Set perched on her arm. Eight pins six inches in length have been drilled into the bone and interconnected. Fifteen pounds of metal rods, screws, and bolts shape the fragments into something resembling an arm.

They tell her it is only the second time such a device has been used on an arm, and they have never saved one so far gone. A year or two earlier, they say, it would be in that proverbial box under the willow tree. Portia never understands if she is to be complimented for managing the injury or impressed at their skill. She understands she is to feel lucky but she doesn't. She just feels pain and isolation. They say in a few days there will be a skin graft; in a few months, a bone graft. A nerve graft. Maybe an artificial elbow. She is not appreciative. It just seems more of the same.

Washing her, the nurses marvel at the persistence of coal dust. Her hair fades back to a dingy red. Black slowly evacuates the pores. Grease and minerals are rubbed away. But the dark half-moons under the fingertips of her mangled hand persist, a personal affront to hospital hygiene and operating sterility. Nurses scrub, fuss, scrape, and cut. It does no good.

The woman's consciousness remains borderline. The pain ebbs and flows. She dips into oblivion and finds it wanting. Nurses try to position her for comfort and end up contortionists. Some become frustrated at their own helplessness, resentful of her pain. Her buzzer is often ignored or answered slowly. Nurses give pain shots with a sigh of relief, knowing for a while the agony will back off and there will be only minor discomforts to deal with.

Through it all, there are visitors. Sympathetic, well-meaning, and conscientious. And one must talk to them. "Now, what did happen? Harry heard . . ."

The companionship she needs is provided by those

few who come and say little, holding her hand and pushing back the dimness. They require no words and generate healing with a light touch.

The two months of hospitalization pass. She recovers quickly, surpassing expectations. Doctors credit her stamina . . . toughness. Always that word: *tough*. "You'll get through okay," they say. "Operations, therapy. You'll make it. You're tough."

But mostly she recovers because of a confused little boy who only understands that his mother has left him.

The baby is slow to accept her again, fearing another betrayal. But they make their peace. The emotional damage is nearly as limiting as the physical. Tasks done with one hand require twice the time. Portia knows she must do them. To become dependent will establish a precedent she will have to live with the rest of her life. She returns, taking care of Pansy and the child, resisting P.J.'s attempts to help. It is easier to do the hard thing and be done with it.

Portia adjusts to the mutilation, beating herself into fatigue each night, hoping exhaustion will bring sleep. But three A.M. is the witching hour. Yesterday's tiredness has mellowed. Dreams wrap, entangle, snare.

From beneath her eyelids, the canopy grabs her arm, chewing it to the consistency of dog food. The hand jerks toward her, yanked by the remembrance of the machine grinding the limb into the rib. *Snap!* A clean cut across the marrow, severing nerves. The hand flops in protest. She thinks of a dead fish. *Snap!*

Jerking awake in her room's blackness, akin to that of the coal, she clutches her right arm. The elbow is frozen in a perpetual half-bend, screwed into place, its skin rough and mottled to the touch. But there, sweet Jesus. Warm and alive. Crippled and unsightly. But there.

Funny. The arm has more personality mutilated than it had as a whole. She is continually aware of it being an extension of herself, having definite wants and needs. Her body caters to its whims. The back has donated skin and bone. Nerves have come from the legs. Tendons . . . where did they come up with the tendons? The left arm works for its partner, attempts to write, performs life's primary functions.

During these long nights she thinks of what she will do and what she can no longer do. Obviously her life in the mines is over. She considers the possibility of a return to teaching. She has rejected that career once but cannot afford to do so again, with the baby to think of. Can she move into a new life with the pull of the old one still upon her?

Physical and mental aches dim as the morning comes strong. Rising, she takes Jesse from his bed. He stirs, then relaxes on her taut left arm. Placing him on the right side of the bed, she slides in beside him and insulates the aching limb with his warmth. Already this child she has so recently nurtured with her body moves to sustain her. She will have to buy a heating pad . . . tomorrow.

But Portia has learned that all her tomorrows will be compressed into minutes, units of emotion to be counted like the beads on Pansy's rosary. Life's beginnings have culminated in Jesse and she has been shown the shadows of its conclusion. The interim has promise.